DISCORD

OTHER FOLLY BEACH MYSTERIES

FOLLY

THE PIER

WASHOUT

THE EDGE

THE MARSH

GHOSTS

MISSING

FINAL CUT

FIRST LIGHT

BONEYARD BEACH

SILENT NIGHT

DEAD CENTER

DISCORD

A Folly Beach Mystery

BILL NOEL

Copyright © 2017 by Bill Noel
All rights reserved.

No part of this book may be reproduced in any form or by any electronic or mechanical means, including information storage and retrieval systems, without written permission from the author, except for the use of brief quotations in a book review.

Front cover photo and design by Bill Noel
Author photo by Susan Noel
Props provided by Jamie McDonell

ISBN: 978-1-942212-80-5

Hydra Publications
Goshen, KY 40026
www.hydrapublications.com

South Butler Community Library
PO Box 454, 240 West Main Street
Saxonburg, PA 16056

PROLOGUE

Midnight had come and gone. The Top Ten Bar had been standing room only two hours earlier yet now was as quiet as a Baptist church on Tuesday morning. Rod, a tall, thin, thirty-something bartender, stood behind the distressed wooden bar wiping dry the last of the clean wine glasses, not difficult since most patrons were beer drinkers. The exhausted employee, who looked more like a history professor with his neatly-trimmed beard and glasses perched on his head, was forty feet from a couple of stragglers. Rod had pulled a double shift and the two customers were all that stood between his aching feet and heading to his girlfriend's condo where he hoped to find sympathetic coos, and with luck, a foot massage and more.

The female customer pushed an empty beer bottle aside and leaned against the table. "Think you can walk away after stomping on my dream?" She was seething and making no effort to hide it. "All your talk, your smiles, your empty promises. You've been lying through your freakin' teeth. You've taken my money. Buddy, let me tell you one thing you're not going to do." She hesitated, glanced toward the bartender who was ignoring her outburst, and turned to her table mate. "You ain't going to get away with it."

The man shrugged. It wasn't the worst reaction from the customer sitting on the other side of the table from the tirade, but it was close. He grinned and things hit rock bottom.

The woman swept her arm across the table and the bottle tumbled to the cracked, beer-stained linoleum floor. The bottle exploded into hundreds of shards and shattered not only the container but the eerie silence in the room. She shoved away from the table and stormed out of the bar.

The bartender's expression switched from boredom to irritation. The man who had been sitting across from the woman turned toward Rod, held his hands out. "I got it. I'll clean it up."

You'd better, thought Rod. He glared at the man, glanced at the door where the companion had stomped out, and reached for the broom and dustpan. He mumbled a profanity and faked a smile as he handed the cleaning tools to the customer. "Thanks, Kevin. I'd appreciate it."

Kevin had been a regular at Top Ten Bar, located a few blocks away from Lower Broadway, Nashville's epicenter of country bars and aspiring singers and songwriters, for the last year and had escorted a constant stream of young women to his evening "office." After the first few months, the bartenders had stopped paying attention to the ladies with Kevin and swore they couldn't recognize any of them even if the room had been lit by klieg lights. The inside joke among the staff had been that Kevin was either a talent scout in futile search for the next star, or a pimp plying his bevy of beauties with liquid encouragement before sending them out to enhance his coffers. Regardless, the less the bartenders knew about Kevin and his activities the better.

There was something else Rod didn't know about Kevin. This would be the last night he would be escorting anyone to the out-of-the-way Music City watering hole.

Rod could spot a cop within a millisecond of one entering his workplace, a talent he'd acquired from standing behind bars for a third of his life. It didn't take years of observation to tell him the two men walking his direction were on the payroll of the Metro Nashville Police Department. They weren't in uniform, yet their poorly-fitting navy blazers with conspicuous firearm bulges made formal introductions unnecessary. They flashed their creds at him anyway. Troy Rogers was the younger of the two; Wayne Lawrence, the more seasoned detective.

Detective Rogers unfolded an enlarged driver's license photo and slid it across the bar. "Recognize him?"

A dozen pre-happy-hour drinkers were spread throughout the warehouse-size room. They were more interested in their drinks than in the detectives.

Rod removed his glasses and laid them on the bar. He squinted at the photo and at the detective. "Sure, it's Kevin. Kevin Starr, at least that's what's on his credit card. What'd he do?"

Detective Lawrence ignored the question. "When was the last time you saw him?"

Rod glanced around the room. No one needed his services nor was paying attention to what was going on with the detectives. "Couple of nights ago. Why?"

Rogers took a notebook out of his jacket pocket. "What time?"

"Didn't see him come in. Had to be after eleven. I was busy. He sat over there." Rod pointed to a table on the far side of the room.

Rogers jotted a note and said, "He alone?"

"No. Had a woman with him. What's going on?"

"Know who she was?" Rogers asked.

Rod smiled. "Hell, I'm not Kevin's secretary. He has a different woman every time he's here. Couldn't tell you one from another."

"So you don't know who she was?"

Ain't it what I said? Rod thought. Instead, he said, "Nope."

"Describe her?"

"I never got a good look. It was busy when they came in and Kevin came to me and got their beers. I was the only employee here. The damned waitress left sick an hour earlier leaving me with all this." He waved his hand around the room.

Rogers said, "Try anyway?"

Rod looked at the table where the couple had been sitting. "Average height. Didn't strike me as tall or short. Figure she was attractive because all of Kevin's *friends* are lookers." He shook his head. "She had her back to me. Sorry, that's it."

Detective Lawrence said, "Don't suppose she paid by credit card?"

"Don't you think I would have mentioned it? Besides, she didn't pay." Rod hesitated and grinned. "Not to me, that is."

"What's that mean?" Lawrence asked.

"Umm, nothing."

"Nothing?"

Rod looked at Rogers and turned to Lawrence. "Don't take this as gospel. Some of us thought Starr was a pimp. All those good-looking gals, you know."

"Any proof?" Lawrence said.

"Just gossip."

Rogers asked, "What time did they leave?"

"Twelve-thirty. Remember because they were the only folks here. Had to wait for them to go to lock up."

"Anyone else here that night who might recognize her?" Lawrence asked.

"Maybe, except I don't know who. I told you it was crowded when they got here. The waitress was gone. Don't know if they talked to anyone. Place was dead when they left; dead until he must've said something to piss her off."

The detectives leaned forward. "Explain."

Rod looked around to see if any customers were listening. "They added fifteen minutes to my already long night when she knocked a bottle off the table. Sticky beer and glass everywhere. I made Kevin clean it up."

"Accident?"

Rod grinned. "If flailing her arm around, knocking the bottle five feet from the table, and storming out of the room was an accident, sure."

Lawrence asked, "Know what she was angry about?"

"Nah, but Kevin was nice about cleaning the mess up. He kept mumbling about the chick not having to break the bottle. Something like he was doing the best he could."

"Any idea what he meant?" Lawrence asked.

Rod shook his head.

Lawrence jotted another note.

"Now your turn. What's going on?"

Detective Rogers glanced at his partner and turned to Rod. "We found the credit card receipt that showed he was in here two nights ago."

"So?"

"We found it on his body. Mr. Starr was murdered sometime Monday night or Tuesday morning."

CHAPTER ONE

I was in Cal's Country Bar and Burgers a block off the literal and figurative center of my slice of heaven in Folly Beach, South Carolina. The lunch crowd, if you call four people a crowd, had settled their checks and headed to the beach. The bar's owner and I were alone.

Cal folded his trim, six-foot-three frame in the chair and scooted up to the table. "Heard from them lately?"

The last four months, when anyone mentioned *them*, it was safe to assume they were referring to my best friend Charles Fowler and his girlfriend Heather Lee, the couple who had moved to Nashville so Heather could pursue her dream of becoming a country music star. Considering her singing voice, to put it gently, stank, the odds on her achieving the lofty goal was worse than me, a man in my sixties and allergic to exercise, running the hundred-meter hurdles in the Olympics.

"Last week," I said. "Charles called excited to tell me Heather made another appearance at open-mic night at the Bluebird."

"Got herself discovered yet?"

Cal, who was in his seventies, would know a thing or two about being discovered. He had a national top-twenty country hit, "End of the Story," that reached number one in his hometown of Lubbock, Texas. Unfortunately, he had reached his pinnacle of success in 1962 at the ripe old age of eighteen.

"Don't believe so."

Cal chuckled. "Suspect Michigan would've mentioned it if his gal had become famous."

Cal had a habit of calling people by their state of origin. Charles and I had come close to breaking him of it. He would occasionally backslide.

I nodded.

Cal continued, "Appearing at the Bluebird Cafe's a big deal. Back in my day, there weren't nearly as many places where someone could be discovered. Because they let Heather croon a tune there don't mean much other than she can say she did."

"She knows it. She's got her heart set on breaking into the music industry."

Cal pushed his ever-present, sweat-stained Stetson back on his head, looked at the front door where nobody entered, and back at me. "How many songs has she penned?"

"Two that I know of. Why?"

"How many times has she appeared at open-mic night at the Bird?"

"Several."

"Has she appeared anywhere else in Nashville?"

"Don't think so."

"Open-mic night at the Bird is for songwriters, not singers."

"I know."

Cal looked toward the stage at the far end of the bar. "My ears have suffered from hearing Heather warble through her two ditties many nights up there." Cal shook his head. "Now I'm no expert on the new-fangled country music. In my day, a songwriter hauled around a satchel with a hundred or more songs he, or sometimes a gal, had put to paper. Heather's two aren't much better than a dolphin could write and her singing's not as good as those swimmin' mammals can croon."

I knew how much Charles cared for Heather, and Lord knows, everyone who knew her understood how much she wanted to find fame and fortune standing behind a microphone. Cal was right. I started to tell him so when the door opened and I was surprised to see Preacher Burl Ives Costello peek his head in. He saw us and headed our way.

Cal said, "Afternoon, Illinois."

"A pleasant afternoon to you, Brother Cal," said the portly minister of First Light, Folly's newest, and most unusual house of worship. "And to you too, Brother Chris."

First Light should be called a place of worship rather than a house since it conducted most of its services on the beach. When bad weather descended, or in the preacher's words, the "Devil took to interferin' with the work of the Lord," the services were held in a storefront on Folly's main street.

Cal looked around the empty room. "Here to save someone? If you are, you're stuck with Kentucky, umm Mr. Landrum here, and me. Don't see much hope for savin' us."

Burl was quite familiar with the aging bar owner and me. We had been embroiled in a deadly situation a couple of years back that involved members of his congregation, or as he called them, his flock. Burl had been the prime suspect in the death of several people, and just as quickly had almost become the victim of the real murderer. Since then, First Light had increased in popularity and its flock had grown, especially among those who were looking for a nontraditional worship experience.

Burl laughed. "My job's to not give up on anyone, although I reckon you might be right about little hope for you two. Truth be told, I wanted to sit a spell and enjoy a cold brew."

Cal tipped his Stetson. "That'll be a lot easier to rustle up than throwing out my demons." He smiled. "Bud, Bud Light, or Miller?"

Cal's range of drink offerings included three beers, and an equal number of wines: red, white, and pink. If he was pushed, which he seldom was, he could find you a glass of water or a Coke.

Burl patted his ample stomach and smiled. "Better stick with Bud Light to maintain my shapely figure." He pulled a chair to our table and lowered his *shapely* body on it.

Cal returned with the beer and held up the bottle before giving it to Burl. "Preacher, I hear rumors you preach about the sins of, what do you call it, the Devil's juice. Don't get this old washed-up singer wrong, I ain't trying to talk you out of sipping this brew and adding to my massive fortune. I'm wondering if this ain't what you preach against?"

Burl nodded. "Brother Cal, you're right … and wrong."

Cal rolled his eyes. "That explains it."

Burl chuckled. "I preach against excess, Brother Cal. Excess."

"Too much beer," Cal said, as if he needed clarification on the meaning of excess.

"Brother Jesus wasn't above sippin' wine. Heavens, if he were in here today, I believe he'd be tasting one of these." He held his Bud Light bottle in the air. "Moderation my friend. Moderation is the key to the good life. Excess is the work of the Devil. It includes this stuff." He hesitated and pointed at the bottle. "Or whiskey, or lovin', or speeding, or even consuming too many M&Ms. Excess, my friend."

"Got it, Preacher," Cal said. "Now if the theological lesson's over, can we commence drinking?"

"I can't help myself. To paraphrase Descartes', 'I preach, therefore I am.'" He chuckled and turned to me. "Brother Chris, my misquoting that French philosopher reminded me of our friend Brother Charles and the way he's always quoting presidents. Have you heard from him and Sister Heather?"

I was stuck on Burl knowing Descartes quote enough to paraphrase it, and asked him to repeat his question.

"Heard from them lately?"

I shared what I had told Cal, and Burl asked if the agent I didn't trust had found Heather any paying gigs. Heather's pilgrimage to Nashville had begun a little over four months ago, when she had been performing during Cal's weekly open-mic night. A man named Kevin Starr said he was in town meeting with record executives at the Tides Hotel and had walked to Cal's to get away from the boring discussions. He heard Heather, asked her to join him after her set, and told her he was an agent and owner of Starr Management, based in Music City. He offered to represent her and said he could get her appearances in Nashville's top venues for discovering talent. That was all it took. A few days later she had packed her belongings lock, stock, and guitar, and she and Charles had moved 560 miles to find her fame and fortune in the country music capital of the world.

Burl sipped his beer and nodded or shook his head during my update on *them*. "Now I know Brother Charles and Sister Heather are your good friends, Brother Chris. I hope you don't take offense at what I am about to say. Umm ..., I'm no expert like our friend Brother Cal here. From my untrained ears, I don't detect the qualities in Sister Heather's voice that would lead her to music stardom. Am I incorrect?"

Cal leaned closer to Burl. "If all those words mean you think Heather's singing sucks, you smacked the truth right on its noggin."

My phone rang before Cal could continue with his in-depth analysis of Heather's vocal talents.

I looked at the screen. "Speaking of the Devil," I said. "Figuratively speaking, Preacher."

CHAPTER TWO

"Is this Chris Landrum?" asked the voice on the phone. "You know, the aging, retired, guy who's bored because he went and shut down his photo gallery."

I grinned and thought of how much I missed my friend. "You got Chris Landrum and retired right. Hi, Charles."

"Nope, I got all of it right. As James Garfield said, 'The truth will set you free, but first it will make you miserable.'"

Telephone courtesies and greetings like *hello* are a thing of the past, or so it seemed. Instead of hitting the *End Call* button, I repeated, "Hi, Charles."

He mumbled, "You're no fun," followed by a moment of silence, and, "Okay, enough foolishness from you. I called to tell you about an epiphany I had in the middle of the night. Think it was brought on when Heather kicked me in her sleep, anyway, here it is—"

"Epiphany," I interrupted. "Who took possession of Charles Fowler's vocabulary?"

"Heather spends her time singing. I spend mine reading and

grabbing a new word every once in a while; need them to talk to the intellectuals here. Stop knocking me off track, you want to hear my epiphany or not?"

I wanted to say "not," yet wasn't ready to incur the wrath of Charles; besides, I did wonder what could possibly have come to him because of being kicked. "I'm waiting."

"Good. It struck me that since you deserted the gallery you've become a retiredaholic."

"Have you thrown that word around those intellectuals?"

"Saved it for you. Stop interrupting. The point is you'll burn yourself out spending all your time retired—day and night, night and day, 24/7. After Heather kicked me awake, we talked about your precarious situation and came to a decision. You ready?"

Cal and Burl stared at me. I sighed. "Sure."

"You need to get away from retirement for a while and take a vacation. Hang on a sec, Heather's trying to say something."

I stared at the phone and realized I hadn't been aware how strenuous being retired was. I also realized Charles had finally gotten over my closing the gallery where he had been my unpaid sales manager. The few years it was open, the shop had done little but drain my net worth. It had given my friend a purpose in life and something he could take pride in. He was hurt, frustrated, and at times angry with my decision. The fact was, he hadn't been the one writing checks every month that exceeded the money I'd taken in.

"I'm back," he said. "Okay, the Charles and Heather Travel Agency have it worked out. This is Thursday, right?"

"Right."

"Take the rest of the day to pack. Tomorrow get in your little Cadillac ATS, set the handy-dandy navigation thingie for Nashville, Tennessee, and zip on over. Here's the best part. We have an extra bedroom—well, it's sort of a storage room. All the stuff in it can be put somewhere else, and you can sleep on the queen mattress the previous renter left on the floor. We won't charge you a single cent to stay here. See, we've already saved you at least a hundred bucks a night. Now get this. On Monday night, Heather will be performing at the Bluebird Cafe, and you can go with us."

"Charles, I—"

"I know, I know. You get a complete vacation package including room and entertainment for only the cost of gas and food. And, if you wanted to take Heather and me to supper to celebrate her Bluebird appearance, we know of a restaurant that has good food at cheap prices. We only have one bedroom left. Can we make your reservation? Besides, there's something important, a problem, we want to bounce off you."

Heather was laughing in the background and saying, "Please come. Please."

Cal and Burl continued to stare at me.

"Sure."

Heather must have been near the phone. She squealed.

Charles gave me the address to plug in my *handy-dandy navigation thingie*, where to park when I got there, and their apartment number. He told me to let them know when I was a few hours away. He said Heather wanted to be there when I arrived and would need time to reschedule some of her many appointments with music executives, and Charles might be at Starbucks reading a thesaurus.

I set the phone on the table, exhaled, as Cal and Burl said, "What?" They had heard my end of the conversation, so I filled in the blanks, omitting why I needed a break from being retired and Charles's made-up malady, retiredaholic, and his real, but totally out of character, word-of-the-day, epiphany.

"You moseying over?" Cal asked.

Burl said, "You miss him, don't you?"

"Sure, I do, Preacher," and realized how true it was. "He's my best friend. I told him I'd come."

Cal headed to the cooler. "Next round's on me. That'll help you pay for your gas."

Burl asked, "When are you going?"

"Tomorrow."

Cal handed each of us a drink. "Had a thought on the way back from the cooler." He took a draw on his beer.

I glanced at Burl and at Cal. He was waiting for one of us to ask about his thought.

Burl didn't disappoint. "Planning on sharing it?"

Cal looked at the preacher and pointed his Bud bottle at me. "Maybe I could tag along. It's been a bunch of years since I sauntered around Music City. I miss the good old days when I would hang around the Opry House; the real one, not the sterile one out by the hotel that's the size of Topeka, Kansas. Willie, Roger, Ernest, Roy—ah, the good ole days. Anyway, how about me going with you?"

I enjoyed spending time with Cal. He was entertaining and fun to be with, but, truth be told, I was more a loner. I wasn't sure I was ready to spend most of the day in the car with him, or for that matter, with anyone. And, I couldn't imagine that Charles and Heather's apartment had enough room for both of us. On the other hand, unless he went, he may never get back to the city that had meant so much to him.

"Sounds good, Cal." I shook my head. "But I couldn't take you away from your bar. I don't know how long I'll be there."

He frowned and looked down at his bottle. "Guess you're right. Wouldn't want to deprive my loveable drunks by locking them out."

Burl had been watching the exchange, and leaned closer to the table. "Perhaps I can offer a passable solution."

Cal said, "What might that be?"

"I mentioned this to Brother Chris a while back, but don't think you know, Brother Cal. Years back, when I was doing most anything—most anything legal—to make ends meet, I spent a year tending bar. I could fill-in for a week or so and you could have your part-time cook come in more shifts to fix food. Don't think your customers' stomachs would take kindly at me frying burgers."

Cal pushed his Stetson back on his head. "A mighty kind offer, Preacher. Now how would it jive with your preaching? Seems like it'd cause a passel of probs."

Burl smiled. "Can't think of a better place to find souls needing saving."

Cal leaned back. "Now Brother Burl, I can't have preaching in—"

Burl faced his palms toward Cal. "Kidding. I'd be glad to watch the bar while you're gone. No preaching, no plugging religion. Let's call it community outreach without the church reaching."

Cal looked at me, I shrugged, and he turned to Burl. "Sounds like a fine idea, Preacher. Not to sound rude and unappreciative, I'd take you up on it if you could do me one favor."

Burl smiled. "I ought to hear it first."

"When you're tendin' bar, would it be possible for you to refrain from calling everyone Brother or Sister? Don't think it sets the proper tone for my customers."

"You drive a hard bargain." Burl reached up and removed an imaginary hat from his head. "When I'm behind the bar, I'll take off my preachin' Panama and put on my beer-belchin' beret."

Cal grinned and stuck out his hand to Burl. "You've got a deal, bartender Burl."

And I had a vacation companion. To think, a mere thirty minutes ago, I hadn't known I was a retiredaholic in need of a vacation. I also wondered what was so important, such a problem, that Charles needed to bounce it off me. I'd known Charles for nine years and knew when he said problem he meant something most people would consider to be a disaster, or some other word Charles could find in a thesaurus.

CHAPTER THREE

Cal was silent the first four hours of our nine-hour drive. When I picked him up at his apartment he had said it was his middle of the night. Nights in the bar often lasted past midnight and during his forty-plus years travelling the country and singing most anywhere that would have him, his performances often didn't start until past dark. I was a morning person and encouraged him to put his seat back and sleep until he was ready to wake up. I didn't have to say it twice.

It wasn't until we were on the Interstate between Asheville and Knoxville that he showed signs of life. He stretched his arms over his head and said he was ready for a hearty breakfast. I reminded him it was noon and lunch would be more appropriate. He said, "tomato, tomahto," as I pulled in a Waffle House near Canton, North Carolina. The only tomatoes, or tomahtoes, I saw were when Cal slathered ketchup on his hash browns.

Forty-five minutes later, breakfast/lunch was finished, and after Cal had started a conversation with everyone who walked by our table, we were back on the road, this time with Cal piloting. I tried to nap, though I would have had as good a chance reciting the first nineteen amendments to the US Constitution. Cal had his left hand on the wheel. His right hand fiddled with the radio controls trying to find the nearest country music station, singing along with each traditional country artist, and complaining about the stations that had the nerve to play contemporary country and hick-hop. Yes, Cal was awake.

Three hours later, we switched drivers at an exit between Knoxville and our destination. Cal grabbed his guitar from the back seat and serenaded me with 7,395 songs in the two hours it took us to get from the stop to the Interstate exit to downtown Nashville. If a country song had been recorded, oh, let's say, between 27 AD and 1975, Cal knew it. I'd heard what he said were the B side of many hits from that period, but when he started strumming B sides of songs he said had barely reached the top two hundred of the day, I was lost. I'm a country fan, although by the time we reached downtown Nashville, I was yearning for some Snoop Dog.

The navigation system did an excellent job of directing us to the address Charles had given me. The lot where he told me to park wasn't as easy to find. With the aid of Cal telling me each way *not* to turn, pointing out the Ryman Auditorium, and getting excited about a vacant building where he said he had performed "back in the day," we managed to find the narrow alley that led to the five-story warehouse that had been converted to apartments, and home of Charles and Heather.

I called Charles a couple of hours out and he said he'd have had Heather cancel any music appointments, except she didn't have any, so they would be home when we arrived. I put the car in park and Charles bounded out a windowless, rusting, steel door at the corner of the apartment building. At five-foot-eight inches, he was a couple of inches shorter than me, twenty pounds lighter, and had long, graying brown hair, mainly on the sides. He and I shared a near hairless top of our heads. Instead of wearing one of his trademark long-sleeve college T-shirts, he wore a charcoal-gray Bluebird Cafe T-Shirt. He hadn't abandoned all traditions, despite being June, it was long-sleeve like his countless other shirts.

Charles had me in a bear hug before I closed the car door. If he'd attempted to shave in the last week, Heather needed to get him a new razor. Regardless of his shaggy face scraping my cheek, I was thrilled to see him. On the scale of world history, four months was merely a nano-speck. To me, it had seemed like an eternity.

Cal was feeling neglected and was on the passenger side of the car. He yelled, "Hey, Michigan, I'm here too."

Charles peeked around my head at Cal. "I ain't Ray Charles, I see you. Just haven't gotten around to huggin' you."

Heather scurried out of the building, made a beeline for the car, and squealed, "Yay, they're here." Cal had come around to where the action was and Heather managed to put her arms around him.

She was approaching her fiftieth birthday and was a five-foot-six bundle of enthusiasm. She greeted us with a wide smile and a giant hug. She's wholesomely attractive with her curly brown hair and freckled nose. She was seasonably attired in a dark-blue V-neck, short-sleeve Bluebird T-shirt and tan shorts.

Heather moved to the rear of the car. "Let us help you carry your stuff."

Cal started to protest until Charles said they were on the third-floor. There was an elevator, although the old-time residents told him it worked about as often as Congress did something smart. The country crooner gave in to Heather's hospitable offer. I carried my suitcase and didn't start regretting it until I was between the second floor and our destination. I hadn't realized how far it was between floors in a high-ceiling, converted warehouse.

"Chuckie saw you pulling in the lot," Heather said as Charles unlocked the apartment. "We've got a great view of the parking lot from our living room."

What more could one ask for? I thought. "That's great."

My friend had spent most of his adult life riling when anyone called him anything other than Charles. Chuck, Charlie, and up until Heather came along, Chuckie, were like waving a Pepsi at a Coke sales rep. My friend would still correct anyone who made such a ghastly error, unless the person's name was Heather Lee. Love was not only blind, it was deaf.

The exterior of the building looked like it hadn't received attention in decades. Rust battled paint for control of most exposed steel surfaces; the fire escape looked like it would struggle to hold more than one person at a time; and, the brick walls had served as canvases to numerous graffiti artists. The stairwell didn't look much better, so I was pleased to see the interior of the apartment had a fresh coat of paint, the hardwood floors had been refinished, and from a glance in the kitchen, the appliances appeared new.

Charles hadn't been back to Folly to get his massive collection of books, yet he had already started a mini-library along one of the living room walls. Bricks that had come from the same era as the building were stacked three-high on each side of a four-foot-long board he had repurposed as a bookshelf. Approximately fifty books, many with library labels, stood at attention on the shelf. Fist-sized rocks served as bookends.

Heather waved her arms around the room. "What do you think?"

We had just entered the apartment and hadn't had much time to think. It didn't stop Cal from saying, "Honey, it's better than anywhere I've ever lived."

It wasn't saying much since Cal had spent much of his adult life living out of his 1971 Cadillac, and since settling in Folly, he lived in a run-down apartment building that had been swept out to sea during a hurricane and was currently residing in an apartment which was a candidate for condemnation.

"I knew you'd love it," she said, responding to words which hadn't been spoken. "How about you, Chris?"

I moved to the corner of the room where I could look at the door leading to the bedrooms and glanced at Heather's black and silver karaoke machine and music stand, items I had helped her load into Charles's car the day they had left the beach. Crystals attached by a thin thread dangled from the top of a chrome picture frame that held a prominent place on a manicurist's table inside their bedroom. In addition to being a massage therapist and alleged singer, Heather prided herself on being a psychic. If true, a fact that's still unproven, her psychic abilities fall somewhere between her massage therapy skills and her singing. A forked, hazel twig, Heather's divining rod, leaned against the bookcase.

"What can I say, Heather, it's you."

"And me too," Charles said, as he leaned over and patted the bookcase. He didn't wait for a response. "Want the rest of the tour?"

Cal said, "You bet."

The entire apartment couldn't have taken up more than 700 square feet of Nashville's 504 square miles of land. The kitchen wasn't large enough for all of us, so I stood in the doorway while Heather pointed out each new appliance. I'm no expert in the kitchen, but had learned over the years what a refrigerator looked like. I was happy to see Heather so excited to show it to us. After moving her guitar case and wide-brimmed, straw hat she wore during most every performance, we were able to get in their *master bedroom*, as Heather proudly proclaimed. Cal and I nodded when she told us how grand the room was. She started to say something about the bed and mattress, when Charles interrupted and said it was time to see our room. She had inched close to *too much information* and I welcomed Charles's interruption.

The best thing about the bedroom Cal and I would be sharing was it had a queen-sized bed and enough space for both of us to be in the room at the same time. Cal said, "Cozy," and we moved past the tiny bathroom back to the tiny living room. By Manhattan apartment standards, the room may have been considered spacious. It made my tiny cottage in Folly seem palatial. Cal and I squeezed together on the mini-couch, Heather sat in the only chair in the room, and Charles moved to the floor.

The awkward moments people experience after arriving at someone's house and having finished the tour were beginning to set in. What do we talk about now? Heather came to the rescue.

"Are you ready to see our city?"

After spending the better part of the day in the car I wasn't anxious to get back in one so I said, "Looks like there are lots of interesting things within walking distance. I'd like to see some of them."

Cal added, "I've got a couple of stories you wouldn't believe about things that happened to me right up the street."

Whether he did it on purpose or not, I was glad he kept us focused on a walking tour.

Heather grabbed her straw hat and waved us toward the door. "What are we waiting for?"

The temperature was mild for June and a walk would do my old muscles good. Tour guide Heather told us we were just three blocks from Lower Broadway, in her words, "The plumb center of the country music entertainment universe." I'm sure many would disagree, but it was a major entertainment area in Nashville. We walked past the Ryman Auditorium, the former church that became the long-time home of the Grand Ole Opry, before the radio show and performing venue moved to its new home in 1974, and Cal started to tell us one of his stories we *wouldn't believe*. Heather would have none of it; it was her tour and we were moving on.

A half block more and we were standing at the corner of Fifth Street South and Broadway. Across the street was the Nashville Visitor's Center and behind it stood the Bridgestone Arena that looked like a giant spaceship plopped down in the middle of a historic district.

"Ain't they something?" Heather said with a wide grin.

No argument from us.

"We're going this way." She turned left on Broadway.

We were standing beside a guitar on the sidewalk that was the size of a Boeing 747. Live music flowed across the street from the second-floor bar at Rippy's Ribs & Bar-B-Q, and from the loud sounds of electrified country from the open door of Legend's Corner fifteen feet away.

"Ain't this something," Heather repeated as we headed down the sidewalk, dodging tourists.

Charles tapped me on the shoulder and motioned for me to wait while Heather continued her tour. Heather stopped in front of Tootsie's Orchid Lounge, Nashville's most famous bar, and Cal finally got to tell one of his stories. He was telling Heather about having spent many late nights in there. "Most of the time in a booth, some on the floor. Ah, the good old days."

Charles took a couple of steps farther away from Cal's story and pulled me with him. He whispered, "Think we've got a problem."

I glanced at Heather who was focused on Cal's story, and asked Charles, "What?"

"Chuckie," Heather said, "you and Chris ain't baskin' in Cal's fascinating story."

She said something else, but was drowned out by "The Race Is On," the George Jones classic, being sung by an overweight, middle-aged man on the stage inside the front door of Tootsie's.

"Later," Charles whispered before he moved closer to Cal, Heather, and the George Jones semi-sound-alike.

Heather continued her tour pointing out the bars and live music venues along Broadway. She appeared cheerful and more in her element than I'd ever seen her. I was happy for her, yet conflicted knowing it would take something approaching a major miracle to convince her—and Charles—to move back to Folly.

We reached Second Avenue North and Heather guided us left where we walked three blocks and left again and back to their apartment. Cal said he needed a nap. He said his seventy-two-year-old body didn't quite have the "get-up-and-go" it had when he closed many of Nashville's bars "a while back."

His nap became our nap, which flowed into bedtime. Heather said she and Charles were going to take in one more bar before "hitting the hay." We wished them well.

Cal's snoring woke me up at three in the morning; he also was occupying more than half of the bed. I stared at the dark ceiling and wondered what problem Charles and Heather had. Although we shared a lot of words after returning to the apartment, his "later" had not been among them.

CHAPTER FOUR

Heather rattled enough pots and pans the next morning to wake Cal and me and probably anyone living nearby. I suspected it was her intention, since she had fixed us a gourmet breakfast of Dunkin' Donuts with the consistency of Styrofoam. Nary a pot nor pan was used in the preparation. She said the donuts would provide us energy for another day of walking around her town.

To a casual observer, our activities would have appeared to be a rerun of yesterday's tour. Lighter crowds and fewer live performances were all that separated the two days. She did listen to more of Cal's reminiscing about his days as a "big star" during his performances at the Grand Ole Opry House, his walking across the alley from the Opry to Tootsie's for a midnight brew and staggering across Broadway to take in the live, midnight radio shows from the Ernest Tubb Record Store. Charles and I had heard most of it before. If Heather had, she feigned enough enthusiasm for Cal to rehash his adventures.

Heather suggested we *check out* the Nashville landmark after hearing Cal's Ernest Tubb Record Store story. Charles said for Heather and Cal to go ahead and he and I would stay and *shoot the breeze* until they got back. Heather seemed hurt we wouldn't be joining them. She got over it and grabbed Cal's hand and led him through the light traffic as they crossed Broadway.

I watched them and turned to Charles. "Is later now?"

"Good memory." He motioned me to join him on a bench in front of the Stage Bar.

Charles grabbed a hot dog wrapper from the bench and dropped it in a nearby trashcan while fifteen feet to our left, a street musician strummed on an old Yamaha guitar. From his straggly, age-stained attire and equally straggly face, he appeared to be a permanent resident of a homeless shelter and from the single, one-dollar bill in an open guitar case at his feet, he wouldn't be moving to the Hyatt anytime soon.

I turned back to Charles. "What's the problem?" We didn't have much time before Cal and Heather would be returning and I wanted to hear what Charles had to say.

He looked at a crumpled napkin on the sidewalk. "Kevin Starr."

I waited for him to pick it up and put it in the trash. He didn't, so I said, "What about him? He's still Heather's agent, isn't he?"

"Think he's ripping her off."

I had thought that from the moment in Folly after he'd heard her sing and said he'd like to represent her. Her bubbly stage personality made up for much of what she lacked vocally. I still didn't think it would be enough for her to be successful. Heather may be many things and no doubt the best thing that had ever happened to Charles, but a singer, she wasn't.

A few days after Charles and Heather had arrived in Nashville he'd called me and said Starr wanted her to cut an expensive demo CD.

"Did she get the demo she paid for?"

Charles waited for a tour bus to pass before continuing. The smell of burnt diesel fuel washed over us.

"Yeah, the demo was pretty good. It showed Heather at her best."

"What's he done to make you suspicious?"

"Chris, we've met with the man four times. Each time was at a Starbucks over on Church Street. Yeah, it's convenient to our apartment, but each time Heather asked him if we could meet at his office, he told her he meets his artists in different public spots around town. Heather is in love with everything about Nashville and wants to add a trip to a real music agent's office. Starr always says something about how he likes his meetings to be convenient for the client." He paused and looked across the street to the record shop and back at me. "I'm wondering if he has an office."

Heather and Cal were still in Ernest Tubb's. "Don't suppose he has to have an office. He could work out of his house."

"Maybe. That's not all. Heather's appeared at the Bluebird five times. Starr—*her agent*—said he'd be there each time."

"And he wasn't?"

He shook his head. "Plus, we've met other songwriters while we've been standing in line at the Bluebird. Heather's gotten to know a couple of them pretty well. They say Starr Management was handling them. It sounds good and impressive until they start talking and their stories are not a hair different than Heather's. None of them have been struck by fame."

A girl around nine dropped another dollar bill into the street singer's guitar case. The musician smiled and started singing "You Are My Sunshine." The child laughed and her parents stood behind her and smiled.

I waited for the song to finish, watched the parents applaud and turned to Charles. "Have you confronted Starr?"

He shook his head. "You know I'm a detective, well, sort of, and I've—we've—gotten pretty good at it." He pointed at me and at his chest.

Now's when I wished Cal and Heather would run back across the street and interrupt the direction Charles was headed.

"We've been lucky," I said.

"You call it luck, I call it superior detecting skills."

"Whatever."

"Anyway," the faux-detective continued, "I thought since you were heading over anyway, we could talk to Starr. Then we could put our heads together and figure out if he's what he says he is, or if he's ripping us off."

Charles's reason for suggesting I needed a vacation was beginning to come into focus. This was as close as he would come to asking for help and he was the best friend I'd ever had.

"What's Heather's take on Starr?"

Charles looked at another tour bus as it rolled by, at the singer, and finally at me. "She's trying to keep her head up and her cute little grin on her face."

"But?"

"She's POed. She doesn't say he's conning her, although she wanders close to it. I've caught her bawling her eyes out twice. She said it was Tennessee allergies. I didn't believe it." He glanced across the street. "She has a temper, you know."

She was high-strung and could be moody. I nodded.

"I think if Starr had come knocking on our door the day before you got here, he would have been greeted by a frying pan to his toothy smile. She's putting on a good front for you and Cal."

"Is she going to talk to Starr?"

"Don't know. On one hand, she's afraid he's taking advantage of her dreams, and she also wants to believe he's on the up-and-up and is going to make her famous. God, Chris, it tears me up seeing her hurt."

"I know. You're leaning toward him ripping her off?"

He nodded.

"Does she know about your plan to *investigate* the agent?"

"Umm, not yet."

"That's what I thought. When are you supposed to talk to Starr again?"

"He told her he was coming to the Bluebird Monday."

"He's said that how many times and failed to show?"

"I'm playing the law of averages. He's bound to show this time."

My law of consistency says *if he hasn't shown the last five times, he won't be there Monday.*

"What if he doesn't?"

"Tuesday morning we'll set out to find him. After all, I am a detective."

Heather and Cal made their way back from the record store.

Cal shook his head and pushed his Stetson back off his forehead. "Fellas, I remember back in the day when ETs was stocked out the door with records and people. Know what I couldn't find over there until your gal Heather showed me?"

My guess would have been records and people. I didn't want to spoil Cal's story, and said, "What?"

"It's chock full of books, CDs, DVDs, photos, songbooks, souvenirs and a danged actual record section the size of Charles book shelf." Cal pointed in the direction of Charles and Heather's apartment. "To top it off, Heather and I were the only customers in there until a gal came in to see if they had guitar strings. Fellas, I'm dee-pressed." He shook his head again. "Should have let my memories do the walking over there instead of these old calloused feet."

Charles began humming "The Times They Are A-Changin'" but Cal was stuck in his memories and didn't appreciate, or hear Charles.

Heather convinced us we needed to spend culture-accumulating time a couple of blocks from where we were standing over a brew or two at the Tin Roof.

The Tin Roof called itself "A Live Music Joint," and looked a lot like a bar. A male-female duet was playing from the stage that had the front windows as its backdrop. The bar had a balcony, but we opted for a table on the first floor. We didn't want Cal's *old calloused feet* to walk more than they had to. As per Heather's suggestion, our brew became two and we added Tennessee Hot Tops, another brew, and to honor my home state, Charles ordered Kentuckyaki Wings, followed by another brew. The band changed once, our conversation changed several times and Heather changed from the venue's typical music fan enjoying the food and music, to a marketer when she asked the server what it took to get a gig playing there.

The mid-thirties, bearded server gave her a big smile and said, "Get in line, honey. Plumb near every server, bartender, and taxi driver here is ahead of you to the line. We're all singers or song scribes waiting for our big break."

"You too?" Heather said.

"You bet." He pointed to the stage. "I was up there yesterday." He laughed. "Had my fifteen minutes of fame, but drug it out to two sets."

Heather looked at the stage and back at the bartender. "How do I get up there? I've got an agent. Can he contact someone here?"

The server nodded. "Could. It won't do much good. Word of mouth is the best way to get in the bars down here. We know who's good or not and tell our bosses; they tell other bosses and time slots are filled. Word of mouth, honey."

Charles leaned close to me. "See. What good's Starr, even if he's on the up-and-up, which I'm doubtin', seriously doubtin'."

The server told Heather he'd love to stay and talk but had other customers.

A new band had begun its set and Heather leaned closer so we could hear her. "It's what Gwen told me."

Cal said, "Who's Gwen?"

"A friend. Met her at the Bluebird. She's also a songwriter and not a bad singer." Heather rolled her eyes. "She's also a client of Starr Management."

Cal asked, "Has Starr made her famous?"

"No. She's been his client for a couple more months than me. Claims he got her a couple of auditions on Music Row. Gwen said auditions meant getting to hand her demo to someone who acted like a receptionist more than someone important. They said they'd get back with her if there was interest. She's never heard a peep. That gal's pissed at Starr." She huffed. "Don't blame her."

Heather's dark side had made a brief appearance until more drinks followed. She cheered up, Charles asked about getting a Tin Roof T-shirt but declined when the server said they all were short sleeve. We called it a day.

CHAPTER FIVE

Thunderstorms punished the area Sunday and we stayed holed up in the apartment most of the day. Cal was back in his comfort zone and regaled us with countless stories of his days hobnobbing with the "biggies" of country music. I had no doubt there was some truth in his stories involving Patsy Cline, Hank Snow, Roy Acuff and of course, Willie, although I suspected his innate ability as a storyteller and songwriter and years of retelling the tales added his personal spin—aka exaggeration. Regardless, Heather gobbled them up like a bat in a cloud of gnats.

Heather said eating three square meals a day was the key to her singing success, so she and Charles went to get pizza for supper. A bowl of corn flakes, a Velveeta cheese sandwich on stale wholewheat bread and now a cheese-laden pizza will be today's three squares. I wondered if they would improve her singing voice; truth be told, I wondered whether anything short of vocal cord surgery could improve it. While they were gone, I filled Cal in on what Charles and I had talked about.

He listened without interrupting, something I wasn't accustomed to, having been friends with Charles for many years.

I finished and he said, "If Heather handing her demo to a secretary is the best Kevin Starr can do, she'd be better off having yesterday's server as her agent."

I told him that was what I feared.

Cal moved to the window with the scenic overlook of the parking lot, gazed out, snapped his fingers. "Tell you what, pard, hand me your phone and I'll try to track down my old bud Johnny Roman. He was a top-shelf A&R man in my day. If he's above ground, he may know something about Starr."

"A&R?"

"Artists and repertoire. It's the guy who handles stuff between the singer and the label. My friend goes by Johnny R and worked for several record labels. He was responsible for talent scouting, putting together songs with artists, booking the musicians and studios and overseeing the development of artists. It's a big job."

I handed him the phone and he stared at it. "Now, how do I use this iThing contraption?"

Ten minutes later, numerous wrong numbers punched in and finally a helpful electronic voice saying it would connect us to a number listed in the name of Johnny Roman, the phone was ringing. I handed it to Cal. I heard his half of the conversation and gathered Johnny R's daughter answered and her dad was in Oak View, a nursing home in Madison, nine miles north of where we were.

"Wonderful, we'll go see him," Cal finished and handed the phone back to me.

He filled me in on the other end of the conversation, most of which I had figured out.

"How long's he been in the nursing home?"

Cal looked at his hands like he was counting the years on his fingers. "She said nine years. He's a mite older than me, around eighty. Had a stroke and they had to put him in the home. His daughter bought his house and keeps his old phone number because he has so many friends who call. She wanted them to be able to find him."

A soaked Charles and Heather returned with pizza along with a six-pack of Budweiser and a bottle of cheap chardonnay, a concession to yours truly. Heather said it was still raining *felines and pups* and they weren't going out again.

∼

The next morning, Heather was up before anyone else. I was next out of bed, awakened by the non-melodious voice of the girl singer, as Cal politically incorrectly calls her. She was standing behind her music stand, strumming a guitar and practicing one of the two songs she'd written.

She stopped strumming and grinned as I came in the living room. "Practicin' for my big performance tonight. Didn't wake you did I?"

Why would she have thought a guitar playing and her singing as loud as she could ten feet away from where I had been sleeping may have awakened me?

Of course, I lied. "Nah, I was awake. Ready for the Bluebird?"

"Not yet." She shook her head. "I will come singin' time. My agent's going to be there. You'll get to see him again."

"Great," I said, not believing for a second that Mr. Starr and I would be shaking hands at Heather's performance.

She looked at her closed bedroom door, turned back to me and whispered, "Got a favor to ask. I've got to get my head ready for tonight, gotta get my good Chi flowing and ready to channel Patsy Cline's voice." She looked back at the bedroom door. "It takes me all day before a performance as important as the Bluebird. Chuckie doesn't understand. He wants to talk or do things. He's trying to be sweet and doesn't know how he's messing with my Chi. Think you and Cal could get him out of the house? Go somewhere, anywhere and let me do my thing?"

I was skeptical that a day of good Chi would make a difference. I wasn't a psychic or a singer, so what did I know? "We'll try."

Cal and Charles came into the living room at the same time—synchronized waking.

Cal rubbed his hands through his thinning, long hair. "What's for breakfast?"

I glanced at Heather and said, "I've got an idea. Why don't we go out and grab something to eat? I could drive and you and Heather could show us some of the sights outside downtown. It's been years since I saw Vanderbilt, or maybe we could go over to the Hermitage."

Charles looked at me like, "When did you take an interest in universities and historic sites?"

Cal said, "Good idea. I don't need to do any walking today." He lifted and wiggled his bare foot like it was nodding.

Heather said, "Great idea. I've already had breakfast. Why don't you boys go ahead and I'll hang around here and practice."

Charles didn't ask her what she'd found in the bare cupboards to eat and said, "Sure, why not?"

Waffle House fed our stomachs, a quick ride past Vanderbilt University fed our intellectual curiosity and Charles making me stop at three used bookstores quenched his, and only his, need to stock up on books he didn't have. Cal asked me to drive by some of the publishing houses he had been familiar with during his times in Nashville. Several wrong turns later, I managed to find Music Row, an area southwest of downtown where Cal said hundreds of music-related businesses were located. Cal pointed out every house that had been converted to "publishing businesses," more traditional looking office buildings, and a few empty lots he swore used to be buildings where everyone knew him. I asked Charles and Cal to keep a look out for a sign indicating

Starr Management was in one of the structures. They said they would. I wasn't optimistic.

We were on Seventeenth Avenue when Cal pointed to a spot in the middle of the street. "Guys, remember when Heather met Starr in Cal's."

Charles said, "Sure, why?"

I said, "You were concerned that he didn't list the address of his agency on his business card."

"Your point, Cal?" said Charles.

"I said he didn't want every Tom, Dick, and nutcase singing wannabe knocking on his door."

Charles rolled his eyes and repeated, "Your point?"

"I remember back in the 1970s, not sure what year. My mind was a bit fluttered back then. Anyway, one of those wannabes wanted to get an appointment with Chet Atkins in his office right over there." Cal pointed across the street. "Chet was one of the biggest of the biggies in this town in those days, yes he was."

Charles said, "Cal."

"Hold your nosy nose, I'm getting there. Well the wannabe stood out in the center of the street, stripped jaybird naked, and stopped traffic until he got his appointment."

Charles said, "Did he get an appointment?"

"He sure did, got himself a ride in a Nashville police car, and an appointment with a judge. Don't think he ever got to show Chet anything other than his naked butt. That my friends is why many record agents and bigshots don't put addresses on their business cards."

I smiled, more at Charles's irritation than at Cal's story, and said, "Cal, thanks for sharing that bit of Nashville history."

After driving in circles, more accurately, rectangles, around the Music Row area for what seemed like hours, Cal said he was getting dizzy and suggested we park and "walk a spell." We walked two blocks down Music Square East and stumbled on a small park named for Owen Bradley. Cal shared that Bradley had been a songwriter, performer, and influential publisher. I wasn't particularly interested in Mr. Bradley, but was interested in the shade-covered benches in the park. I'd told Heather I would keep Charles and Cal away a few more hours, and was tired of driving.

Charles tapped his ever-present, handmade, wooden cane on the back of the bench. "Fellas, Heather's sure hyped you'll be there tonight. It didn't keep her tears from flowing after you hit the hay last night."

Cal asked, "Why?"

"She's afraid she's been snookered. After the server told her he didn't think an agent could help her get gigs at those restaurants and bars, she's wondering if Starr can do anything for her. That's if he's on the level." He looked over at a homeless man shaving on the next bench, and back at us. "If he's a fraud, she's afraid she'll end up like that poor guy." He nodded his head in the direction of the man shaving.

Cal pushed his Stetson back. "That's just one singing server's opinion. A good agent can work wonders."

A good legitimate agent, I thought.

Charles said, "I'm sure you're right, Cal."

"I know I am. Music's a tough industry to get a toe-hold in and Nashville'll chew up and spit out thousands of aspiring young'uns each year. Heather won't be able to make it on her own; she'll need all the help she can get. It don't come quick, no it don't."

"Cal," Charles said. "You're an expert on this stuff. Be honest. Does Heather have what it takes to make it?"

I looked toward the front of the park at the life-size statue of Owen Bradley seated at a piano and imagined his head shaking.

Cal took off his hat and set it on the bench and took a deep breath before speaking.

Charles said, "Well?"

"There's a history of untalented folks making it here, not many, but a few. Some guys and gals with limited talent have succeeded, again, only a few. And there are numbers too large to count of singers who have talent out their ears and mouths, who never make it. Can I say your gal will? Absolutely not. Can—"

Charles interrupted, "But."

Cal waved his hand in Charles's face. "Let me finish."

Charles stopped in mid-interruption.

"On the other hand, can I say Heather won't succeed? Nope."

Charles waited for Cal to continue. He didn't and Charles said, "The odds are against it."

Cal looked at the Bradley statue and at Charles. "A billion to one."

CHAPTER SIX

We returned to the apartment and Heather's moods swung from euphoric to morose and back again. One minute she was a few feet above cloud nine about her pending performance; the next, her expression said she was ready to bite the head off anyone who dared speak to her. Cal, who had been around performers all his life, understood her fluctuations and said he needed to get some fresh air and "mosey around lower Broadway." He told Heather he knew she had to mentally prepare and would rather be alone. She said it was a good idea and Charles, Cal and I took a leave of absence.

"Heather ain't the Heather I knew," Cal said as we walked along Broadway. "I saw her every time she was in the bar and on the stage. Always happy, always bouncy. And, how about those times she'd sing at the farmers' market back when it was held in that parking lot beside The Washout restaurant. I can still see her standing by the restaurant's wall singing and strummin'. Her beaming personality charmed whoever stopped to listen."

I was glad he'd said it first. I had noticed the change in her moods and behavior. She was quieter, sullener and did something I'd never imagined from her, she leaned toward the negative. She had been one of the most positive people I'd encountered. It was a big part of her endearing charm.

Charles stopped walking and pointed his cane at Cal. "You can say that again."

Cal grinned. "Heather ain't—"

"Got it," Charles said. "You're right. Half the time she's happier than a mouse in a cheese factory. She's lived all her life for this." He waved his cane at the bars on either side of the street. "Now she's pissed at the world."

"What's the problem?" Cal asked.

Charles lowered his cane. "Two words: Kevin Starr."

Cal shook his head and pointed at Charles's cane. "Don't hit me with that thing. It strikes me that it may be a couple of other words."

Charles said, "What?"

"Can't sing."

I took a step away from Charles and his wooden weapon. Instead of swinging it at Cal's head, Charles lowered his head. "I know. She's put all her eggs, and a lot of our bucks, in Starr's basket. Now it's up to more than six-thousand dollars. She thinks he can—"

"Whoa," I interrupted. "Last I heard you'd given him $2,900 for a demo."

"Yeah," Charles said. "I've been afraid to mention the other expenses. Knew you'd blow a gasket."

Cal moved closer to Charles, no longer afraid of his cane. "What'd it go for?"

"Full-service marketing campaign."

"What in Sam Houston does that mean," the Texan asked. "Marketing what? The gal ain't even got a record."

"Starr told us it was the latest in getting word around Nashville, heck, even getting to the music industry big-wigs in New York and

Los Angeles. He said all the newcomers who make it bought the service. He told us because Heather was special, he could swing the deal for *only* $3,700. He said other agents charge more than five grand for the same thing."

"What's the pot load of money get her?" Cal asked. "I've been out of the business for a long time. I ain't ever heard of it. Back in my day, hawking singers meant an eight-by-ten glossy and a howdy."

Charles shrugged. "It gives Starr access to the inner-offices of the publishing and recording companies; gives him money to create marketing materials, mostly digital and electronic, called an EPK. For you newcomers to the music biz, that's an electronic press kit. It's to accentuate her strengths for the potential publishers and recording companies; and ..." Charles hesitated and looked around to see if anyone was listening. "To grease a few palms to get Heather past some of what Starr called *gatekeepers* who'd keep her out."

Cal leaned against the brick wall in front of Jimmy Buffett's Margaritaville Restaurant, glanced at me, and turned to Charles. "When I was growing up in Texas, we called that a crock of shit. Those things are what agents bankroll. Hell's bells, it's what agents do. I think we need to have a confab with this Kevin Starr."

"That's what we're planning to do tonight," I shared.

Cal said, "If the slime bucket shows."

The Bluebird Cafe hosted an open-mic night on Mondays and five times in the last three months Heather was, in her mind, the featured performer. Each week between thirty and forty aspiring songwriters have their three and a half minutes of fame in front of a packed audience. The event began at six o'clock so I wondered why we had to leave at three-thirty for the five-mile drive.

We weaved our way out of downtown and past churches, a residential section, and several suburban shopping areas, and pulled into the parking lot of a large furniture store near the Bluebird. I realized why we had to leave early. Two security guards stood in front of a faded blue awning with *The Bluebird Cafe* in script on it. If Charles hadn't pointed it out, I wouldn't have noticed the iconic venue in the nondescript strip center sandwiched between a Chinese massage parlor, and a hair salon. What I did notice was a line of thirty people standing in the parking lot.

Charles said, "Good, we beat the crowd."

"Are they here for open-mic night?" I asked.

"They sure are," Heather said. "In an hour, there'll be three times that many. Now we'll be able to get in."

Charles explained the Bluebird only held about ninety patrons and most every Monday there were more in line than its capacity. Charles also said since we were in the furniture store's lot a couple of us should do some furniture shopping or we'd get kicked out of the parking space. He said he and I looked the most like we could afford a couch so we went shopping while Heather and Cal got in line. None of the couches were to our liking, nor would fit in Charles and Heather's apartment, so we joined the others in the line which had grown in the short time we'd been couch hunting. The number exceeded the occupancy limit of the building.

"Hey, Gwen!" Heather shouted. She looked at the people near us and back at the woman at the end of the line. "Here we are. Get up here. What took you so long?"

I glanced at Charles who gave a slight shrug. The newcomer strolled past forty people in line behind us, and sidled up to Heather. The group behind us appeared far from happy at the line breaker.

Heather ignored those around us and said to the woman who was around Heather's age, trim, and attractive. "You singing tonight?"

I thought the guitar case in her hand would have given it away.

The newest member of our group said, "You bet."

Heather said, "Meet my friends. You know my guy, Charles. That tall drink of water's Cal Ballew. He's also a country singer. Honest to God, he had a hit record."

"Cool," Heather's friend said. "Have I heard it?"

How would Cal know? I wondered.

Cal tipped his Stetson at Gwen. "It's called 'End of the Story,' hit number seventeen on the national charts."

Gwen said, "Don't recall it."

Heather leaned closer to Gwen and whispered, "It was before you were born."

Cal smiled. "A classic."

Gwen repeated, "Cool."

Heather pointed to me. "The other guy there is Chris Landrum. He's Chuckie's best friend. Him and Cal are over from the beach for a few days. Drove all the way to hear me sing."

"Cool," said Heather's articulate friend.

Heather looked toward Cal and me. "Fellas, Gwen here—Gwen Parsons—is a friend of mine. She's written a whole basket full of tunes and is here as often as I am."

Gwen said, "Pleased to meet all of you."

Cool, I thought.

"Gwen is also handled by Starr Management."

Gwen's smile disappeared. "For what that's worth. You heard from him lately?" she said aimed at Heather.

"No, but he's supposed to be here." Heather hesitated and looked around the gathered group. "Got a few things to iron out with him."

Gwen looked at her guitar case at her feet and at the Bluebird. "I'd like to take an iron to his conniving skull. He'd better show."

"Hadn't made you a star yet?" Charles said, I suspect because he'd been ignored for three minutes.

"Chuckie—umm, Charles—Starr's been my agent for going on

half a year, and all he's done for me is charge me out the ear for a demo tape, tried to get me to buy a freakin' marketing package for more than I could sell my car for, and got me three gigs I later learned I could've gotten myself by asking the bar owners." She pointed to the Bluebird. "This here being one of them." She shook her head. "A star, right."

Gwen's ringing endorsement of her agent was interrupted when a short, chunky man in his thirties tapped Heather on the shoulder. "Yo, Heather, brought that guitar you wanted to try out." He held a guitar case in Heather's face.

Heather hugged the guitar wielding stranger. "Thanks, Joey. Hey guys, this is my friend, Joey."

Cal and I nodded, Charles said, "Hey, Joey," and Gwen looked irritated that he'd interrupted her rant.

"Would you mind putting it in my car?" Heather asked.

"No problem."

"It's the red Toyota Venza that's not supposed to be parked at the furniture store. The lock's broken so slip it in the back seat and cover it with the green blanket. Don't let the furniture guy see you."

"No problem," Joey repeated as he headed to the adjacent lot.

"Joey's a good guy, but not much of a songwriter. His singing's a bit on the weak side, too. You'll get to hear him tonight."

That's something to look forward to.

Heather said, "Seen Jessica?"

I assumed she was talking to either Charles or Gwen since neither Cal nor I would know Jessica.

"Don't think she's around. She usually beats me here. The last time—"

Gwen was interrupted again. This time by a man talking into a megaphone telling the group if they wanted to perform, they needed to sign a slip of paper he was handing out, and a drawing would be held to determine the order of their appearances. Several aspiring stars groaned when he said that since there was a large number of singers, each would be limited to one song. It seemed about every fifth person in line had a guitar case, so there would be a full complement of singers. Heather grabbed one of the sheets and put her name on it in big, block letters so there could be no mistake who she was.

The papers were collected and Gwen yelled, "There's Jessica."

We turned in the direction of a tall, thin woman, in her late-twenties walking toward us with a guitar case in hand and a scowl on her face.

"Seen Starr?" Gwen asked.

The woman standing behind us in line said, "Humph. No breaking line."

Jessica turned to her. "Hold your water, lady. I'm just talking to my friends. Somebody's holding a place for me in the back of the line." She turned to Gwen. "Starr was supposed to meet me yesterday at his *Starbucks office*. I waited two hours, made me late for my waitressing gig. He never showed."

Heather said, "Haven't seen him here."

"He'd better show," Jessica said. "I've got a piece of my mind to give him."

"Get in line," Heather said, not referring to the line to sing.

I suspected Jessica had similar experiences with the illusive and probable con artist who pawns himself off as a music agent. I wondered how many more gullible wannabe singers and songwriters had fallen for his line. And I wondered how Heather's story would end with Starr. I couldn't picture it ending well.

CHAPTER SEVEN

Heather had drawn number thirty-six, Gwen twelve, and Jessica two slots ahead of Heather. Charles told me if songwriters who drew a high number didn't want to wait long to sing, they could have first shot at performing at future open-mic nights. Heather said "no way." Her beach friends were here to hear her and that's what she was going to do even if it took all night.

The door to the Bluebird was opened and the crowd filed in and was seated at vinyl table-cloth covered tables surrounded by wooden chairs. The space was tiny by bar standards and so cramped I doubted everyone in the room could exhale at the same time. A server was at our table as soon as we were seated and took our drink order. The menu was typical bar-fare except for edamame, something I'd never heard of. Charles, the trivia king, said it was young green soybeans in the shell. It sounded too healthy for my taste and I ordered a chicken-fingers basket.

Singer number one was called to the stage before our drinks arrived. She plugged her guitar into the sound system, said her name, her composition, and began singing. Over the next thirty minutes, a steady stream of songwriters moved to the tiny stage with assembly-line efficiency and stood, or sat at a keyboard the bar provided and sang. Talking was close to impossible because of the music, and was discouraged out of respect for the performers. Charles tried to tell me about the photos along the wall, the history of the cafe, and what famous entertainers had performed before the packed-in audiences. I couldn't hear what he was saying. I nodded as if I understood.

I was surprised by the high quality of the performers and their songs, and was even more discouraged about Heather's chances. I was also impressed one of the songwriters was from Australia, two were from England, and one even from far-away, exotic Minnesota.

Gwen's number was called between our first and second round of drinks. She took the stage, gave her name, and said she was from McAlester, Oklahoma, and added it was the hometown of Reba McEntire. Her song was a lilting love song, her voice was pleasant, but nowhere near the quality of her fellow McAlesterian. Heather applauded when Gwen finished, with hopes it would be reciprocated when she finished her song some twenty-two performers later.

An hour and a half passed before Jessica's number was called. Heather, who was scheduled to sing two artists away, was having trouble containing her excitement and nerves. Gwen had stayed after her song to hear Jessica and Heather and applauded when Jessica finished. Heather took her guitar out of the case and bit her fingernails as the next singer performed an up-tempo song accompanying herself on the keyboard.

Heather took the stage, said who she was, and that she was from Nashville. I glanced at Charles who mouthed, "She is now." She sang one of her two compositions, a song I'd heard dozens of times. After three torturous verses, she strummed the last notes to the sounds of applause from everyone at our table, and from no more than four others in the room. Heather smiled as if she had received a standing ovation and thanked the crowd. My heart bled for her. She made it back to the table and received pats on the back from Gwen and Jessica. Charles reached over and gave her a hug. Cal said, "Good job, gal." I nodded and bought her another beer.

We filed out and stood in the parking lot looking at a line stretching past three stores in the shopping center waiting to get in the next show. Three of the people we heard perform were exchanging demo CDs. Two taxis were letting people out and a limo blocked the entrance. Heather stretched her neck to see if its occupants were famous or only people who had enough money to arrive in style.

Gwen and Heather were bragging on each other's set when Jessica approached and whispered something to the other two. They talked for a couple of minutes and Gwen grabbed her guitar case, waved bye to Charles, Cal, and me, and patted Heather on the rear and walked toward the McDonald's a block away.

Cal was telling us a couple of the people in the group, especially one of the "gals" in line before we entered, looked familiar. He wondered if she was someone famous, and Charles said it was no telling who we might see taking in the show, when Heather came over to Charles and waved for Jessica to follow.

"Jess wants me to head downtown with her to a bar so we can "put back a few" and unwind after our performances. Wasn't she great guys?"

We agreed Jessica was great and Charles said if Jessica would have her, he'd let her borrow Heather for a while. Heather gave a wide grin, pecked Charles on the cheek, and handed him her guitar case and wide-brimmed straw hat to put in the car. She told him not to wait up, and headed off with Jessica *to put back a few*.

Cal wiped sleep from his eyes and joined Charles and me in the kitchen. "What time did Heather mosey back to the bunk?"

It was a couple of hours after sunrise and I'd already taken a walk around the neighborhood. Charles was up when I returned and was trying to figure out how many eggs to put in an omelet he was struggling with. He said he'd made omelets although Heather was always around to supervise. She hadn't made an appearance.

"Could've been two-thirty, maybe three-thirty," Charles said without taking his eye off the stove. "Don't know for certain other than it had thirty in it."

Cal said, "Guess you didn't talk a bunch when she got here."

"Think I said 'ugg,' and she may've said, 'Go back to sleep.'"

Charles had finished making breakfast and the smell of burnt omelet filled the air, Cal and I had eaten it and commented on how "interesting" Charles's masterpieces of culinary delight had been and Heather still hadn't ventured out of the bedroom.

Cal glanced at the closed door to Charles and Heather's bedroom. "Think I need to go see my old bud Johnny R today. This Starr Management stuff's getting smellier and smellier. Don't take offense, Charles. It'd be best if she didn't go. No telling what Johnny R might say. He ain't known for beating around the burning bush."

"I'll stay here, and—"

The door of the bedroom creaked open. We turned toward the sound, which was fortunate since Heather whispered, "Morning guys," in a voice we wouldn't have heard unless we were looking. In muted voices, we agreed.

She walked to the table at about the speed of a snail, lowered her body on a chair, and sighed. "Any of y'all see the tour bus that hit me?"

Cal and I shook our head and Charles said, "Feeling poorly, sweetie?"

"If you call a headache that feels like I had three teeth pulled without any knock-out stuff feeling poorly, yeah."

Cal said, "Good show last night?"

Interesting use of the term show, I thought. Heather sang one song, so I suppose Cal was trying to get her mind off her headache.

Heather's eyes were bloodshot and her hand trembled as she lifted her coffee mug. "Thanks, Cal. You don't have to blow smoke up my, umm, posterior. I saw where the clapping came from. I thought I did pretty good, but other than y'all, I bet there weren't three people putting their hands together."

Cal nodded. "Believe you me, I know the feeling, H. Sometimes folks just don't appreciate good music. I've done shows where I thought I knocked it out of the park and the folks sitting out there must've been sitting on their hands."

Her face tried to smile. It was forced, looked painful, and didn't last long. "I'm frustrated Cal. I ain't giving up. I know it'll happen; just wish it'd get here soon."

"You never know, H," Cal said. "You never know."

I thought I did.

Charles looked at Cal, glanced at me, and turned to Heather. "The guys here want to do some sightseeing today, maybe go to the Hall of Fame. You and I could stay here while you're recuperating."

Heather blinked like that was too much information for her ailing head to comprehend. "No, Chuckie, you go. You're a good tour guide and I could use some meditating time."

Cal smiled. "Thanks, H. He could show us the way around."

Cal had achieved his goal of visiting his friend without Heather.

The Country Music Hall of Fame and Museum was five blocks from the apartment so we walked rather than paying to park. According to Charles, the massive building complex with an exterior covered with symbolic images of music replaced the original Hall of Fame in 2001. Its windows mirror the configuration of piano keys and the overall façade seemed overwhelming. The sights and sounds inside were as impressive. Cal added his personal narrative to many of the displays. Walking through the museum with him felt like I was living part of country music history. The tour lasted two hours longer than necessary after we paused to hear each of Cal's "fascinating" stories.

We returned to the apartment and Charles checked on Heather before we headed to Madison to find Johnny R. She said she wasn't any better and for us to take our time. The nine-mile trip took longer than expected. A four-car accident had the road closed and we had to take a detour.

While Madison was easy to find, the nursing home presented a more difficult challenge since it was a mile outside town on a road that had befuddled the car's navigation system. Charles finally ran in Shoney's to ask for directions while Cal strummed on an imaginary guitar and sang Hank Snow's "I've Been Everywhere." It felt like a piece of the Hall of Fame had escaped and was sitting in a car entertaining the driver.

We walked through the double door of the nursing home that didn't look younger than its residents, and were slapped by the ever-present smell that must be sold only to nursing homes. Nothing about the odor said welcome. No one was at the desk, but a man sweeping the floor pointed us in the direction of Johnny R's room, smiled and said, "Get ready. He's having a mood."

Cal's friend must've been huge in his better days. He was lying on his side and the droopy skin of a three-hundred-pound man dangled from a body that couldn't have topped one seventy. Johnny R glanced at the visitors, dropped a copy of *People Magazine*, and smiled.

"Holy shit. I must have died and landed in the bad place. If it ain't my buddy Country Cal right here in Hillbilly Hell." He tried to sit, and fell back in the bed.

Cal moved to his side, bent over, and gave him a hug. They

exchanged a couple of insults and Johnny R tilted his head my direction and asked Cal who his roadies were.

Cal introduced us to the man he'd told us was eighty, but looked to be pushing triple digits. "What'd you do horrible enough to my bud Cal to get him to drag you out here?"

Charles, in his best suck-up voice, said, "We're friends of Cal and were visiting the high points of Nashville. He said unless we met his good friend Johnny R our tour would've been wasted."

Johnny R looked at the stained ceiling, at me, and finally at Charles. "See why y'all are friends. You're as full of shit as Cal. You a singer? You have that beat-down look."

I figured he wasn't talking to me since I didn't think I looked beat-down. I answered anyway and told him we were from South Carolina and visiting a friend of ours.

"So why are you really in this old man's castle in the heart of Geezerland?"

"Johnny R ain't never been strong about editin' his words," Cal said in my direction. He turned to Johnny R. "Wantin' to pick your brain."

Johnny R chuckled. "Good luck with that. My old thought-machine's being starved in here. Not much left. Know what they won't let me do?"

Trivia-collector Charles asked, "What?"

"I can't smoke. The nicotine police say it's bad for my health. Do I look like I have enough health to worry about?" He hesitated and caught his breath. "And, get this, they won't let me have sex with the nurses. Can you believe it?"

None of us responded.

"They have more rules than the IRS. Anyway, I'm sure you didn't drive out in the middle of nowhere to talk about my sex life."

Cal knew what to say and how to say it, so we deferred to him. Cal shared that Charles's main squeeze had signed with Starr Management and had become disappointed with the results. He didn't put it like that. That's my translation of his country-music insider lingo.

Johnny R waited for Cal to finish and continued to stare at him. "Cal, look around. Do I strike you like I'm in the center of anything related to the music industry? How in the name of Jimmy Rogers am I supposed to know anything about moon, planet, star, or whatever the guy's name is you're talking about?" Johnny R was getting louder by the word. "Hell, most of the people in here think Al Jolson just recorded 'Mammy.'"

"Don't blow a gasket." Cal put his hand on his friend's shoulder. "We knew you wouldn't know Starr, but I have a suspicion you still have contacts and maybe you could check around." Cal leaned closer to Johnny R. "You're the man. Think you can help out an old buddy?"

Johnny R leaned back in bed and smiled. "Give me a few days and a number where I can reach you. I'll see what I can find."

"Much obliged, my friend. Much obliged."

Cal gave his old friend his number and another hug. Charles and I shook his emaciated hand before we headed to the door.

Johnny R said, "On your way out, fellas, see if any of the nurses out there are hankering to have sex with me. There's one cutie, Mildred, couldn't be a day over seventy, but hey, I'm not above robbin' the cradle. Let her know I won't tell on her."

Cal said he would. To Charles and my relief, he didn't.

On the way to town, Cal said that in his heyday, there wasn't anything Johnny R couldn't find out. Charles astutely observed that Cal's friend didn't appear to be involved like he once was. Cal agreed, and said even though Johnny R seemed out of it, he probably still had more connections than some insiders. I doubted it, although Cal knew his friend and I didn't. Charles also suggested instead of waiting for Johnny R, we should call Starr and ask what he was doing for Heather.

Cal and I didn't enthusiastically jump at the idea. That didn't stop Charles from looking up the agent's number and dialing. He listened and instead of talking to someone or leaving a message, Charles hit *End Call* and shook his head.

"What?" Cal asked.

Charles looked at the phone. "Machine said the boy's message contraption's full."

Cal asked, "What do we do now?"

"Head to his house, knock, and say, *Surprise, we caught you.*"

It was nearing my bedtime and I suggested we save the surprise for tomorrow.

Charles said, "Suppose we can wait." Cal said, "Hallelujah!" It was after ten when we traipsed into the apartment. Heather wasn't there but had left a note on the table telling us not to wait up.

I was exhausted and it didn't take a note for me to not wait up. I did wonder what tomorrow and a trip to Kevin Starr's house would bring.

CHAPTER EIGHT

The day started much like yesterday. Charles was in the kitchen attempting to fix breakfast. This time it was toast and scrambled eggs. I knew it was Charles's toast because I was familiar with the aroma of burnt bread as it drifted through the apartment. Also, as was the case yesterday, Heather was nowhere to be seen and her bedroom door was closed.

I looked at the clump of eggs in the skillet. "Heather teach you to do that?"

"Tried to teach me how to fix them over easy. I taught myself that when they plop out of the shell all a mess, I can slush them around and say they were supposed to be scrambled."

"Your secret's good with me." I scraped the blackened coating off the toast. "Heather sleeping in?"

Charles glanced at the bedroom door and back at the skillet. "Yeah. Don't know when she got in this morning. Didn't hear a thing." He again looked at the door. "Chris, I'm worried about her. She's moping around and on the verge of tears more often. Her temper's getting as short as a speck of dust."

"Think she's worried her dreams will never be more than dreams?"

Charles scraped the eggs on two plates, looked at his bedroom door and at the closed door to Cal's and my room, and put the plates on the table. "Guess it's you and me feasting alone."

"Their loss," I said as I wondered how Heather and Cal would survive without burnt toast and over-scrambled eggs.

"Think it's more about Kevin Starr than her dreams. She's growing a hate for that man, I'm afraid."

I had learned Charles's answers could come any time after a question. He'd gone days before getting around to the answer. Yet, if he asked something and the response didn't come before a breath could be taken, he'd be asking again.

"She's a lot like you," I said. "She tries to like everyone and looks for the good in the worst folks."

Charles took a bite of toast. "Yuck." He dropped it on his plate. "President Garfield said, 'I am a poor hater.' He and I agree. Heather used to be; now I'm afraid she's getting pretty good at hating."

"What's that about me, Chuckie?" Heather's sleepy voice asked as she opened the door.

She had a smile on her face and wore a long red, white, and blue striped nightgown that looked like an American flag. She pecked Charles on the forehead.

"Nothing, sweetie. We were wondering if you got enough sleep."

She looked at his plate. "See you were playing Emeril LaChuckie again."

LaChuckie said, "Want me to fix you some?"

"Not hungry. Had some food late. What are we doing today, fellas?"

For whatever reason, Heather appeared to be either over or taking a break from hating and being depressed. I didn't know if

Charles had wanted her to go with us to find Starr, I deferred to him.

"Umm, Cal wanted to see Kevin Starr since he didn't get a chance to talk to him in Folly or at the Bluebird. They have a lot in common, being they're both in the music business."

Heather said, "Oh."

"Yeah," Charles continued. "Cal thought it'd be good to see if Starr was at home where they could talk without being interrupted."

"I'll be back," I said. "Got to get something out of the bedroom." I neglected to say I had to get to Cal before he talked to Heather so he'd know who he wanted to see today, along with why, and where. "Don't eat all my breakfast, Heather."

She turned up her nose at the eggs.

I shook Cal awake, told him *his* plans, and returned to the kitchen and my one-star breakfast.

An hour later, we were following the car's automated GPS directions across the Cumberland River and six miles away from the apartment through the East Nashville section of the county. Charles had finagled Starr's home address from someone he had met at one of Heather's open-mic appearances. Signs on a building indicated we had reached Five Points where, you guessed it, five roads converged. The navigation system led us through the confusing intersection and had us turn right at Three Crow Bar. From the looks of the small, well-maintained homes, East Nashville and Five Points was made up of a mix of artsy and eclectic residents. Several of the houses were colorfully painted, a few had large sculptures in the yard.

"Cute as a cricket," Heather chirped, as she pointed to a yellow, converted VW minibus that was home to a hotdog stand named I Dream of Weenie. It wasn't open or Heather would have made us stop for lunch and would have forgotten about our destination. The mechanized voice from the navigation system wasn't impressed by I Dream of Weenie and led us another block before announcing: "You have reached your destination." A decorative wrought-iron gate greeted us in front of a light-green bungalow. It was situated on a narrow, deep lot. A concrete-block building was at the back of the lot with a swing set between the structures. The house and its surroundings were idyllic and looked like a set for a Hallmark movie. It was the last place I would expect to find a con artist.

Charles knocked four times and I was about to think we wouldn't be finding a con artist, or anyone else at home. Heather had walked around the side of the house and returned and waved for us. We followed her toward the building where I heard a whooshing noise and what sounded like steel striking steel.

Charles, who'd never feared to tread most anywhere, looked in the open door. The rest of us stood behind him.

"Yo, hello!" he yelled over the loud whooshing. Heat rolled out the entry, adding to the already hot morning.

The hammering stopped and Charles stepped back. We were greeted by an attractive, petite woman. She was no more than five-foot-two, in her thirties, had her hair tied in a bun and wore a black leather blacksmith apron over jeans and a white T-shirt. Black streaks mixing with perspiration covered part of her face. She had an oversized ball-peen hammer in her leather-gloved hand, and if she hadn't been so short and attractive would have looked like someone I wouldn't want to meet in a haunted house.

"May I help you?" she said in a throaty voice. "We didn't have an appointment, did we?"

Charles asked, "Are you Mrs. Starr?"

She glanced at the rest of us; her gloved hand tightly gripped the hammer. "Yes. Again, may I help you?"

I didn't blame her for being leery of four strangers at her door, particularly when one was tall and wore a Stetson, two others wore tan Tilleys, and the fourth person had on a yellow dress brighter than a caution light.

I stepped beside Charles. "Pardon our rudeness, let me introduce everyone." I proceeded to tell her who we were and that Heather was one of her husband's clients.

Mrs. Starr removed her leather glove, set the hammer on the ground, told us to call her Sandy, and shook hands. She said she was a blacksmith and sculptor and asked us to join her on the porch after saying the studio was too hot for normal humans.

"I've never met a blacksmith," Charles said, a statement most of us could make, as Sandy pointed to chairs on the porch. The porch was shaded by the house and more comfortable than her studio or standing in the sun. Neat and quaint were the words that kept coming to mind. Again, not the home of a con artist.

Cal asked, "What kind of blacksmithin' do you do?"

Sandy pointed at a metal table with a glass top in the corner of the porch. Its legs were wrapped in decorative, metal vines with leaves on them, and a framed photo with three children posed in white shirts and huge smiles sat on the glass top.

"That kind of stuff. Do mainly commission work for high-end builders. Stair railings and such, and tables for designers."

Heather pointed at the photo. "Them your young'uns?"

Sandy looked at the photo. "Getting older by the day. Steve, Kevin Jr., and Dolly; four, five, and seven."

Heather said, "Cute as crickets."

I wondered what Sandy would have thought if she knew Heather had said the same thing about the hotdog stand.

Sandy smiled. "Thanks. I don't suppose you came out here to see what I make back there." She nodded toward her studio. "Or to hear about the kids."

Heather leaned forward in her chair ready to respond. Charles beat her to it. "No, but it was interesting hearing about your work, and your kids are adorable."

Sandy nodded. "But?"

Charles said, "We were looking for Kevin. Heather was performing a couple of nights ago at the Bluebird and Kevin was supposed to be there and was going to talk to us about her career. We were worried when he didn't show and his phone message machine's full up."

Sandy's smile faded. "Oh, I'm so sorry. That must be why I got the other calls."

Charles tilted his head to the side. "Other calls?"

"Yes, two women called the last couple of days asking for Kevin. It was strange because all his clients have his cell number and he doesn't give out our home phone. Maybe he was supposed to meet them too. I asked if I could take a message and they said no."

"Did you get their names?" I asked.

"They didn't give them. One sounded young and the other older, about your age, Heather."

Charles asked, "Did you tell your husband?"

Sandy looked at her studio and at the floor. "No. He's, umm, been away for a few days and I haven't had a chance to tell him."

"Oh," Charles said. "Where is he?"

Sandy hesitated and looked at the porch floor. "Don't know. Haven't seen him since Sunday morning. I was working on a project for a builder in Franklin and had to get it done by Monday. The kids are with my parents over in Hendersonville, and to be honest, I didn't miss Kevin until that night."

Charles said, "Does he leave often?"

Sandy tried to smile. "There's a lot of travel with his business. Sometimes he has to go to Memphis, or up to Kentucky, and North and South Carolina to meet with potential clients and other music execs. It's a demanding business. I'd rather be pounding steel." She nodded toward the outbuilding.

"He doesn't tell you where he goes?" I said.

"I get caught up in my work and block out everything but the kids. He tells me, but it's in one ear, out the other." She chuckled. "He usually calls a couple of times when he's on the road."

"Not this time?" I said.

Sandy continued to look at the floor. "No. You don't even know me and I don't want to burden you, but I'm worried. It's not like him to be gone three days without calling."

Cal asked, "Did he take a holdall with him?"

"A what?" Sandy asked.

Good question, I thought.

Cal said, "Suitcase."

"Oh, no. He keeps a travel bag in his car. Says he has to leave from downtown sometimes and doesn't want to have to come out here to pack."

"Tell you what," Charles said. "Let me give you my number. Give me a holler when you hear from him. In the meantime, we'll check around. We'll find him."

Sandy took the number, said she'd call Charles when she heard from him, and said she was sorry we missed her husband.

"Check around. We'll find him," I parroted Charles as we piled in the car.

Charles looked back at the Starr house. "Maybe the boy's not quite the rip-off, con man I thought he was. Nice wife, *cute as cricket* kids, maybe the boy's in trouble. Who wouldn't call them if everything was okay?"

"Now Chuckie," Heather said. "It's none of our business."

That'd never stopped Charles before. It wouldn't now.

CHAPTER NINE

On the drive to town, Charles, Cal, and I talked about where we could look for Starr. After ten red traffic lights, and a near collision with a garbage truck, we didn't have any more idea where to find him than we did finding an Eskimo in Nashville. Heather proved to be the smartest person in the car; she slept the entire trip.

"Got an idea," Cal said as he climbed the stairs with the aid of the handrail. "Got another buddy here, name's Vern Watson. I'll catch my breath, pop open a beer, and give him a holler."

That meant I'd have to find Vern Watson's number.

Heather declined a beer and said her headache had returned and she was going to catch more shuteye. The only name close to Vern Watson that directory assistance knew about was V. Watson, who turned out to be a woman named Veronica who worked at a Nashville bank and had never heard of Cal's friend.

"Got another idea," Cal said. "Vern's a retired steel guitar player, was in the Opry house band for a spell. The boy played steel guitar and the ponies—better at the guitar. I'll call the union and see if they still have his card."

That meant another number to find for my connected friend. The offices were closed so Cal would have to wait until morning. None of us wanted to, or had the energy to wander out, so we spent a couple of hours staring at the walls before heading to bed.

Cal managed to get a real person on the phone the next morning. The woman he talked to was helpful—sort of. Vern Watson was no longer in the musician's union; no longer a member because he'd gone to the great recording studio in the sky seven years ago. I could almost see the wheels turning in Charles's head where he was going to tell Cal that learning anything from Watson was a dead end.

A knock on the door prevented Charles from making the tasteless joke.

Cal was nearest to the door, opened it, and was greeted by two dour-faced men, one tall at around six-foot three, the other a half foot shorter, although he carried about the same weight except much of it drooped over his belt. Both wore dress slacks, wrinkled blazers, and cheap-looking ties. They weren't starving musicians.

"I'm Detective Lawrence," the tall one said. "This is Detective Rogers." Lawrence looked at a note in his hand. "Is this where Eileen Gordon Smith lives?"

"You've got the wrong crib," Cal said. "No Eileen—"

Charles stepped in front of Cal. "She lives here. Why?"

The detectives looked at each other and then Lawrence glared at Cal. "Need to get your story straight, cowboy."

Cal still had on his Stetson and started to speak.

"Cal," Charles said, "It's Heather's name. She stopped using it a few years back when she wanted to reinvent herself."

The shorter, and younger detective, held his hand between Charles and Cal. "Is Ms. Smith here?"

Charles turned to the detective. "Heather—Eileen—isn't up yet. Why?"

Lawrence looked at his watch. "Please get her. May we come in? You don't want us standing out here talking to her."

I didn't know why they were here, yet I doubted we wanted them talking to her in the hall or anywhere else. Charles opened the bedroom door and whispered something. A long minute later Heather walked in, blinked a couple of times, and wiped her eyes. Charles told her the two detectives wanted to talk to her and Detective Lawrence took the lead and introduced himself and his partner. Lawrence asked if she had a few minutes to talk. It was apparent she didn't have a choice. Heather nodded and kept glancing over at Charles. Lawrence suggested that he, his partner, and Heather have seats in the living room and the rest of us "might be more comfortable in the kitchen." Again, it wasn't a suggestion, and Cal, Charles, and I moved to the kitchen and gathered around the table.

Cal removed his Stetson and set in on the table and whispered to Charles, "What's going on?"

Charles looked at the door leading to the living room and shrugged.

There were many drawbacks to the tiny size of the apartment. One plus became apparent when we heard everything being said in the other room. Charles's chair was farthest from the living room and he scooted it around the table to be closer.

"Ms. Smith," Detective Lawrence said, "where were you Monday night?"

"I go by Heather Lee now. Think you could call me that?"

"But you are the Eileen Gordon Smith, in the system for grand theft auto?" Detective Rogers said.

Heather sighed. "It was a long time ago, and all I did was borrow my ex-boyfriend's car and it wasn't my fault that a deer ran across the road and I tried to miss it and ended up in the river. The car didn't even sink. The ex got himself pissed and called the cops and—"

"Enough," Lawrence interrupted. "The point is you are Ms. Smith."

"Umm, yes."

Cal leaned close to Charles. "You knew that?"

"Sure."

Cal turned to me and held out his hand. "You too?"

I whispered, "Yes. She likes telling that story and that she changed her name."

Cal looked at the ceiling. "I could've written a song about it."

"Shh," Charles whispered. "I'm trying to listen."

"To my question, Ms. Smith—Heather. Where were you Monday night?"

"That's easy. I was singing at the Bluebird Cafe. I'm a country singer and it was open-mic night. My friends in there were with me."

She must have pointed toward the kitchen. Cal and Charles nodded when she told the detectives where she was.

"When did you leave the Bluebird?" Lawrence asked.

"Let's see, it was going on nine o'clock. Why?"

"Then what did you do?"

"Oh yeah, I hitched up with one of my singing buddies and came downtown for a couple of brews. We were celebrating our performances."

Rogers asked, "Who was your singing buddy?"

Heather told them Jessica Sayre, the detectives had her spell it, and asked where they went. Heather gave them the name of a lower Broadway bar.

"What time did you leave the bar?"

"Ten-thirty or so. Jess got a call and said she had to meet up with someone, her boyfriend. I'm guessing it was him; she didn't tell me."

"Then where'd you go?"

"Why?"

Rogers said, "Answer, please."

"Okay, okay. I was still hyped from singing and walked around downtown a couple of hours or so. Not certain exactly how long. Everyone was asleep when I got back here."

"Anybody see you during that time?"

"Why sure. There were a bunch of people out and about."

Lawrence said, "Anybody who was able to vouch for where you were?"

There was a long pause before Heather said, "Don't reckon. I didn't talk to anyone. I stopped in a couple of the bars but spent most of the time walking around. I love this city, don't you?"

Lawrence asked, "Do you know Kevin Starr?"

"Sure. He's my agent."

"Did you see him Monday night?"

"No sir. He was supposed to be at my performance but didn't show. Are you looking for him too?"

"What do you mean?"

"Me and my friends went out to his house yesterday looking for him. Talked to Sandy, that's his wife, a cute little gal. Did you know she's a blacksmith? Can you believe that? Sandy said he'd been gone for a few days and didn't know where he was. Guess she told you. Whew, I'm glad y'all are looking for him."

There were a few seconds of silence and finally Rogers said, "When was the last time you saw Mr. Starr?"

"Must've been a week. Met him at Starbucks."

"You haven't seen him since?" Rogers said.

Charles was tapping his fingers on the table, Cal was leaning toward the door to hear everything, and I was getting a bad feeling.

"No sir. Any good leads on where he's gone to?"

"Your friends in there were with you at the Bluebird but not later, and they were with you at Mr. Starr's house yesterday?"

"That's what I said."

A few seconds later, Detective Lawrence stepped in the kitchen and asked us to join him in the living room. There was only room for one of us to sit so Charles and I deferred to age and motioned for Cal to take the chair. Lawrence waited for us to get situated and asked about Monday night, rehashing all the details he had covered with Heather. We acted like we hadn't heard their conversation and acted surprised by the questions. He asked about our trip to Starr's house. Charles did most of the talking and talked way more than the detectives wanted to hear about the kiln, the building behind the house, and Sandy's clients. Heather interrupted once to tell Charles to make sure he tells about the hotdog stand.

Detective Lawrence maintained eye contact but his partner kept looking around the room and appeared like he would be happier being somewhere else. Charles's trivia-infused conversations can have that effect on people.

"One more question," Lawrence said after Charles paused for a breath. "Whose idea was it to go to Starr's house?"

Strange, I thought, and turned to Charles who told the detectives it was his idea.

Cal pointed at the lead detective. "Now, Mr. Detective, I think we've answered all your questions. How about answering one for us?"

"What?"

"Where do you think Starr's gone? Seems strange his wife didn't know."

Lawrence glanced over at his partner and turned back to Cal. "I'm afraid he didn't go anywhere. Mr. Starr's dead."

"Oh, my God!" Heather shrieked. She started to stand and fell back on the couch.

"When? What happened?" I asked. "Car accident?"

"Afraid not, sir," Lawrence said. "Mr. Starr was murdered."

"Oh, my God!" Heather repeated.

The detectives stood and Lawrence handed Heather his card. "Thank you for your time. If you think of anything else, please call. And, please don't leave town."

Heather took the card and tilted her head toward Lawrence. "Am I a—"

Lawrence cut her off. "Again, thank you for your time."

And they were gone, sucking all the air out of the room with them.

CHAPTER TEN

"Oh, my God," Heather repeated for the tenth time after the detectives ruined our morning. "Do they think I had something to do with...with his murder?" she asked no one in particular.

From the line of questioning she was without doubt a suspect, if not the prime suspect. Instead of reminding her of the obvious, I said they were talking to anyone who had a connection to Starr, and that had to be many people.

"Especially if he was a con man," Cal added.

A tear rolled down Heather's cheek. "But he was my agent. He was going to make me a star. He was going to … now he's dead."

It was clear Mr. Starr had met his demise sometime Monday evening after Heather had left the Bluebird with Jessica. Since his wife didn't know anything about it during our visit, he must not have been found until yesterday. His death could have been mentioned in today's paper, on television, or the radio.

"Charles, where can I get a newspaper?"

He thought there was a stand by the coffee shop on the next

block, and I asked if anyone wanted to go with me. My question was met with blank stares.

I found the stand and grabbed a paper. A perusal of the Local section of the *Tennessean* made me realize we were probably the only people in town who didn't know about Kevin Starr's demise. The headline read: "Music Executive Murdered." I skimmed the article before taking it back to the apartment where I knew I'd be battling the others over it. The article revealed Starr was found yesterday morning in an industrial trash dumpster a block east of lower Broadway, no more than three blocks from the apartment. The body was found through luck and a habit of the worker emptying the dumpster. The truck driver said he had seen a television story a couple of years ago where a body was found in a dumpster. Since then, he'd been careful to watch the contents of the dumpsters he'd emptied into his truck. He said he couldn't live knowing he may have dumped someone without knowing it. The reporter speculated if it weren't for an obsessed employee, Mr. Starr would have never been found. The article went on to tell about Starr's business and his wife and three children. My stomach sank when the article said the coroner revealed his death was caused by a gunshot wound and placed the time of death between late Monday evening and Tuesday sunrise. Much of that time Heather was with Jessica or walking around Nashville by herself. She'd told the detectives that she'd not been seen by anyone who would remember her.

All eyes were glued to the paper when I entered the apartment. I folded it so the article was on top and dropped it on the table. Cal, Charles, and Heather surrounded the table and started reading.

A couple of profanities later, and Cal saying something about excrement hitting a fan, Heather said, "I feel terrible about poor Sandy and those three chillens. What'll they do?"

Charles reassured her the Starr family would be okay, Cal said being stuffed in a dumpster was a terrible way to leave this world, and I wondered if everyone in the room—particularly Heather—

realized the aspiring singer could be the prime suspect. A suspect with motive and no alibi.

Heather moved to the living room and plopped down on the couch and Charles sat beside her. Cal stayed in the kitchen and continued reading, and I moved to the window and stared at the parking lot three floors below. Charles had his arm around Heather and I heard him saying she hadn't done anything wrong and had nothing to fear from the police. I had known the psychic/massage therapist/country crooner since the day she and Charles had met seven years ago. She was as quirky as a one-armed, albino one-man-band, as friendly as an Irish setter, and from everything I had seen, as harmless as a ladybug.

Then again, there had been a marked change in her demeanor since she'd arrived in Nashville. She was moody, shown an explosive temper I hadn't seen before, and while she masked it in front of Cal and me, was irate at Kevin Starr. Was she capable of putting a bullet in him and stuffing him in a dumpster? Capable, I suppose; likely, I honestly didn't know. What I did know was Charles was in no position to assure her she had nothing to worry about.

Cal was still in the kitchen when Heather grabbed Charles's phone and punched in some numbers. She waited a few seconds, and rolled her eyes, "Gwen, this is Heather. Listen, some cops just left. Did you hear someone killed our agent? Umm, there's more, call me when you get this."

She slammed the phone on the table. "Danged answering machines. The devil's gift to people who want to irritate other people."

Charles said, "You've got that right, sweetie."

She went in the bedroom, returned with a scrap piece of paper, and called the number on it.

"Hey, Jess, this is Heather … yeah. Did you hear about Kevin Starr?" There was a long pause and Heather flopped down on the couch. "Yeah, okay, the cops were here and said it happened after we left the Bluebird." Another pause. "Yes, it could have been after we split. Where did you say you were going after I left you?" A longer pause. "Oh, that's too bad. Seen him since then?" This time a shorter pause. "Sorry. What'd the cops ask?" A long pause. "Me too. Wasn't it scary when they told you not to leave town?" By now Charles was pointing to the phone and imitating someone talking into a megaphone; Charles-speak for put it on speaker. Heather ignored him. "They didn't." Another pause. "Oh, okay, talk to ya later."

She ended the call and flipped the phone in Charles's lap. "Shit."

I wasn't a psychic like Heather. I had heard enough to figure out Jessie had already talked to the police and was warned to not leave town. Not a good sign. I also didn't know what her alibi was, since from what I'd heard earlier, she was as unhappy with Starr as Heather was.

I asked, "Where did she say she went after you parted company?"

"Her boyfriend called and asked her to meet him at the Wildhorse Saloon but he wasn't there when she got there. Said she didn't wait and went home."

Charles said, "Isn't it weird he calls and asks her to meet him and doesn't show?"

"Not really. Her fella's kind of erratic. I think she ought to dump him." She sighed. "You know how blind love is."

If he wasn't there, I wondered what Jessica's alibi was for the time Starr was killed. "She live by herself?"

"She's got a cat. Cute little calico named Kitty."

I doubted her cat would be much of an alibi. "Anybody live with her?"

"Nah."

On the surface, Jessica would have had as much reason to kill

Starr as Heather had. What if the call she received was from Starr and not her boyfriend and she left Heather to meet the agent?

Cal asked, "Was the Jessica gal pissed enough at Starr to shoot him?"

Heather bowed her head and tapped her foot on the floor. She whispered, "Don't know, she was pretty angry. He was about all we talked about the other night. Could have, I suppose."

If that's the case, I wondered why the police hadn't told her not to leave town. Or did they?

My phone rang.

"Good morning, Brother Chris. Is this a bad time?"

The reference to Brother Chris and the polite way he asked if it was a bad time, told me it was Preacher Burl. I lied and said it was a good time.

"Good. Is Brother Cal in the vicinity? I'd like to speak with him."

I said he was five feet away and started to hand him the phone. Burl said I could listen if I wanted to, and he joked he wasn't going to say anything horrible about me. I tapped the speaker icon and told Burl that Cal was listening. So was nosy Charles, but I didn't mention that.

Cal said, "Hey, Preacher Burl. Is everything okay at the bar?"

"Fine. I tried your number—"

"Dead battery; forgot to charge it. Sorry. Is everything okay?"

"Yes, sir. It's busy. I—"

Cal held up his hand, and interrupted, "Not trying to convert my pickled patrons, are you?"

"Heavens no," Burl said, with an emphasis on *heavens*. "Everyone in last night said they were coming to the service Sunday and starting a choir. I think it was because they were reading the Bibles I put on each table, or maybe because I switched out all your old country songs in the jukebox with hymns."

"What?" Cal shouted.

I covered a smile with my palm.

"Kidding, Brother Cal. Preachers can have a sense of humor."

"Thank Go—goodness. You made my heart upchuck."

"Yes. Your customers don't have to listen to hymns. I turn the jukebox off during each evening's prayer meeting."

"Amen," Charles said.

"Hi, Brother Charles," Burl said. "I figured you'd be nearby. Is Sister Heather there as well?"

"I'm here." She smiled for the first time this morning.

Cal said, "Preacher Burl, you didn't call to stop my heart, did you?"

The preacher chuckled. "No, but doing so brought a touch of joy to my soul."

"Well?" Cal said.

"Brother Caldwell was in last night and wanted to know when you will be returning."

Caldwell Ramsey was my friend Mel Evan's significant other. I had known Mel, the owner of Mad Mel's Magical Marsh Machine, a marsh tour boat, for several years. He was a retired marine who found a niche in the tour business by taking groups of college students on excursions with the objective of his customers hiding out in the marsh and consuming alcoholic beverages. I didn't know Caldwell as well as I did Mel, but he seemed like a great person, somehow put up with Mel's rough edges, which encompassed most of his edges, and was a concert promoter in Charleston who worked with small venues and lesser-known bands.

Cal said, "Not certain when I'll be back. What's Caldwell want?"

"He didn't give me details but it has something to do with someone wanting to convert a failing bar to a country music location. Brother Caldwell said he wants to pick your brain about what would work best."

Cal said, "Hope the bar ain't in Folly."

"It's in Charleston. I don't picture it interfering with my nightly prayer meetings in Cal's."

"Funny. Tell him I don't know when I'll be back. It'll be in a few days; I'll call him when I get there, and after I run the Holy Spirit out of Cal's."

"Funny," Burl said, with more enthusiasm than Cal had. "One more thing. This bartending, cleaning, opening and closing, and using my limited bouncer skills are taking a toll on this old, chubby body. The sooner you return the better."

"I'm working on it Preacher."

"Much obliged. I'll pray for your safe return during tonight's free beer and preaching at Cal's."

He ended the call, but it didn't stop Cal from mumbling, "Funny."

CHAPTER ELEVEN

I woke the next morning to Cal strumming his much-travelled guitar and singing, "I'm So Lonesome I Could Cry." I yawned, opened the door and looked around the living room and only saw Cal. Heather and Charles's door was closed. Cal stopped strumming and asked if his singing was the reason I was up. I said no and asked if anyone else was moving around. The country crooner reported Heather was "sawing logs" and her Chuckie was "strollin' around Music City."

Cal looked at the closed bedroom door and waved for me to join him on the couch. "I do my best thinking when I'm singing songs that I've sung a few thousand times. My mind wanders out past the words to where they don't get in the way."

"What are you thinking about?"

He glanced again at the bedroom door and leaned closer to me. "Think Heather's in a cow pie field full of trouble."

Cal must be as psychic as Heather, and I wondered why it took singing to figure out she was in trouble. I also wondered what he was referring to, so I asked.

Cal leaned his guitar against the couch. "Let's see, first, she's got a pent-up load of anger at that so-called agent. Second, she thinks he ripped her off on the demo and the stupid-ass PR package. Third, out of all the nights she's finagled her way to the stage at the Bluebird, he's managed to show up zero times. And cripes, it almost slipped my mind, fourth, two cops showed up giving her the third degree." He looked at her door, lowered his head. "Chris, her alibi holds as much water as a tennis racket."

"You think she killed him?"

"Don't matter a termite turd what I think. I ain't the police, judge, or jury."

"That didn't answer my question."

"Don't seem like Heather, but these old bloodshot eyes have seen stranger things. Tell you what I do know."

He paused. I figured I wouldn't have to ask.

"We've been here going on a week and I can't continue to impose on the good preacher to keep running the bar. I need to mosey back."

I hated to leave Charles with everything going on, but couldn't think of anything I could do to help. I offered to head home today if Cal was ready. He told me I didn't need to go and he could take a bus or hitchhike. I told him those were two of the dumbest ideas I'd heard from him, and said we'd leave once Charles returned and we could say bye to Heather.

He strummed and sang, "Thaaaank you."

Charles returned an hour later and said he loved the sweet aroma of stale beer along the sidewalks of Broadway. Heather made her appearance and I nearly saluted her in her patriotic gown. I shared that Cal needed to get home and I was taking him. Charles and Heather protested, yet I could hear relief in their voices. The apartment was barely large enough for the two of them, and houseguests, regardless how much we tried to stay out of the way, got old fast. Heather said she had another headache and said goodbye from the apartment and Charles walked us to the car.

Cal and I were on the Interstate headed to Folly by ten o'clock and pulled on the island a little before nine that evening. Burl had called for Cal when we were two hours out and said Mel and Caldwell were at the bar and since we were close, they'd wait for us. Cal would rather have gone home, but didn't want to disappoint Caldwell.

"Hallelujah, praise the Lord, I'm free at last!" Preacher Burl exclaimed as Cal and I entered Cal's.

I thought he was going to break into the chorus of Handel's *Messiah*. Instead, he rushed out from behind the bar and hugged Cal so tightly it knocked his Stetson off. Cal and Burl exchanged a couple more pleasantries and Burl asked how Charles and Heather were. Cal told him about Kevin Starr's death and the visit by the police.

"Oh my." Burl's grin became a frown. "Why would the officials think she could have had anything to do with his graduation from this earth?"

Cal gave a vague answer and it appeared to alleviate the preacher's fear. Cal didn't get in a discussion about Heather's lack of an alibi and how angry she had been with the agent.

The conversation was interrupted by a growl and "Umm" from someone who had moved behind Cal. If I hadn't seen who it was, I still would've recognized the abrupt, rude interruption as coming from Mel Evans. The six-foot-one, bald, former marine wore a leather bomber jacket with its sleeves cut off even though it was in the eighties outside, camo field pants with the legs cut off below the knees, and a snarl designed to intimidate. I knew him well, so his expression was wasted on me.

Cal turned, smiled, and said, "MM, how in grouchy-world are you?"

"It's about damn time you got your sorry country ass back."

Cal opened his mouth to respond, when Caldwell Ramsey, who had been standing beside the former marine pushed him aside. "Give the man a break, Mel. He's been on the road all day." He turned to Cal. "Welcome back. We've been waiting for you."

"For hours," Mel interjected.

Cal ignored Mel, "Thanks Caldwell, it's been a long day."

Caldwell was three inches taller than his partner, was several years younger, and looked in as good a condition as he had been in when he played basketball for Clemson in the 80s. Mel had described their relationship as the twenty-first century version of the odd couple. In addition to being gay, Caldwell was African-American, polite, and didn't treat everyone he met with disdain, one of Mel's less popular but often displayed traits.

"Let me buy you and Chris a beer," Caldwell said. He twisted around and looked at bartender Burl, pointed at an empty beer bottle, and turned back to Cal. "There's something I'd like your advice on."

Burl said, "Go ahead, I'll get your drinks. Might as well finish my shift." He grinned. "Wouldn't want my boss to think I'm slacking off."

Cal tipped his hat to Burl and pointed to the ceiling. "Don't know about your boss up there, this one appreciates it. Much obliged, my holy friend."

Curiosity prevented me from wishing them well and heading home to a familiar bed. I joined the group at the table, one of only three with occupants. It wasn't a hymn coming from the jukebox, but close, as Johnny Cash sang "Sunday Morning Coming Down."

We settled around the table, Mel brought Cal and my drinks, and what appeared to be the fourth round for Mel and the second for Caldwell.

Cal turned to Caldwell. "What can I do for you, pard?"

Caldwell stretched his long legs out beside the table. "Need to pick your brain."

"May need a shovel to find anything in it tonight."

"I've got a client who has a bar on Folly Road near Savannah Highway. Name's SHADES. The owner's done well with it. I've worked with her the last year or so finding entertainment on the weekend. The bands have been good, the crowds not so good. Most of the bands have leaned toward pop, occasional hard rock, some alternative rock. She's wanting to shake things up, completely remodel both the inside and the outside, and repackage the place."

"Don't blame her," Cal said. "That music can cause brain cancer and retardation."

Caldwell smiled. "Figured you'd say something like that. She has this bee in her bonnet and wants to switch to country. She thinks she could get it kick-started by having open-mic nights one or two nights a week, and bring in better-known country acts on weekends."

"She have the dough to do it?" Cal asked.

"Money's not the problem."

"What do you need from me?" Cal waved his hand around the room. "Don't think I'm the person to be asking about interior design."

Caldwell chuckled. "She has a designer to take care of the looks, and I can handle the acts, it's what I do. When it comes to open-mic events, I'm a fish out of water."

"I'm still confused," Cal said. "What's there to know about open-mic nights? Tell her anyone can show up, sing, and sit down."

"She's heard about places that have those kinds of nights and only terrible singers show up. It ends up like karaoke rather than a good draw. She wants an event that pulls audiences, not just relatives and friends of the singers. She's hoping to attract others who want to hear good music."

"And drink," Cal said.

"And drink. If she's available, can you meet me there tomorrow night so we can talk to her and see what she needs? Country's not my strong suit."

Cal turned to me. "Will you go?"

It wouldn't have been at the top of my priority list. Cal had spent a week with me, so it was the least I could do. I nodded.

Cal asked, "What time?"

Caldwell told him and Cal went to the bar to ask Burl if he could cover a few more hours. The preacher agreed and Cal said his brain, or what's left of it, and his broken-down body would be there.

Mel said, "Now can we get out of here?" He pointed to the jukebox where George Jones was sharing the downside of whiskey. "This country music moaning-and-groaning crap's giving me heartburn."

I got home a little after eleven. Other than a week's worth of dust and a temperature higher than I would have preferred because I had turned the A/C off before leaving, everything looked the same. I thought how soothing it would have been if an enthusiastic canine greeted me with a lick on my face, or a warm female body received me with an even more enthusiastic kiss. It was not to be. I loved most animals, while the selfish part of me couldn't handle their care and feeding. I lavished my animal appreciation on other people's pets.

The warm female issue was more complicated. I had been-there, done-that with a wife, but it was many years ago. Since I had been in Folly, I had been in three relationships not counting a few dates with Amber, none of which had approached fiancée level. I had dated Karen Lawson, a former detective with the Charleston County Sheriff's Office and daughter of Folly's mayor, Brian Newman, for four years before she took a high-paying position handling corporate security for a company headquartered in Charlotte. I had shared a few meals with her when she was back in Charleston working with one of the company's satellite offices, until we both had realized a long-distance relationship wouldn't work. Yes, I could have moved to Charlotte, but hadn't. That decision could have been one of the worst I'd ever made—or not.

Since Karen's been gone, I'd had three dinner dates with Barbara Deanelli, owner of Barb's Books which was in the space that had been my photo gallery for several years. Barb was close to my age, had spent much of her life as a practicing attorney in Pennsylvania, and because of illegal activities on the part of her ex-husband, she had given up law and moved to be closer to her half-brother, Dude Sloan, a good friend of mine and owner of Folly's surf shop. Barb was fun to be with, intelligent, and easy on the eyes. I didn't know where our relationship was headed, and neither of us appeared in a hurry to move it along.

With that said, it would have been nice to know someone was glad I was home. After a glass of chardonnay, I realized I had no business feeling sorry for myself. I had good friends in Folly and despite its shortcomings, I considered this island my heaven on earth. Besides, I was in a much better place, physically and emotionally, than Charles and Heather, Kevin Starr, and his wife and three children. I had much to be thankful for.

CHAPTER TWELVE

After a twelve-mile drive up Folly Road, Cal and I walked across a large parking lot to an attractive, stone building with a neon sign above the door that said SHADES with under it in script "Where you're always cool."

Cal said, "Stupid name."

I didn't think it was that bad. A handful of vehicles were in the lot.

The deep, thumping sounds of a bass guitar, eardrum pounding drums, and a vocalist who sounded like a cross between a screeching owl and a roaring tiger with a sore throat greeted us before we reached the entry.

Cal yelled, "Think this is the wrong place?"

"No such luck," I yelled and reached for the door. The handle vibrated in time with the "music."

Yellow and red strobe lights were doing their thing in time with the blaring sounds from refrigerator-sized speakers. Three couples were gyrating in time to the lights and music. To these old eyes, they seemed to be in excruciating pain or being attacked by killer bees. I assumed they were having a good time. The interior décor was as opposite to Cal's Country Bar and Burgers as a hummingbird to a Ferris wheel. The only similarity was the approximate number of customers. There couldn't have been more than a dozen people in the bar, and that included Cal and me.

Caldwell was standing beside the shiny, black and red-trimmed aluminum bar talking to a woman I figured to be the owner. She was tall, although a few inches shorter than Caldwell, trim, with curly-brown hair and appeared to be in her late thirties. The music promoter saw us and waved us over. Cal and I skirted the dancefloor and moved close to the two. Caldwell started to introduce us when the woman pointed to a door behind the bar and motioned for us to follow. She didn't have to ask twice since anywhere but this sound chamber on steroids would be an improvement.

We followed her to an office that would have been the envy of many CEOs.

"Room's soundproofed," she said and closed the door. They were the first words she said that I understood. "Only thing that keeps me sane. Excuse my rudeness, I'm Olivia Anderson, owner of this cornucopia of blaring bands."

Cal said, "If that means ear-splitting loud, I agree." He stuck a finger in each ear.

Olivia laughed. "You must be Cal. I looked you up on the Internet and saw where you had a hit or two a while back."

Cal tipped his Stetson. "That would be one hit, and it was probably before you were hatched."

"Maybe."

Cal told her who I was and she said something like it was nice to meet me. I had never had a hit record so she didn't seem to care about me one way or the other.

In the better light, I would guess her age to be older than I first thought. She looked more like a corporate executive than a bar owner. Her light-gray suit looked tailored, she wore expensive shoes, and her wrists must think God created them to hold bracelets. She had four wide, gold bracelets on her left arm and three on her right wrist. On her left ring finger, a diamond sparkled, and if real, she should have an armed escort following her around.

She offered whatever we wanted from the bar and we declined. Her finely-appointed office had more chairs than I had in my house and we moved to the grouping on the far side of the room. Olivia excused herself to get a drink and I looked around the walls at the multiple photos of Olivia with a variety of people who I probably would have recognized if my musical tastes hadn't stagnated three decades ago. I was also drawn to two framed diplomas beside her large mahogany desk, both from Wake Forest University.

Olivia returned carrying a tumbler nearly overflowing with an amber liquid. "Don't mind if I drink, do you?"

Caldwell and I shook our heads. Cal said, "We're in a bar."

"Demon Deacons," I said and nodded toward the diplomas. I thanked Charles for that bit of trivia I'd learned from one of his college T-shirts.

She glanced at the diplomas. "Wake Forest. Best years of my life; worst years of my life. Got a degree in Latin and one in English. Means I couldn't get a job using either one of them, but I could read all the words on a dollar bill." She laughed at what I suspected was the often-told joke.

Caldwell laughed with her. He was here to get her business.

The name on the diplomas was Mona O. Alliendre, probably her maiden name.

"Gentlemen, why don't we get down to why you're here? Let me give you some background. Caldwell knows most of this."

Her husband opened SHADES four years ago. He had been a successful businessman and wanted to "diversify his assets." He was a few years older than Olivia, and wasn't a fan of the hard-rock music the bar was known for, yet he was smart enough to know it was hot at the time. He died of a brain aneurysm two years ago, and she was in a funk for the next year and walked through the motions without giving thought to changing anything.

Cal said, "Sorry to hear about your husband."

"Thank you." She paused and took a sip. "Sure you don't want anything?"

The room was soundproofed yet the thumping bass could be felt in the office. The sweet smell of a citrus candle on a mahogany credenza permeated the space. I thought how pleasant it smelled as compared to the stale beer and burgers aroma that greeted Cal's patrons.

We again declined.

"About a year ago, Edwina Robinson mentioned redoing the place to me. She's one of the gals who sings here regularly and fills in when one of the other bands Caldwell books arrives late or is 'under the weather'—high, in other words."

Caldwell shrugged. "Musicians."

"Edwina's good," Olivia continued. "She prefers country but can rock with the best of them. The gal's going to make it big one of these days."

"Name sounds familiar," Cal said. "She ever sing in Folly?"

Olivia tilted her head toward Cal. "Don't know. She could have. Edwina started talking to me about redoing the place, calming the music down, and going country." She giggled. "As you can see from the crowd out there, a change couldn't hurt."

Cal smiled. "Got it."

Olivia waited for him to say more. He didn't. "I told Edwina it wasn't a bad idea and started working with a consultant on the changes and the concepts. That didn't work out, and Edwina said I should talk to Caldwell who suggested that since you were in the country bar business, he'd see if you'd share your opinion. If I can get it off the ground, I'd like to expand to other cities, and maybe to Knoxville, Nashville, and Atlanta."

"I'll try, but I'm no expert on the business side."

Caldwell must not have told Olivia the only reason Cal now owned his bar was because he happened to be singing there when the man who owned it killed the co-owner, an action frowned on by the police. Cal took over by default and knew as much about the business end or running a bar as I did about the cholesterol level of a Jurassic dinosaur.

"I have a handle on the business," Olivia said. "Edwina said from what she's seen that a good way to get the crowds in early on would be to have one or two open-mic nights during the week and let Caldwell get us well-known entertainment on weekends. Edwina said she's played several of them, not only here but in other states, and they pack the venue. She also said her agent told her it was the way to go. So, Cal, how do I get good singers to show up? I don't want the ones who would be booed off the stage karaoke night. That won't bring in the type of customers I'm looking for."

Cal nodded. "Don't want the suckees."

Olivia took the final sip and grinned at him. "Couldn't have said it better."

Caldwell leaned closer. "Olivia's already scouted out a couple of open-mic venues in town."

The owner said, "I've been to the East Bay Meeting House where they have poetry and music and Parson Jack's Cafe."

I hadn't been to either. From what I knew of Cal's approach, they were probably better and had fewer "suckees" than Cal's attracted.

"Tell you what, Olivia," Caldwell said. "Let me work with Cal and I'll get back with a plan."

My phone rang before I heard her response. The screen said it was Charles and I interrupted and said I had to take the call. Olivia said for me to go out the back door where I would have some privacy and not be blasted by the music.

I would have been better off having the music burst my eardrums.

CHAPTER THIRTEEN

Charles screamed, "They took her!"

It took a second to realize what he'd said. "Who took who?"

"Cops. They took Heather. They just left. They got her. Gone, they—"

"Slow down," I interrupted. "Start at the beginning."

Charles was out of breath and struggled to breathe. I should have stayed in Nashville.

"Give me a second. Let me sit."

I heard a chair scrape the floor and a calmer voice. "They came pounding on the door an hour ago. Same detectives. There were two uniformed cops with them and the older detective handed Heather a search warrant; told us it was for the apartment and the car. I hadn't read all of it when they said for us to go downstairs while they searched the apartment." He sighed. "Crap, they had one of the cops go with us. What'd they think, we were going to try to run? It's horrible, Chris. Horrible."

"It's okay, Charles." I realized it was not only a lie, but a terrible response to his pain. "Go slow. What happened next?"

"We weren't down there a half hour. The cop got a call and escorted us back to the apartment. Chris, they tore the place apart. Our stuff was everywhere. They even flipped through my books and threw them on the floor. Thank God we don't have much."

"Then what?"

"They told us to stay in the apartment; left a cop at the door like we were going to, I don't know what. They were gone a long time searching the car. Then the detectives came back with sour looks on their faces. The younger one stuck a clear plastic bag in Heather's face. He stared at her and said, 'Is this yours?'"

The pulsating rhythms of the sound system reverberated in the air. I waited for him to continue. After what seemed like an eternity, I said, "What was in it?"

"A gun."

I was stunned. I'd never known Charles or Heather to have a firearm. Charles hated them and would've been shocked if he'd known it was in their car. "Where'd they get it?"

"It was a little thing. The detective said it was a twenty-two caliber Derringer. I'd never seen it before."

"Was it in the car?"

"Said he found it under the registration papers in the glove box." I heard the chair scooting around and Charles taking a drink.

"Did you know it was there?"

"No." He paused. "Heather did."

"Oh."

"My honey looked at the gun, and said, 'That's mine.' The detectives stared at her. I nearly fell out of the chair. Chris, the cops hadn't even asked before Heather said her friend Gwen sold it to her a few weeks back. Gwen told her she wasn't in Kansas, or Folly, anymore and needed some girlie protection—it was her word, *girlie*. Gwen said it was more dangerous here in the big city and

Heather needed something to keep her safe. Keep her safe. Now she's in jail. How damned safe is that?"

"I'm sorry. Then what happened?"

"The older detective took a card out of his pocket and read Heather her rights, and said she was … she was under arrest for the murder of Kevin Starr. Said she'd be able to call an attorney once she was booked. They made her put her hands behind her back and slapped cuffs on her." He hesitated. "Chris, they wouldn't let me wipe the tears off her face before they hauled her away."

My head began to throb in time with the music from the bar. "Charles, I'll leave now and try to get there in the morning."

"No. They said I could see her for a few minutes tomorrow. Let me talk to her before you come. You need to get some sleep anyway. Driving all night ain't going to do Heather any good."

I made him promise he'd call the second he left the jail.

I was better off not leaving for Nashville last night, but not much. I couldn't have gotten more than three hours' sleep, for worrying about my friend, wondering what Heather was doing with a gun, and if the gun was the murder weapon. If it was, had Heather pulled the trigger? I also wondered why the police had focused on Heather in the first place. I knew of a few, and there were probably more, people who were mad at the agent. Someone was angry enough to kill him. What had Heather done to merit a search of the apartment and the car? Did the police know ahead of time about the gun? I also knew none of these questions would be answered in the middle of the night.

By six, I had given up on sleep and shuffled to the kitchen and fired up Mr. Coffee, filled a Roasted mug with steaming hot coffee, and moved to the screened-in front porch. I watched a steady stream of traffic head to work, both on-island and headed to Charleston.

One of my secret pleasures since retiring had been watching people go to work. This morning it wasn't the least bit pleasurable; it simply killed time waiting for Charles to call.

After three cups of coffee, a hundred or so cars passing the house, and a clock that read nine-thirty, the phone rang. Charles was calmer, but was again out of breath. I asked where he was and he said he had just left the jail and was sitting in the car. They only let him see Heather for ten minutes. She looked like she hadn't slept, and was as scared as he'd ever seen her. She'd told the detectives she didn't think it was a good idea to talk to them without an attorney. They asked her if she had any money for a lawyer; she told them no, and they said a public defender would be assigned.

Charles hesitated. A large truck or bus moved past his car and he continued, "Chris, I have money I could give her. I don't think it would be enough to get a good lawyer. I also hate to have her fate in the hands of a public defender. Some of them are good. How do I know hers will be? Chris, how do I know anything?" There was a long pause. "Didn't even know she had a gun. What if it's the one that killed him? What do I do?"

"Let me get with Sean Aker and see what he says. Maybe he knows someone over there, or is able to find out more about the public defender she'll have."

Sean Aker was one of four practicing attorneys in Folly. A few years back, he had been accused of killing his law partner and Charles and I had helped prove him innocent. He said he owed us big-time, and we'd withdrawn from that bank several times. He was also a friend.

It wasn't yet ten o'clock and there was little chance he would be in. I called anyway. Marlene, his receptionist and only other employee in the one-lawyer office, answered and told me of course he wasn't there. "Chris, haven't you figured out after all these years, the boy doesn't start thinking or doing legal work until afternoon?"

I knew that. "I also know he comes in early some days so he can get a peaceful mid-morning nap."

Marlene laughed. "Yes, you do have him figured out. He's not in his opulent office snoozing. I can tell you where he is if you need him."

I told her that intel would be helpful.

"He's at the Dog, probably thinking he will be having a peaceful breakfast, until you show up. Be sure and tell him I wasn't going to tell where he was until you tortured me."

I assured her I would and thanked her for ratting him out. I wasn't in any mood to tease as much as I had, yet Marlene has a way of defusing difficult clients who venture into Sean's office. She had brought a smile to my face, something I needed. Now I needed to see if Sean could bring some advice to what had started as a terrible morning.

CHAPTER FOURTEEN

The Lost Dog Cafe was Folly's most popular breakfast spot and hangout for several locals and a must-visit restaurant for the thousands of vacationers who wander the streets and beaches of the barrier island each year. I had eaten countless more meals there than I had in my kitchen and had met and talked to more locals and learned more about the character and characters of the island than anywhere else in Folly.

Most days I found an excuse to drive rather than walk the short distance. Today, with the temperature in low seventies, nary a raincloud within a hundred miles, and feeling a need to continue the walking I had started while visiting Nashville, I hoofed the ten-minute trek. It proved to be a wise choice. There wouldn't have been a parking place near the restaurant and twenty people waited outside for a table.

Sean was at a table on the front patio. He spotted me heading his way, waved, and pointed to the empty chair across from him. I ignored the angry glare of two men in line and walked to the far end of the patio and opened the fence that led to Sean's table.

"Marlene told you I was here, didn't she?" said the thin, sickeningly handsome, and at age forty-six, sickeningly young attorney.

I nodded.

"Going to have to fire her." He rolled his eyes. "Again."

"She told me where you were. You invited me to the table."

He pointed to my chair. "So, it's my fault you're here?"

I nodded again.

"Since I'm stuck with you, are you going to ruin my peaceful morning?"

Nod number three.

Before he asked how I was going to ruin his morning, Amber appeared carrying a hot mug of coffee for me, and wearing her most endearing smile. Amber was five-foot-five, had long auburn hair tied in a ponytail, and was a little older than Sean. She was one of the first people I'd met when I arrived in Folly and we had dated for a couple of years, and after that we'd remained friends. She was the best source of rumors, and occasional facts, on the island.

She turned her back to the glaring customers who were waiting for us to leave. "Hear you decided to become a country music star and went to visit Charles and Heather."

I grinned. "For being such a good rumor collector, you were led astray with the star story. Yes, Cal and I were over there."

"How're they doing?"

This wasn't the time and place to talk to Amber about Heather's problem and said they were adjusting to their new home.

Amber shook her head. "Hate to hear it. I miss the crap out of him. It's not the same without Charles clanking around with his cane, wearing those silly college T-shirts, and pestering me."

I told her she was right—again.

"Next time you talk to him tell him to get his sorry rear end back where it belongs."

She started to leave when Sean gently grabbed her arm and

turned to me. "Is this visit going to have me doing work and not getting paid for it?"

I nodded. If the reason for my visit wasn't so serious, this would be fun.

He let go of Amber. "Put my breakfast on his check."

I stopped nodding as Amber headed inside.

"Spill it," Sean said.

When he switched gears to lawyer mode, Sean was an excellent listener and was quick to assimilate what was being said. He didn't interrupt as I gave him an abbreviated version of why Charles and Heather had moved to Nashville, the trip Cal and I had made to their new home, learning about Starr's death, and the unsettling news that Heather had been arrested."

Sean, like most everyone who lived or worked in Folly, knew Charles but had only met Heather a couple of times.

He shook his head. "You never cease to amaze me. How do you manage to turn a simple life of retirement into a constant stream of murder, mayhem, and madness?"

"It's a gift."

Sean sipped his coffee, stared at the real estate office across the street, discreetly glanced at the throng of people waiting for our table, and turned to me. "What can I do?"

"Do you know any attorneys in Nashville?"

Sean grinned. "Darnell G. Edelen, Esquire, the best criminal defense attorney in Music City. I know he's the best because he tells me so each time I talk to him."

"Could he help Heather? I doubt her court-appointed public defender will do the kind of job she may need."

Sean took his phone out of his pocket and started scrolling through his contacts. "One way to find out. Darnell owes me." He tapped in the number. A few seconds later, he said, "Mr. Edelen, please." A short pause later. "No, but tell him his savior is calling." Another brief pause. "Not that one. That savior wouldn't call on the phone. Your boss will know who it is." Sean took a sip and I heard mumbling on the phone. Sean blew at the phone, and said, "Hear the wind howling? I'm getting ready to jump and thought of you. Want to come over and step out of a plane with me?" Sean laughed. "Okay, your loss. I need a favor."

Sean gave his friend a shorter version of what I had told him about Heather's situation, and answered a few questions. "Need I remind you about Chattanooga?" One more pause. "Great, here's my good friend Chris with details. Thanks, *amigo*."

Sean handed me the phone and I introduced myself to Darnell.

"Sean taken you skydiving yet?"

I said, "No," and thought it was a strange way to handle introductions.

He asked for Heather's name, Charles's name and phone number, name of the person she allegedly killed, and my number. He said he'd make a few calls and get with Charles. I thanked him and handed the phone to Sean who listened to something Darnell said, laughed, and ended the call.

"Sean, Heather can't afford the *best criminal defense attorney in Music City*, even if he exaggerates."

"Doesn't have to. Won't cost her a penny unless it goes to trial. If that happens, we'll figure something out."

I was stunned. "What'd you do, save his life?"

Sean smiled. "He thinks I did."

"Want to explain?"

"We went to law school at Alabama. Couple of years back, we had a class reunion and some of our buddies decided we needed to celebrate by skydiving. It sounded like a great plan at two in the morning after a night of, shall I say, enjoying the liquid fruits of our success."

I wasn't surprised. Sean was an experienced skydiver as well as a scuba diver and surfer.

"I reserved a plane at a skydiving school a few miles from the hotel and when we got there, Darnell was a lima bean shade of green. I figured it was from overindulging the night before. By the time the plane reached jumping altitude of twelve thousand feet, he was petrified. If he could've curled up and died, he would have. The other guys were stuck on themselves and didn't notice Darnell." Sean took another sip.

"What happened?"

"I fiddled with his chute, acted serious, and said there was something wrong with the way it was packed and he shouldn't jump. The other guys told him they were sorry he'd have to stay with the plane. Darnell told them he was disappointed. Lying's a skill we learned in law school. The rest of us jumped and caught up with him on the ground."

"He knew what you were doing?"

"When we met up after the jump, I was afraid he was going to kiss me; would've ruined my macho image in front of my classmates. Instead of a smooch, he said he owed me his life, the life that had a lifelong fear of heights. He thought he was over it until we got in the air. He said if I ever needed anything, he'd do it." Sean nodded. "I just cashed in."

I thanked him. He said he needed to get to the office before Marlene sent the police out after him, and I told him she was a good nanny. He joked I was nothing but trouble, and got serious. "Do you think she did it?"

"I'd love to say no. To be honest, I don't know. She's changed since moving. She was always kind, sweet to a fault, and found good in everyone. The Heather I saw in Nashville was angry, bitter, and depressed." I paused and shook my head. "She had motive, no alibi, and if ballistic matches her gun with the bullet, there'd be a strong case against her. Sean, I don't know."

He said he hoped not and told me to let him know what Darnell learns. I said I would and he left to incur the wrath of Marlene, and

I left so not to further incur the wrath of the line of customers drooling over the table.

Instead of heading home and pacing the floor, I stopped at Barb's Books, located on Center Street in a retail building that for seven years had housed my ill-fated photo gallery. My fine-art photos had never reached "necessity" status along with milk, bread, gas, and lottery tickets.

I was greeted by a smile. "Good morning. What brings you out this early? I know it's not to buy a book."

The store's owner, Barbara Deanelli, had short, black hair, hazel eyes, and was thin—almost too thin, although she said *too thin* was not possible. She had been slow to adjust to the laid-back lifestyle and friendliness of Folly's residents. After having a few months to experience us first-hand, she had warmed.

"Thought I'd stop and see my favorite bookstore owner."

"How many bookstore owners do you know?"

"Counting you?"

She nodded.

I held up my forefinger.

"Thought so. Interest you in coffee?"

I didn't tell her I'd had several cups and said sure as I followed her to the backroom and her ultra-fancy, single-cup Keurig coffeemaker—a major upgrade from the Mr. Coffee machine that had provided caffeine for visitors to Landrum Gallery.

We waited for the coffee to brew, and killed time talking about the weather, fickle vacationers, and the high turnover in the police department. She also shared she didn't know why she bothered to open on weekday mornings, and it seemed people who bought books stayed in bed until noon. I recounted some of my bad-old-days and said people who bought photographs must have never gotten out of bed.

She took a sip of some exotic coffee blend. "What really brings you in?"

I told her most of what I'd told Sean. Barb had been a successful attorney in Harrisburg, Pennsylvania, before giving it all up and moving to Folly. She understood what I was talking about without me having to explain.

"Kevin Starr. Didn't you say he was the reason Charles and Heather moved?"

"Yes."

"If memory serves, she met him when he heard her singing at Cal's."

I told her yes and that they only met one time before she moved. He had convinced her he could get her gigs in Nashville.

"What was he doing here?"

"He was at the Tides on a retreat with record executives. Why?"

"I find it interesting that he heard her sing, got her to move, and then she killed him. I never heard her, but from what I've been told, Heather's no Taylor Swift."

"Kindly put. I have no doubt he was ripping her off."

"Doesn't bolster her case, does it?"

I shook my head.

"You think there are other gullible hopefuls he was ripping off?"

"Yes, I met a couple in the brief time I was in Nashville."

"Other than Heather, any of them from around here?"

"Not that I know of. Why?"

"If he conned Heather into following her dream into his wallet, there may have been others from places he travelled. Just a thought."

I told her about Sean's friend who would be handling it and she seemed pleased it wasn't going to be a public defender. I asked what she thought about the case against Heather.

"Unless ballistics can tie her gun to the murder or someone saw her pull the trigger, a good attorney could throw enough crap at the jury to establish doubt. How much doubt will be the key."

I told her I hoped she was right and that the lawyer could throw whatever amount of doubt would reach the "reasonable doubt" threshold. Someone came in the front door and she started to see who it was.

"I also wanted to see if you wanted to have supper tonight?"

"Sure," she said and went to wait on the latest arrival.

CHAPTER FIFTEEN

I called Charles before I was to meet Barb at Rita's Seaside Grill. Good to his promise, Sean's friend had called and Charles said he felt a glimmer of hope with a big-shot attorney representing Heather. Darnell was going to meet with her this evening and try to find someone in the district attorney's office in the morning to see what they were basing the charge on. He had hoped my call was the attorney. I said I wouldn't tie up the line and that I wanted to know if the attorney had contacted him and to see how he was holding up. I told him I'd head to Nashville in the morning.

The temperature was still pleasant so I managed to commandeer the next to last vacant patio table. I wasn't nearly as obsessed about arriving early as Charles was, yet it was still fifteen minutes before I was to meet Barb. Since I'd moved to Folly, the restaurant had had three names and even more owners. Rita's had undergone a major remodel a few years ago, and featured one of Folly's most attractive outdoor seating areas, and arguably the best location on the island. It faced Center Street and the Sand Dollar, Folly's iconic bar; was directly across Arctic Avenue from the Folly Pier; and, catty-corner from the Tides, a nine-story hotel. The restaurant was often filled with conventioneers dressed in their best beachwear, sharing the patio with groups who had come directly from the nearby beach and were surf-attired in bathing suits and cover-ups.

I felt guilty. Charles was hundreds of miles away worrying about his girlfriend sitting in a jail cell and wondering when, or if, she would ever walk the sidewalks of her dream city as a free woman, while I was sitting on the patio, sipping a chardonnay, and watching a steady stream of people strolling along the sidewalks, and waiting to have a pleasant dinner with an interesting, attractive woman.

I saw Barb walking this way from her large condo complex on the far side of the hotel. She had on one of her trademark red blouses and tan shorts. She had gone home and changed for supper while I was sitting here in the same faded-blue polo shirt and shorts I'd worn all day.

I opened the patio gate so Barb wouldn't have to walk through the restaurant. She thanked me with a kiss on the cheek.

"Thanks for the invite," she said, as she sat and looked for the server. "I wasn't looking forward to cooking tonight. Today's been a bear."

"Grizzly or Teddy?"

She chuckled. "Folks talk strange here. Whatever bear it is when I've been as busy as a ticket-taker at a Bruce Springsteen concert."

"And you think we talk strange," I joked. "That'd be a black bear."

"I'll add that to my Folly vocab." Her smile faded. "Any news on Heather?"

I shared my conversation with Charles. She said she was glad the attorney was on it, and we glanced at the menu before Barb ordered the seafood Cobb salad, which explained her thinness; I ordered a burger, which by one look at me said it was my favorite food at Rita's.

"Speaking of Folly vocab," I said.

"Is that what we were speaking about?"

"Before food ordering got in the way. Have you seen Dude lately?"

Dude is Barb's half-brother and was as opposite of her as a duck was to a dandelion. He owned the surf shop, one of the island's most successful businesses. They had little contact during her years practicing law and had come back in her life when he suggested she move to Folly where she could escape her past. He had been wrong about that. It nearly got her killed a few months ago, when she crossed paths with her past. The best thing that had come from the traumatic events was Barb had reconnected with Dude and I got to know her.

"He stops in the store occasionally. I love him to death, but we don't have much in common, and as you know, his conversational skills are only exceeded by his ability to flap his arms and fly."

Dude was known to murder, mangle, and shred the English language, or as Charles had said, "The old surfer had never met a sentence he couldn't screw up." To Dude's credit, he would also never use twelve words when one would do—almost. Understanding him was an acquired skill.

Barb was in a cheerful mood, one that was appreciated after what I had been dealing with. After what seemed like only minutes, I realized the sun had set and most of the tables around us had changed occupants. It was Tuesday and open-mic night at Cal's so I asked Barb if she wanted to go. She said she'd never been in Cal's, which didn't surprise me, and that she'd love to, which was a surprise.

The good thing about Folly's main business, restaurant, and bar district was it would fit inside the Georgia Dome with room left over for a cattle ranch. Barb and I walked two blocks to Cal's and were greeted by the smell of fries and sounds of a long-haired, tat-covered, forty-year old standing behind an antique mic on the stage singing a passable version of John Anderson's "Would You Catch a Falling Star."

Cal's wasn't nearly as crowded as Rita's, and we had no trouble grabbing a table against the wall.

Barb looked around. "Retro."

I waved toward the furnishings. "Yard sale."

Cal arrived at the table at the same time, tipped his sweat-stained Stetson at Barb. "Chris, I see you managed to lasso the most fetching bookstore owner in Folly for a night of good singing and hospitality." He smiled and tipped his hat again in case Barb missed it the first time. "Welcome Miss Barb. First drink's on the house."

Barb returned his smile. The singer belted out "Okie from Muskogee," and Barb said, "Only bookstore owner."

"You'd still be fetching even if there were fifty bookstores. What's your medicine?"

"Got Corona?"

"Miss Barb, I'm from Texas. We fought a war many moons ago so we wouldn't have to be drinking Mexican beers. How about a Bud?"

Barb grinned. "My second choice."

"Good, because it's all I got. Gotta introduce a girl singer. Be back in a jiff."

Cal headed to the mic and Barb turned to me. "A character, isn't he?"

I watched Cal thank the singer for sharing his talents and called for the next in line to head to the stage.

"Never heard him call anyone fetching. You must've charmed the crooner."

"He's been in three times asking if I have songbooks. Gave him the same answer each time. Seems like a nice fellow."

"One of the best."

"Ladies and gentlemen," Cal's Texas accent blared through the sound system. "Put your hands together and welcome one of the finest gal singers around. Edwina."

The bar was about one-third full so the applause for the newest aspiring star didn't quite reach deafening proportions. It didn't stop her from covering Tammy Wynette's "Stand by Your Man."

Cal returned with Barb's second-choice beer and a chardonnay for me.

Barb looked at the stage and leaned close to Cal. "Is she really one of the finest singers around? She sounds okay, not great."

"She's not bad," Cal faced the stage and said. "She's only been in once or twice and is far better than most. I say they're all *fine* singers when I introduce them. It's the only good thing most of them ever hear about their singing coming from someone other than tone-deaf relatives. It takes guts standing up there and a good word won't hurt any of them." He turned back to Barb. "What're you doing out with this old codger?"

Asked Cal, who was four years older than this old codger, and Barb was only a couple of years younger than I.

She punched Cal in the forearm. "Figured he needed someone to lean on after the long walk over. You know how old folks are."

Cal saw more humor in it than I did.

The Tammy Wynette imitator finished "Stand by Your Man," and moved right into Lea Ann Womack's "I Hope You Dance."

Cal leaned over and put his arm on Barb's hand. "Better drink it up quick and get another one."

"Why?"

"Next guy up. Good country songs are played with only a few chords. He's so bad, I call him *discord*...not to his face, of course. Don't say I didn't warn you."

She patted his hand. "Think I'll have another Bud."

"Wise decision, Miss Barb."

Barb watched Cal head to the cooler and leaned against my shoulder. "Bet he was a charmer back in his day."

"He thinks his day's still here."

She squeezed my arm. "Don't think so."

"At least he was right about your being fetching."

"Thank you," she said, and "Thank you," the singer said, after Cal introduced him as David, "one of the finest guy singers around." He went into his version of "Behind Closed Doors." He will never be confused with Charlie Rich, nor will he get rich from his singing.

Cal returned with our drinks and we listened to David struggle through two songs, before Barb said it had been a long day and she had listened to all the *finest singers* she could stomach.

I walked her to her condo. She thanked me for the escort home, gave me a lingering hug, a kiss on the cheek, and said we needed to do it again. I said I'd like that.

My phone rang while I was on my way down the stairs. I stubbed my toe on the next step as I glanced at the screen and saw it was Charles.

"So, here's the story," he said. There was no one around and I sat on the last step leading to the parking area under the condos.

For several years, I had been on a futile campaign to encourage my friends to start phone conversations with openings like, "Hello," or "Hi, Chris." I might as well have been trying to teach them how to build a nuclear reactor with LEGOS.

"Let's have it," I said, in the spirit of his opening statement.

"The whole thing sucks."

"Okay." Clarification would follow—I hoped.

"I talked with the attorney."

"Public defender or Sean's friend?"

"Darnell G. Edelen, Sean's friend, thank God. He met with Heather and talked to the district attorney. It sucks, Chris."

"What did he learn?"

"Heather's gun killed him."

"You're right, that sucks."

Charles sighed. "There's more. They have a witness who saw her arguing with Starr the night he was killed."

"Is the witness positive?"

"Almost. The cops showed him photos of several women, including some of Starr's clients, and he picked Heather."

"Where were they arguing?"

"In a bar in an old warehouse a couple of blocks from the action on Broadway. The witness tends bar there. Edelen says he doesn't think he has a chance at getting her bail, something about Heather being a flight risk, not being in Nashville long, and her record." He hesitated. "Chris, she's not going to get out."

"What can I do?"

"Come back. Please."

I reminded him I was leaving in the morning.

"Thank you," he mumbled, and then dead air.

I detoured from my path home and returned to Cal's to see if he wanted to go with me. He was on stage introducing another *fine singer*.

"Come back to pick up another chick? One's not enough?" Cal said as he waved to the near empty room. "Past bedtime for old gals who'd be attracted to you."

"Funny." I told him about Charles's call and asked if he wanted to return to Nashville.

He said he would, but didn't want to ask Burl to man the bar again. He said the preacher had done a good job, although he didn't bring quite the country flavor the bar needed. Cal said he was afraid some of his "serious sinners" stayed away because of having to buy beer from a preacher and they were his "biggest booze buyers." He made me promise to call every day with the lowdown.

CHAPTER SIXTEEN

The distance from Folly Beach to Nashville was identical whether Cal was in the car or not, yet with only my satellite radio to entertain me, it felt about seven thousand miles farther. It didn't help that I was awake most of the night. I saw too many hours on my clock as I tossed, turned, and wondered if Heather was guilty. And if she wasn't, how was her gun, the gun that none of us knew she had, the murder weapon? All I concluded was that trying to think at three in the morning was futile.

Somewhere on the west side of Asheville, I remembered something that could have explained her gun being the murder weapon. When we had been outside the Bluebird, someone had loaned Heather a guitar. She told the man to put it in Charles's car and he wouldn't need a key because the lock was broken. I suppose someone could have taken her gun, shot Starr, and returned the weapon to the unlocked car. If true, how would the killer have known about the gun and broken lock?

A hundred miles later, my mind wandered from the road and the radio, and I rehashed my overnight thoughts about someone identifying Heather arguing with Starr. If they'd been arguing, it still didn't prove she'd killed him, yet Heather had denied seeing Starr that night. If she argued with him, wouldn't she have admitted it? Could the bartender have been mistaken? Could Charles and I find the bartender and see how sure he was?

To say I was exhausted when I knocked on Charles's door would be an understatement. I was tired, my eyes felt like if they had to look at another Interstate sign they would beg for cataracts, and my arthritic hands ached from gripping the steering wheel. I thought I was in bad shape until I saw Charles. His long-sleeve, gray Vanderbilt T-shirt had a pancake-sized mustard stain on the front and his shorts looked as though he'd slept in them. His hair, never poised for a model shoot, looked like a mouse had taken up residence. His eyes were red and his expression would have made a Basset Hound look gleeful.

I wrapped my arms around my friend and felt his body go limp. I helped him to the couch. He sat, put his head down, and tears rolled down his cheeks. I moved beside him and didn't say anything. I felt helpless. He sat motionless for fifteen minutes. The sounds of traffic three stories below and someone walking in the apartment directly above us, broke the silence.

"Chris, she killed him." He didn't raise his head.

"You can't be certain."

He glanced at me. "She did it."

"What makes you so sure?"

He slowly stood and walked to the window. "She's not the Heather I fell in love with."

"In what way?"

"You know she's always been as strange as a drunken, red-eyed tree frog. She was always a loveable goofball, and as sweet as a Hershey bar floating in a bowl of maple syrup." He paused. "No more."

I had no idea how strange a red-eyed tree frog was much less a drunken one. I was aware of Heather's loveable quirks, and knew when Cal and I were here, she was moody and angry. Was that all he was talking about? Moody and angry don't equal murder.

"How so?"

He continued to stare out the window. "You know how depressed she was when you were here, and she was being good because she had company. Before you got here and after you left she was in a funk. She seldom slept and was up all hours."

That was still nothing that would make her a killer. "Anything else?"

Charles returned to the couch and looked everywhere but at me. "She left the apartment several times and was gone for hours. Day and night. Never knew where she went, and when I asked, she stomped around and wouldn't say. I also heard her on the phone with her friends, the ones who were supposed to be represented by Starr. I couldn't hear what the other person was saying, but Heather moaned, groaned, and bemoaned how Starr had screwed them. How he was the incarnate of evil." He faced me. "I heard her telling one of the friends, I'm not sure which one, that something needed to be done. She was furious."

"You think she meant killing him?"

He hesitated and nodded. "Yeah."

"You know her better than I do. We know she was angry with Starr. Doing something about it doesn't mean shooting him. She could've meant going to the Better Business Bureau or reporting him to some agency that regulates what he does. When we get mad we often say things we don't mean."

"You didn't hear the way she was talking. You didn't see the hate in her eyes. She did it, Chris."

After the long drive, I needed to stretch my legs and thought it would do Charles good to get out of the apartment. I suggested a walk.

He looked around the room like he had something to do there.

He finally said it might help. He grabbed his cane, smoothed his hair back with his fingers. "Where are we going?"

I said nowhere in particular and suggested we get some fresh air.

He whispered, "Whatever."

The neon lights from the downtown bars gave the appearance of an amusement park rather than a city street. The sounds of country music ranging from traditional country, bluegrass, and contemporary country, which sounded more like rock, leaked out of the bars and restaurants and often melded into conflicting beats. Charles, the consummate observer of people, began to relax as he watched the steady stream of tourists jamming the sidewalks.

We'd walked three blocks when I remembered that Charles said the witness who claimed to have seen Heather arguing with Starr worked in a bar a couple of blocks off Broadway.

"Charles, do you remember where the bar was where someone saw Heather with Starr?"

He stopped in the middle of the sidewalk and a man carrying a guitar case stepped on his heel. Charles said, "Sorry," and the musician said the same and went on his way. He reminded me of Heather doing the same thing on her quest for stardom. I hoped the man had better luck.

Charles reached in his pocket and pulled out a folded piece of paper. "Notes I took when talking to her lawyer," he explained. "Let's see. Yeah, the Top Tan, no, Top Ten Bar, three blocks off Broadway." He looked around and pointed to the opposite side of the street from his apartment. "That way. The bartender's name's Rod, umm, can't read my writing on his last name. Doesn't matter, bartenders don't need last names."

"Let's get a drink."

The festive sights and sounds on Broadway faded as we walked the three blocks. Lively, music-filled venues gave way to an empty lot, a medical supply house, and a vacant warehouse with a for sale sign in front that looked like it had been there forever. The Top Ten Bar was in a deteriorating brick building with the name Top Ten painted on the brick. It didn't get its name for being one of Music City's top ten watering holes.

We stepped in the cave-like dark building and once my eyes adjusted to the near-black environment, I was surprised how large it was. In its previous life, it must've been a storage building or factory. The structure wasn't wide, but was deep. A rustic bar was along the back wall and we had to walk past fifteen tables before reaching it. I thought Cal's Bar had seen its better days, but it was ultra-modern by Top Ten standards. This place's better days hadn't been in the last twenty years. I was also surprised to see how many customers there were. It was nowhere near the constant flow of visitors to the city, but there must have been fifty people enjoying libations and the rock music blasting from the speakers.

There were nine bar stools in front of the waist-high bar; three were occupied. The bartender had his back to us and was pulling beers out of a large cooler. We sat at the stools farthest from the three men and Charles swiveled back toward the tables we had passed on the way to our seats.

"Why in holy Hell would Heather have been here with Starr? For that matter, why would Starr have been hanging around this dungy place?"

I was wondering the same thing and told him I didn't know.

The beanpole-thin, six-foot-tall, mid-thirties bartender gave the beers from the cooler to a bored looking, middle-aged woman who appeared to be the sole server. He came over and asked what we needed. Charles said Budweiser and since I didn't figure there was an extensive wine list, I said white wine. He brought the drinks and said his name was Rod and for us to yell if we needed anything. Charles sat up straight and started to say something. I grabbed his arm and turned to the bartender. "Thanks, we will."

Rod left to do bartender things, and Charles leaned closer.

"Why'd you stop me? I was going to make him say he was lying about Heather."

I looked at Rod who was at the far end of the bar and turned to Charles. "That's why I stopped you. We can't come off strong or he'll clam up. Give it a few minutes, order a second drink, and we'll strike up a conversation."

I sipped my drink and wondered what possible motive Rod could have for lying about Heather. Charles, as impatient as an expecting father in a maternity ward, huffed, took a gulp of beer, and said, "Drink fast."

I patted him on the shoulder and swiveled the barstool so I could get a better look at the rest of the room. The customers at the tables closest to us were in their thirties or forties. They were casually dressed and several shared something on their tablet computers with their tablemates. A few of them wore headsets attached to laptops. They didn't look like salespeople but seemed to be working. I squinted to see the rest of the people in the room but it was near impossible. The room was dark and a couple of the overhead lights were burned out making many of the customers' silhouettes.

Charles finished guzzling his beer and waved for Rod to bring another. Impatience at its finest. Rod returned with a Bud for Charles and although I hadn't asked for it, another wine for me. The three men from the other end of the bar left cash on the counter and told Rod they'd see him later. He waved bye, took off his glasses and threw them on the back bar. He wiped his face with the towel he had over his shoulder, and said, "I hate those damned things. Sweat and eyeglasses don't mix."

Charles said, "Know what you mean, Rod."

To my knowledge, Charles had never worn glasses. In addition to impatience, he had an innate ability to mimic those around him, putting them at ease, and getting them to talk about things they wouldn't think of telling their priest. Heather had once said,

"Chuckie would make a chameleon turn whatever color envy is with envy."

"This is our first time in," I said to break the ice. "Looks busy."

"Welcome. Music biz?"

"Tourist visiting my friend." I tilted my head toward Charles. "Most of your customers in the music industry?"

"Mostly." Rod wiped his eyes again. "Back of the house guys: production, engineers, songwriters." He chuckled. "Not quite Blake Shelton's go-to drinking spot."

"Why here?" Charles asked.

Rod put his elbows on the bar and lowered his voice. "They can get away from the tourists on Broadway—no offense—and far enough away from Music Row to be able to let their hair down, sip a brew, and get work done while doing it, without the suits looking over their shoulder."

Charles shook his head. "Was Kevin Starr one of your regulars?"

Rod gazed at the counter, frowned, and looked at Charles. "Tragic about what happened. Was he a friend?"

"Nah. Met him a time or two."

Rod leaned closer to us. "He was here right before he was killed."

"Wow," Charles said. "That had to feel weird."

"What's weirder, he was with the gal who killed him."

Charles hands balled into fists.

"How do you know?" I said before Charles could climb over the bar and grab Rod's throat.

Someone at a nearby table hollered for more beer. Rod said he'd be back.

"You hear what he said?" Charles said through gritted teeth.

"Yes, but we knew that. Stay calm. Let's see what else he has to say."

Charles sighed, relaxed his fingers, and nodded.

Rod returned. "Sorry about that. Waitresses are getting sorrier and sorrier, and that's if they show up at all. Where was I?"

"You were telling us how you knew the person with Starr killed him," I said before Charles went off on a tangent.

"The police figured it out. They knew Kevin was in here before he was shot. Suppose I was the last person who saw him alive—other than that gal. The cops came in with a fistful of photos, those publicity shots singers pass out. Some of them looked almost alike, real young, big smiles, long hair. Two were older, not as old as you, but maybe in their forties, maybe fifty."

Now I was ready to strangle him. "One of them was the person who was with Starr?"

"Yes, sir. They were sitting back there, that table on the side of the room." He pointed to a table at the far corner of the room where three men were focused on a laptop.

"Did you talk to her?" I asked.

"No, it was crowded when they got here and the waitress got herself sick and went home leaving me with a crowd. Most of my customers are regulars and understood so they came up here when they needed drinks so I didn't have to leave the bar. Kevin got their drinks."

"You're certain it was the woman in the photo?"

"Looked like her. Why are you asking so many questions?"

Charles glared at Rod. "I'm—"

"We're curious," I interrupted. "It was good talking to you. How much do we owe?"

He told me and I paid and said we'd better be going. Charles gave me one of his patented evil looks and followed me to the exit. Sunlight assaulted my eyes and I had to squint to let them adjust from the darkness.

Charles barked, "Why didn't you let me make him say it wasn't Heather?"

"That's her attorney's job. You saw how dark it was. When we were sitting at the bar and he pointed to the table where Starr and Hea—where Starr and whoever he was with were. Could you tell much about the guys in there today?"

"Not really."

"He said he never went to their table and Starr went to Rod for their drinks, so he never got a close look at the woman."

Charles looked at me and back toward Top Ten. "He also hates his glasses and probably didn't have them on."

"It wouldn't do any good for us to try to get him to change his story. He has nothing to gain by lying. He saw what he thinks he saw. If Heather's attorney is half as good as Sean says he is, he'll tear Rod's testimony to shreds. If Rod sticks to his story, because Heather was there arguing with Starr, it doesn't mean she killed him."

We were back on lower Broadway, surrounded by groups of people walking and smiling as they listened to sad songs coming from multiple bars.

"Nothing personal," Charles said. "This ain't as much fun as it is with Heather. Let's go home."

We were headed up the steps to the apartment when Charles stopped. "Chris, I can't shake it. I'm afraid she's guilty."

"I know. We can't give up. Until I hear her confess, I'm assuming she's innocent. Let's say we find out who did kill him?"

CHAPTER SEVENTEEN

Charles asked an excellent question before we had settled in the apartment. "How are we going to find the killer?"

Since I had known him, he prided himself on being an amateur detective. He'd considered doing it as a career until he learned he would have to have formal training and spend years apprenticing under a licensed investigator. He said that seemed like overkill and he had received years of "observational training" watching a plethora of TV detective shows and reading novels written by Agatha Christie, Arthur Conan Doyle, and Erle Stanley Gardner. His detective career was mainly in his warped brain, although he and I had stumbled upon several untimely deaths. Through a bit of luck and being at the right place, or one could argue, wrong place at the right time, we had helped the police. He kept forgetting we nearly lost our lives more than once in the process.

Charles had usually been the first person who suggested, or demanded, we get involved in what should have been none of our business. Today, he was reluctant to, or incapable of, pursuing what had occurred. His surprising belief she was guilty clouded his need to prove otherwise. Charles and Heather meant too much to me to let that happen.

When he asked how we could find the murderer, I hesitated, and said, "Motive. We know Heather had a motive. He also agented other people Heather knew. Wouldn't they have the same reasons?"

"Yes, but they didn't have the murder weapon in their car."

I stood at the window and looked down at Charles's Toyota. "Your door lock's broken so anyone could have taken it out, shot him, and returned it."

"I guess," he said, with little enthusiasm.

"If Cal's right, Heather and all of Starr's other clients paid too much for their demos. Let's find out who the others were. Do you have the name of the studio where she cut the demos?"

Charles went in the bedroom and brought back Heather's business card folder and began thumbing through it. "Crap."

"What?"

"The card's not here."

"Can you find the building?"

"Maybe."

I reached for my Tilley. "What are we waiting for?"

"You mean now?"

"Why not?"

"What if it's not open?"

"What else do we have to do?"

Charles shrugged, grabbed his hat and cane, and followed me out.

He drove since he thought he knew how to get to the studio. The trip to the Music Row area of Nashville was only a couple of miles from the apartment. Because of a wrong turn and a one-way street going the wrong direction, it took us twenty minutes to find what we were looking for.

The studio was a bungalow style house on Eighteenth Avenue

South. If it weren't for the tiny *DK Studios* sign in the front yard, it could have been a well-kept middle-class brick house in most any city. The front yard was manicured and had three large landscaped areas with shrubs and annuals which displayed their summer blooms.

We stepped on the wide front porch and I noticed something else that set it apart from most residences. There was a speaker box next to the door and a note under it that said to push the button and do not knock. There was a security camera looking down at us from the ceiling like a raptor eyeing a squirrel.

Charles saw me reading the sign "Noise from knockin' can mess with recording in here."

I looked at him.

He pointed to the door. "That's what the guy told me."

He pushed the button and was rewarded by a female voice asking if she could be of assistance. Charles said who he was, looked at the camera, and pointed at me and said I was his friend. He reminded her he had been there with Heather Lee.

The voice said, "One moment please."

I don't know the definition of moment, though I knew it should have been fewer than ten minutes, the time it took for the door to open.

We were greeted by a short, to be kind, full-bodied woman with long, stringy, gray hair, around my age. "Sorry for the delay. Got a phone call from one of our famous clients. Sorry, can't disclose her name. You know how stars are. Think they come first. I'm Dale, by the way."

I wondered if she said that to everyone who came to her door so she could convey the feel of success. Regardless, she invited us in and pointed toward what once had been a living room. A residential couch and chairs had been replaced by what looked like used office furniture. Four side chairs bookended two tables holding copies of *Rolling Stone*, *Billboard*, and *Country Weekly*.

"Let me see if my husband's finished with his session so he can join us."

She was gone before she gave us a chance to respond. The most recent magazine was a year old and decades newer than anything else in the room. Charles shared that the studio was in the basement and they used the rest of the rooms for their offices and place for artists to rest while waiting to record. I heard several voices coming from the back of the house and a door slam. Dale returned followed by a man about her age. He was a few inches taller than Dale. What little hair he had left looked like it had been waxed with black shoe polish, and his face was pale like he had spent his life in a recording studio or a cave.

He introduced himself as Kelly Windsor, the *much worse half* of DK Studios. We smiled like we were expected to and Charles reintroduced himself and told them who I was and that I was visiting from South Carolina. We returned to our chairs and Dale and Kelly sat opposite us.

"Heather Lee, Heather Lee," Kelly said. "Remind me again who she is."

Charles frowned like he thought, *who could possibly not remember Heather Lee?* He held his thoughts and told Kelly that Heather recorded a demo there a few months ago. "Kevin Starr set it up. He's her agent."

Kelly leaned forward, his face turned red, Dale put her hand on his forearm, glanced at him before turning back to Charles. "Mr. Starr sends numerous singers to cut demos. I do believe I remember, Ms. Lee." She described her.

Charles nodded.

Dale said, "Starr—"

"Ms. Lee," Kelly interrupted, "had a rather distinct sound. If I remember correctly, she was here for our standard demo package with an electric guitar, bass, acoustic guitar, and drums. That's all I recall."

Dale's face had returned to an ashen pale. "What about her?"

Perhaps word of Starr's demise hadn't reached DK Studios. I turned to the Windsors. "Are you aware Kevin Starr was found dead the other morning?"

Dale gasped and put her hand in front of her mouth.

Kelly made a slight nod and said, "Murdered, no doubt."

"Why?" I asked and noted that I hadn't said murdered.

Kelly said, "Because it's long overdue."

Dale said, "Now dear, that's terrible. What happened?"

"And what's it got to do with us?" Kelly said. "Why ask about this Lee person?"

Saddened about the death would be the opposite of how I'd describe Kelly's reaction. "Why do you think it was overdue, Mr. Windsor?"

"Call me Kelly, please."

"Kelly, what was wrong with Kevin Starr?"

He glanced at his wife and to Charles and me. "Let me make some guesses. Stop me if I'm wrong."

Charles started to speak I held out my hand and told Kelly to continue. I didn't want to cloud whatever he had to say with the thought Heather may be involved.

"First, I don't remember her well. I'll say Heather Lee wasn't from around here. I'd guess Starr 'discovered' her singing in some out of the way place and told her he'd like to be her agent. She moved to Nashville to follow her dream. Starr told her he needed a demo to get her 'unique vocal styling'—punctuated with air quotes—in front of the big recording companies. And, oh yeah, the demo would only cost a few thousand bucks." He paused and stared at Charles. "How am I doing?"

"Not bad," I said. "I take it Heather wasn't the first to go down that path."

"My friends," Dale said, "it's a path so worn and bumpy you couldn't ride a bike down it." She waved her hand around the room.

"As you can see, DK Studios is not one of what would be considered Nashville's biggest or most-prestigious recording venues. Our bread-and-butter is demo recordings and an occasional limited pressing product. We've owned the building for years and keep our expenses down." She looked at Kelly, smiled, and once again put her hand on his arm. "Kelly gets riled when Kevin Starr's name comes up. Don't get us wrong, we're sorry he's dead, hmm, for more reasons than one."

"What are they?" Charles said, asking the kind of question only he can get away with.

Dale shook her head. "We are saddened by the premature death of anyone."

Kelly's face turned red, and he blurted, "The bastard owes us seven-thousand dollars."

"Why?" Charles asked, again skating on thin ice.

"Seven demo sessions he never paid for plus two big-ticket sessions, six musicians, hours of post-production, need I go on?"

Charles said, "So you didn't get Heather's twenty-nine hundred bucks?"

Kelly laughed, not an ounce of humor oozed from his mouth. "Do you know what we charge for our standard demo package?"

Until a few seconds ago, I thought I had. I shook my head.

Kelly said, "Seven hundred twenty-five dollars. That beats most studios in town. In other words, not only did we not get what Starr charged her, but we never even got our paltry fee. Bet there was a line of wannabes waiting to kill the basta…the agent. I hope he had a whale of a life insurance police. Maybe we can get our money that way."

I asked, "Do you often let your customers build up such a large debt?"

"No. Our sessions were light and Starr had several artists lined up. He said he had a deep-pockets backer and he'd clear up the debt at the end of the month."

Charles asked, "You believed him?"

Kelly started to answer and Dale put her arm in front of him and turned to us. "Why are you here? Does Ms. Lee have something to do with Mr. Starr's death?"

I waited for Charles to respond. He looked at me.

I said, "Heather Lee has been arrested for his murder."

Kelly grinned. "Good for her."

"I'm sorry to hear that," Dale said as she stared at Charles. "I take it you and she were close."

Charles mumbled, "We're engaged."

"Oh," Dale said. She leaned close to Charles.

"We're trying to find out who else may have had motive to kill him," I said, like it was the most logical thing we could be doing.

Kelly said, "Too many to count."

"I've known Heather Lee for a long time," I said. "I don't believe she killed Starr." I paused and waited for Charles to pitch in. He didn't. "We came to ask if you could give us the names of Starr's other clients who recorded demos here. We'd like to talk to them and see if they knew anyone who would have been angry enough to kill him."

Dale's expression hardened. "Since this is a police matter, and you're close to the accused murderer, perhaps we shouldn't be talking with you. Our attorney would frown on it. I'm sorry we can't be more help."

Dale stood, nearly pulled Kelly out of his chair, and started walking to the door.

We had exceeded our welcome.

We walked to the car, and Charles stopped and looked back at the studio. "Don't know about Starr's clients, I now do hereby park those two at the top of my suspect list."

From what they, especially Kelly, had said, it would have been hard to argue with my friend. Kelly appeared angry enough to do it. Also, Kelly had said murder even though I'd only said Starr was dead. It seemed they had two things working for their being guilty. Seven thousand dollars would have been a chunk of change for what appears to be a struggling business. So first, how would they have had a chance to get paid from a corpse? Second, and the most difficult to explain, was how would they have known about Heather's gun, Charles's broken door lock, and how to get and return the gun to the car?

I shared my misgivings as we sat in the car. "Don't forget," Charles said, "Kelly said he hoped Starr had a large insurance policy. He would have killed Starr figuring the only way he could get his money was from that."

I conceded that point and asked how he figured the studio owners knew about Heather's gun and Charles's broken lock.

"Don't know, but they did."

I didn't remind him that hours earlier he'd been convinced of her guilt. Since I didn't think she was guilty, I wanted to push on with our unauthorized and amateurish investigation. Kelly and Dale didn't give us a list of Starr's clients, but we knew two of them.

"Charles, what're the names of Heather's friends from the Bluebird?"

"Gwen Parsons and Jessica something. Good point, they were both pissed at Starr. I think Gwen even said something about wanting to conk him in the head."

"Was she the one who left with Heather after their performance when we were there?"

"No, that was Jessica."

"Where can we find them?"

He didn't know. "Their phone numbers should be at the apartment."

CHAPTER EIGHTEEN

Charles found Gwen and Jessica's numbers in Heather's notebook. He left a message for Gwen, had talked to Jessica, and we were on our way to meet her where she was a server at a Cracker Barrel near the Opryland Hotel.

We had maneuvered through the maze of items ranging from pottery, candy, clothing, and thousands of other knickknacks with our goal being to reach the nostalgia-bathed restaurant's hostess station, when Jessica appeared at our side.

"Got a fifteen-minute break. Let's go outside."

She had her arm through Charles's arm before he could get to a revolving book rack and was leading him out. I followed them past the row of rocking chairs and around the side of the building. Jessica was puffing on a cigarette as soon as we reached a shaded spot and a paint-chipped bench at the employees break area. She was not the only smoker who worked there. The ground was littered with butts and the smell of smoke hung in the air even though no one else was nearby.

"How's Heather holding up? Can she get bail? I feel terrible about telling those horrible detectives I left her the night he was killed. I figured I must've set them sniffin' after her. OMG, I feel sick about it." She took a deep breath and another drag on her cigarette.

She was so hyper I didn't know what question to answer first or if she would hear or understand them. Charles didn't have any reservations. "She's miserable and won't get out unless we find who killed Starr. Do you know who did it?"

I wouldn't have been that direct, although it did cut through a lot of other questions.

She looked toward the front of the building, lit another cigarette, and looked at her watch. "Heather."

That wasn't the answer I'd hoped for. "Why do you think that?"

"God, I hate to say this. I had to tell the cops, you know. She said she'd like to kill him. Honest, she did. She said it to me after we left the Bluebird." She lowered her head. "I hated to tell them. Honest to God."

I glanced at Charles who had closed his eyes.

I asked, "Was she serious or letting off steam?"

"I don't know. Like how do you know for certain if someone means something? She had hateful feelings about him, you know."

Charles tapped his cane on the ground. "So, did you?"

Jessica had started to her mouth with the cigarette, hesitated, and glared at Charles. "What are you saying?"

"We're not saying anything," I said trying to defuse the situation enough to keep her talking. "We're trying to figure out what happened."

"Good luck with that one. He had a whole shit-pot full of people who wanted him dead. I don't think any of them did it. Sure, I was one of them, and I didn't shoot him. Your Heather did. She was pissed. She had the gun. The cops said she was with him before he was shot. Duh." She shook her head. "I've got to get back."

She pivoted, threw her cigarette butt on the ground, and stomped away.

Charles watched her and turned to me and shook his head. "That went well. Any other brilliant plans to get Heather off the hook?"

"When's his funeral?"

"Should be soon if he's not already planted. Why?"

"I thought we might go to the visitation."

"Of that SOB?"

"Unless you have better ideas. If we could talk to widow Starr, she might help."

Charles pointed to my phone. "Look it up on that thingy."

A search of the Nashville area obituaries revealed Kevin Starr's interment was still in the future…tomorrow, in fact. Visitation was to begin in an hour at a funeral home a couple of miles from his house. We were on that side of town and decided we were dressed well enough to stop by. I pulled in the parking lot of the white-painted brick funeral home thirty minutes before visitation was to begin, on time, per Charles.

Gwen Parsons returned my call while we waited. I put the phone on speaker, and after a minute of her expressing sympathy for Heather, I asked if we could meet and talk about Starr. She surprised me when she said no, that she was busy and didn't have time, and she said it after I'd said it could be a time and location of her choice in the next couple of days. I gave up on meeting and asked if she had any idea who killed him. She said there could have been any number of people who wanted Starr dead. She couldn't or wouldn't narrow it down. She wished she could help her "good friend" Heather, but didn't know what she could do. She again said she was sorry, and had to go.

"Quick question," I said and hoped she hadn't hung up. "Who else knew you sold Heather the gun?"

She was silent, and I figured the next sound would be the electronic buzz after a hang up. "You there?"

"Sorry, I was thinking. A lot of people know. It wasn't a big secret. We were at the Bird when I gave it to her, standing out front with a ton of people around. Umm, Jessica was there, so was, oh what's his name, Joey, and two or three other pickers I sort of know." She giggled. "The only guys who didn't know were the fuddy-duddy security guards. Didn't think it would be wise to wave it in front of them."

"Who's Joey?" I asked.

"Some guy letting Heather try his guitar. He's always trying to sell something. Says he needs the money to write songs, calls it plying his craft. Can you believe that?"

I remembered him from our visit to the Bluebird. "Was Starr his agent?"

"Nah, he doesn't have one. He wanted us to introduce him to Starr, but the son of…uh, he never showed up at our gigs."

"Are you sure—"

"Sorry, have to go."

Everything in the funeral home was muted: muted music from the funeral home version of Muzak; muted-color, thick carpeting muted our footsteps, through the muted corridors covered with muted wallcovering. What wasn't muted as we stepped into a viewing room, was the robust fragrance of floral arrangements. I sneezed and told Charles, in muted tones, of course, how much the smell in funeral homes bothered me and how it always got my allergies in an uproar. Charles, being the fount of everything trivial, proceeded to tell me that in the pre-air-conditioned, pre-embalming days, flowers at funerals were to mask the smell of the corpse. I asked him if funeral directors realized those days were long gone and he suggested this would be a good time to ask a funeral director. I said never mind.

Much to my relief, the steel-gray coffin housing Kevin Starr was closed. Open coffins bothered me more than the stench of funeral flowers. The room was near empty. I assumed because the visitation had just begun and people were still at work. A man in his late-sixties asked if we were friends of Kevin. We lied and said yes and he shared that he was Kevin's father. He didn't know any of his son's friends since he lived in California, and told us he was the reason the funeral had been delayed. He had been in Italy and got back in the country last night and flew to Nashville. We listened to his long-winded story until he started telling us about his "holiday" in Tuscany. I interrupted and said it was nice to meet him and that we wanted to pay our condolences to his daughter-in-law.

Sandy was in one of the chairs with a muted geometric pattern on the seat, and talking to a woman who appeared to be about her age. We walked over to them, and Sandy glanced up at us like she recognized our faces but couldn't recall from where. The other lady leaned down and gave Sandy a hug and said she'd let her talk to the new arrivals.

The grieving widow stood and held out her hand. She wore a black dress that looked new. It was loose on her shoulders and I suspected was probably bought for her by someone else. Makeup covered most of the red around her eyes. I told her who we were and reminded her about the visit to her house.

"Oh yes." Her voice was hoarse and soft. If the room hadn't been so empty, I wouldn't have heard what she said.

Sandy didn't give any indication that she remembered who was with us or that she knew one of the visitors to her house was accused of murdering her husband. I told her we were sorry for her loss. She nodded, and glanced around the room and noticed there was no one waiting to talk to her.

"I'm being rude," she whispered, and pointed to the chairs beside her. "Please have a seat."

I said, "How are the children?"

Charles glanced at me and gave an expression that screamed, "That's not why we're here."

Sandy looked toward the door to the corridor. "They're in a little room out there where they have toys and books. Kevin's mom is with them."

She continued to look at the door and hadn't answered my question. Perhaps she was in shock and didn't want to, or couldn't, deal with their condition. If I didn't know it was the same person, I never would have suspected this was the same lady we'd met pounding on red-hot steel in her blacksmith shop.

Sandy turned back to us. "I apologize. This has been rough, and I'm not thinking straight, please tell me again how you know—knew, Kevin."

Charles said, "He met my fiancée when he was at Folly Beach a few months ago. He heard her sing and wanted to be her agent,"

He hadn't used Heather's name.

"Folly Beach," Sandy said like she was rolling the words around in her mouth. "Where's that?"

She still hadn't put two-and-two together and connected us with Kevin's alleged murderer. I explained that Folly Beach was a tiny island near Charleston, South Carolina, and we had met—sort of met—Kevin there.

Sandy looked at me like I'd said we hooked up with her husband on the North Pole. "I'm sorry," she whispered, "I'm confused. Kevin's never been to Charleston, a least not since we met ten years ago."

And she was confused, I thought.

"It was five months ago," Charles said, like that would make things clear.

She shook her head and stared at him.

"He told my fiancée he was staying at the hotel and was meeting with record executives from New York. Think he said it was a retreat. He—"

Sandy pulled her shoulders back and clinched her fists. "I don't know why you think that. It couldn't have been."

I said, "When we met you at your house, you said he was gone a lot." Today must be horrible for the young widow and I could understand how she may have forgotten. "You mentioned trips to North and South Carolina. Couldn't the trip to Folly have been one of those times?"

"No. I distinctly remember the two trips he made to South Carolina were to Columbia. I remember because that's where one of my best friends in college was from."

I didn't want to argue while she was sitting a dozen feet from her husband's coffin. I was certain I'd seen Kevin Starr in Cal's Bar, in Folly Beach. "I'm a little confused myself. You're certain he hasn't been there?"

"Kevin called me most every night he was on the road. He always talked to the kids if they were awake, and told me where he was." She hesitated, and continued, "He brought them souvenirs from each of the cities he visited. Nothing big, you know, little cheap stuff with the city's name on it." A tear appeared in the corner of her eye. "He did it so they would learn about other places and so … and so they'd want to visit the cities with us when they got older."

When we had been at her house, she'd told us about his calling from the trips. It wasn't many years ago that saying where he had called from would have meant something. Now, with ubiquitous cell phones, his calls could have been from anywhere. I was as certain as I was sitting here, if he called her that often, one or more of them had originated from Folly, regardless what he'd told her.

Sandy wiped the tear from her cheek. Her hands began to fidget, she shredded a tissue, and squeezed it in her fist. It didn't take a psychiatrist to see we had started a conversation she didn't want to be part of. I started to excuse us when she snapped out of her reverie and glared at Charles.

"What did you say your fiancée's name was?"

"Heather."

Sandy pushed out of the chair, stood and looked down at us. If she had her blacksmith hammer, I suspected she would have treated us like a lump of molten steel.

"The bitch who killed Kevin?"

A handful of others had arrived while we were talking. All conversation stopped, and Kevin's father started toward us.

"We're sorry to have bothered you," I said and eased Charles toward the exit. The only smell I detected on the way out was that of hate.

"What do you think?" Charles asked. We were driving through rush-hour traffic on the way to the apartment.

"She either had lied to us about knowing he'd been in Folly or he had lied to her."

Charles looked at his imaginary watch and at the traffic stopped in front of us. We had nowhere to be, yet he was in a hurry to get there. He sighed like we were going to be late. "She didn't throw off any vibes she was fibbing. I can't see any reason she would have for not admitting he'd been in Folly."

For the next fifteen minutes, we traveled five blocks in traffic that was more akin to stop-and-stop rather than stop-and-go. We talked about why he may not have been telling her the truth and what it could've meant to getting him killed.

Starr had made several out of town trips looking for talent or doing whatever he could to increase his business, so I didn't understand why he'd lie about being in the Charleston area. Why would it have been different than being in Columbia, or anywhere else? Could he have been having an affair? The simple answer was yes. If true, there could have been two more people who may have wanted him dead: whoever he was having the affair with and the lady we had just left wearing a poorly-fitting black dress. I couldn't see Sandy as the murderer. She was hurting, and her reaction when she found out about Heather hadn't been faked. Besides, no one could have mistaken her for Heather, not even in a dark bar. The person Starr could have been having an affair with was another story. If she was one of Starr's aspiring singers, he probably conned her into moving here and since we had no idea who she might be, she could have looked enough like Heather to have fooled the bartender in a dimly-lit room.

We pulled into the parking lot and Charles once again asked the question for which I had no reasonable answer.

"What about the gun?"

"I don't know."

"That's what I thought."

"What I do know is Starr had a reason for lying about being in Folly, a reason which may have gotten him killed. We need to find what it was. We also know the police aren't looking beyond Heather. I need to head home and see what I can learn."

"What time are *we* leaving?"

I told Charles we should leave in the morning. He asked why we couldn't leave now. I asked if he wanted to drive all night; he said on second thought, leaving in the morning was a good idea.

I couldn't have been asleep more than an hour and wondered why the alarm clock was going off. It took me a few seconds to escape from the sound sleep and to realize I didn't have an alarm clock. It was the phone. By the time I was awake enough to answer, whoever had called had been sent to voicemail.

It was after midnight so whoever had called must have had a good reason for calling. I tapped the voicemail icon.

"Yo, Chris," Cal said. "It's—oh, oh—past your beddy-bye time. Sorry. Anyway, if you get this and aren't going to give me a scolding for calling late, call me back. The number is—hell, you know the number."

I wasn't going to rule out scolding, but knew it had to be important for him to call. I tapped his number.

"Hello," he yelled, above the sound of George Jones bemoaning something from the jukebox, and a few patrons who sounded like they had consumed a few beers on the other side of sober.

I told him who it was and said it sounded like he was busy. He said something about overflow from a property-managers' convention at the Tides and said he was glad I had called.

"Didn't wake you up, did I?"

I said he hadn't and asked what was so important.

"Think I've figured out something about shyster Starr's trips over this way."

Someone in the background yelled, "Another round, cowboy." I heard other voices but couldn't tell what they were saying.

"You still there, Kentucky?"

I said I was and that I didn't catch what he'd said.

"When're you moseying this way?"

I told him Charles and I were heading to Folly in the morning.

"Hold your jackass," Cal shouted.

I told myself he was talking to a soused property manager and not me.

There was more mumbling in the background and Cal said, "Holler when you unsaddle at your bunkhouse."

I went out on a limb and assumed he meant for me to get with him when we got home. "You got it, pard."

It was another hour before I stopped wondering what he had learned and returned to sleep.

CHAPTER NINETEEN

After one Starbucks' stop, a Dunkin' Donuts' detour, and yawns that made the inside of the car sound like a six-a.m. commuter train, Charles and I were on the Interstate headed to Folly Beach.

Between yawns Charles asked, "What do you think Cal wants to tell you?"

"Don't know. He doesn't call often, so it's important."

Charles nodded, took another bite of doughnut, and mumbled, "Maybe you ought to call him."

I explained that Cal didn't get home from work not that long ago. If he wasn't asleep, he should be. It could wait until we got back. Charles said I was right about Cal being asleep and I could wait another couple of hours to call. The *wait until we got back* part slipped past him. I pretended it was a good idea.

The trip was all Interstate and except for several miles of winding roads on each side of Asheville, was easy driving. My age and having made the trip so many times in the last couple of weeks was taking its toll on my aching bones and my posterior. Despite his constant babbling about things trivial and irrelevant, having Charles with me made it go quicker. I would have been less patient if I hadn't suspected he was trying to distract me, as well as himself, from thinking about Heather's problems. He wasn't successful. Several times he repeated his belief she was guilty and wondered how he had fallen for a killer. I still couldn't wrap my arms around her guilt and tried to tell him we would do everything possible to find the real killer. I tried to be convincing, yet wasn't certain he was wrong.

Two hours later, Charles remembered his brilliant idea for me to call Cal. Unless I called, I would hear it repeated each mile marker, so I had him punch in the number. He did and handed me the phone. I got Cal's brief voicemail message and left him an equally brief request to call.

Cal hadn't returned my call when we reached the bridge over the Folly River. I was exhausted and suspected Charles was too, yet he insisted we go to Cal's and find the inconsiderate crooner before doing anything else. I parked a block from the bar in an empty spot in front of Cal's classic Cadillac.

I smiled, albeit an exhausted smile, as I entered Cal's. I felt at home. The aging singer greeted us in his Stetson. In the spirit of Folly, he wore a faded, black Nike golf shirt, yellow shorts, and mismatched tennis shoes. Charles had done better in his orange Clemson University National Champions long-sleeve T-shirt, blue shorts, as he tapped his cane on the worn carpeting. As usual, I was the most boring and least Folly-attired of the three in my light-blue golf shirt and navy shorts. The familiar, welcoming smell of frying hamburgers and seeing Cal made the long, exhausting trip worth it.

There were a couple of dozen others in the bar, a good crowd for a weeknight. I knew several of them and they waved at us. We reciprocated and Charles lit into Cal.

"We called you a thousand times. Got your danged machine. You never called back. We could have been turned upside down on

I-26 and you didn't even listen to our messages to save our lives." He paused and took a breath. "Well, what do you say for yourself?"

Cal pushed his hat back and leaned against the bar. "Well, former Folly resident," Cal said in a calm voice he'd perfected during his years entertaining in bars to defuse difficult situations. "Seems to this old-timer that if you were ass up on the side of the road, you would've been better off calling 911 than this old barkeep."

Charles huffed. "Not the point."

I thought it was a good point and hugged Cal and said it was good to be home.

He thanked me, walked behind the bar, got us drinks, and said, "Sorry, Charles, didn't know you called. Must've left my phone in the car. What'd you need?"

Charles smiled. "Apology accepted. Chris wanted to hear what you learned and couldn't wait until we got back to ask."

I must have forgotten that part.

"Think I've got it figured out. It's gonna get Heather off the bucking bronco, and lasso the real killer." He put Charles's beer on the bar, looked around and saw no one was waiting for a drink, "Hang on a sec. Let me get the phone before I forget."

Charles started to object. It wouldn't have mattered since Cal was already headed to the door.

Caldwell Ramsey moved up to the bar and stood beside us. "Hello, Charles, Chris."

"Howdy, Caldwell," Charles said and looked behind the music promoter. "Where's Mad Mel?"

Caldwell nodded toward the empty bar stool. "May I join you?"

I waved for him to have a seat.

He sat and looked at his watch. "Mel should be pulling in to the dock about now. He had a group of college students who wanted to enjoy the marsh, privacy, and a few drinks. I was supposed to meet a client here but she called and said she wasn't going to make it."

"So, you're slummin' with Chris and me."

Caldwell smiled. "I've spent time with worse." His smile disappeared. "Cal told me about Heather—terrible. How's she doing?"

Charles gave a sanitized update on Heather's condition, how she was handling jail, and about her lawyer.

Caldwell leaned his tall, trim body close to Charles, listened, and nodded, before saying in a low voice, "Please let me know if there's anything I can do."

"I will. Thanks for asking. Can we buy you a drink?"

Caldwell looked down at his watch again. "Think I could throw back one more." He looked around the room. "Where's Cal?"

"Went to the car to get his phone," I said. "Should be back soon."

Caldwell smiled. "Suppose I can wait a little longer for my beer."

John Anderson's "Swingin'" blasted from the jukebox and one of the patrons I didn't recognize accidentally elbowed me on his way to the bar. "Excuse me," he said with a beer-breath slur. "Where's the cowboy?"

Charles told him to cool his jets and the bartender would be right back.

Caldwell looked toward the door and at Charles. "Where'd he park, Mt. Pleasant?"

Charles looked at Caldwell, and at the other man who was staggering around waiting for another beer. "Let's check on him. He should've been back."

I wasn't nearly as nosy as Charles, and it felt good to be relaxing at the bar after a day on the road. Still, I followed Charles outside.

We'd parked in front of Cal's car, so we knew where it was. The area was poorly lit and from a distance everything looked fine; fine except no Cal.

"Where'd he get to?" Charles asked. He stopped and shouted,

"Cal!" Charles pointed to a body on the ground beside the car's rear door. I was behind Charles and couldn't see who it was until I recognized our friend's unmistakable attire. Cal was on his stomach and splayed out on the sandy berm. His Stetson was upside down beside his arm and it looked like it had been stomped on. So did Cal's head. His long hair was covered with blood and a trickle of it ran down the side of his face.

I rushed past Charles and bent down to see if Cal was breathing. At first, I didn't think so, until I saw his hand twitch. Charles moved to my side and bent over to get a better view. He asked if Cal was alive. I said barely, and told Charles to run get a medic and a cop. City Hall was across the street from Cal's and housed both its police and fire departments.

Charles rushed off and I kept asking Cal if he could hear me. He didn't respond. I was afraid to move him so I yanked off my shirt and pressed it against the head wound. I prayed an EMT would arrive in time to help. Blood was still oozing from his head, but seemed to be slowing as I kept pressing on the shirt. I hoped it wasn't wishful thinking on my part.

I realized that whoever had hit him could be nearby. I craned my head around while maintaining pressure on his wound. Laughter from a group walking on the other side of the road was all I heard. I didn't see anyone else.

Charles must have made quite a ruckus at the public safety building. Two minutes later, he was back with two EMTs and two police officers. I stood and on wobbly legs stepped aside for the medics to do their thing. One of them asked one of the cops to call for an ambulance. He said he already had. The other police officer pulled Charles and me away from the life-saving efforts and asked what had happened. We said we wouldn't be much help and explained how we had been with Cal in the bar when he left to get his phone out of his car. Officer Kasper took our names, contact numbers, and told us a detective would be contacting us in the morning. He said that was all he needed and waited for us to leave.

I wasn't going to be dismissed. "Is his wallet on him?" Cal always carried an oversized wallet.

Kasper walked over to the paramedic who was watching his partner work on Cal and asked if there was a wallet. The paramedic bent over and felt the back of Cal's pants.

"Don't think so."

The officer shook his head. "Looks like a mugging. Thanks again, gentlemen."

I was polite but firm and told him Cal didn't have any relatives, Charles and I were his good friends, and we weren't going anywhere until he was on his way to the hospital. I also told him we would follow the ambulance. From our vantage point, it didn't appear Cal had moved since we'd found him.

We waited for the ambulance, and I grabbed a clean shirt from my suitcase, before realizing there was no one in charge of the bar. I called Preacher Burl who agreed to play bartender and close for the night. He said he would pray for Cal. I prayed he would be successful. After watching the seventy-two-year-old lay motionless on the berm, I wasn't optimistic.

CHAPTER TWENTY

I had spent so much time at the hospital in Charleston, I should have been given access to the doctor's parking lot and the employee's discount at the restaurant. I'd been here as a patient, and often had visited friends in varying degrees of medical distress. I was never comfortable with the annoying odor of the antiseptic cleaning fluids and the sad sight of sick and injured people in the emergency room.

"When are they going to tell us something?" Charles asked, for a third time. He had stopped pacing the room, and flopped down in a chair.

"When they know something," I said, for a third time.

It had been an hour since the EMTs wheeled our friend through the door into the bowels of the hospital. One of the medics who transported him told us he had a concussion and had lost a lot of blood. His vitals were adequate, although nothing to brag about. I had asked if Cal would make it and was told it wasn't up to him to say.

Preacher Burl called to ask about Cal, when a middle-aged,

overweight doctor with a face that hadn't seen a razor for a few days walked out of the treatment area, looked around, and plodded over to Charles and me. I told Burl I'd call him back and shook hands with the doc. His face didn't give anything away except fatigue.

I explained Cal didn't have any family and we were his best friends. He hesitated before saying anything, but said, "He's fortunate. His skull isn't fractured. His brain's taken quite a jarring. To put it in simple terms, he was hit with a heavy object, maybe a ball bat or piece of wood or metal." He hesitated and rubbed his temples. "The blow caused his brain to rattle around in his head. It bounced off his skull, causing bruising."

Charles stepped closer to the doctor. "Is he conscious?"

The doctor grimaced. "He's mumbling and not making sense. Is he in the music business?"

I said he was a singer and had been for decades.

"Country music?" the doc asked.

I nodded.

"Makes more sense. Mr. Ballew tried to sit up in bed and started talking to someone he called Roy about singing 'Wabash Cannonball.' Then he said something about seeing her in Nashville and how much he missed Patsy." He smiled. "My dad was a big country fan and was always talking about Roy Acuff and Patsy Cline. Figured that may've been who your friend was referring to."

"Is it normal for him to be talking about ancient history?" I asked.

"Not unusual," the doctor said, back in his medical-professional voice. "A head trauma can cause a plethora of distinct and nonlinear reactions within the brain. He may not be able to remember what happened tonight, while he's as clear as day about incidents fifty years ago. It's possible to confuse periods of time."

Charles said, "Will he be okay?"

"His vitals are strong for someone his age. It may take time, but the odds of a full recovery are decent."

"Can we see him?" I asked.

The doctor shook his head. "The fewer distractions he has over the next twenty-four hours the better. He needs to stay calm. Maybe tomorrow afternoon. Leave your number at the desk in case we need to get in touch with you. Sorry about whatever happened."

We thanked him and he headed back to the treatment rooms.

"He's fortunate to be alive," Charles said. "No matter what you say, being hardheaded's a good thing."

"Hardheaded and wearing a Stetson."

"Huh?"

"Did you see his hat? It was crushed; must have taken some of the steam out of the blow. If he didn't have it on, I bet he wouldn't be with us."

"Fortunate," Charles said. He turned his attention to two men entering the room.

One was in a sport coat but with no tie and the other in a white polo shirt. Regardless of their dress, their gait and the way they surveyed the room screamed official, detective official. It also didn't hurt the identification to see each had a holstered firearm attached to his belt. The emergency room was nearly vacant, a rare sight, so the detectives focused on Charles and me.

The one in the sport coat asked, "Are you the ones who found the guy by his car?"

I was irked by his impersonal attitude, and told him yes, we found "Mr. Ballew."

He introduced himself and his partner as detectives from the Charleston County Sheriff's Office, didn't bother to show identification, and said they had a few questions.

The other detective nodded toward the treatment rooms. "He going to make it?"

"The doctor said Mr. Ballew has a good chance of recovering," I said, with an emphasis on Mr. I also told them what the doc had said about visitors in case they'd planned to barge in the treatment room.

"Oh great, now we'll have to wait until tomorrow to talk to him," the first detective said, and hesitated like he had realized how callused he'd sounded. "Glad he's going to pull through. The cops in Folly didn't think he was going to live. They told us what you told them. Let's hear it from you."

"I doubt we can add to what you already know," I said, and repeated what we had told the responding officers.

"Before the vic...umm, Mr. Ballew, left the bar to get his phone, did you notice anyone paying particular attention to him or if anyone left when he did?"

"We hadn't been there long," I said. "I didn't see anyone paying attention to him. Did you, Charles?"

"There was a crowd. Would've been hard to notice anyone in particular."

"Anyone leave when he did?"

Charles rubbed his chin. "Can't say yea, can't say nay."

"So, you didn't see anyone leave?"

Charles glared at the casually-dressed detective. "That's what I said."

Charles had taken great pride in getting along with everyone. Heather's experience with the police was shortening his fuse when it came to law enforcement.

I said, "We didn't see anyone leave. Sorry." I hoped Charles wouldn't say anything else.

"Did he carry large sums of money?"

"Not unless he was taking home the night's revenue," I said. "He was going to the car to get his phone, so I doubt he had much."

"Did he have enemies?" the detective in the sport coat asked.

"Not really," I said. "Everyone got along with him."

"Other than robbery, can you think of any reason someone would want to harm him?"

For a second, I thought about Cal's comment that he had figured something out about Starr's murder. Could it have had something to do with that? I couldn't see how, and didn't want to get into the Heather/Starr situation with the insensitive detectives.

"Not really."

Charles nodded and kept his mouth closed.

The detectives gave us their cards and asked us to call if we thought of anything.

We returned to the island and swung by Cal's to see if Burl needed help closing. He had shooed the last customer out, finished a cursory clean-up, and was locking the door. We updated him, and thanked him for coming to our friend's rescue. He said he would open the bar tomorrow night, actually tonight, since it was well past midnight. I dropped Charles at his apartment and drove home. My eyes watered from exhaustion and staring at pavement all day.

"What a day," I said to myself as I fell into my familiar bed for the first time in several days. Ride ten hours with my best friend who was in the most depressed condition I had ever seen him in; find Cal motionless on the side of the road; spend two hours in the hospital, a building I had come to hate; and now I lay here, eyes wide open staring at the ceiling faintly illuminated by the green digital numerals from my bedside clock. Yes, what a day.

Did Cal know something about the murder? If he did, how could he have learned whatever it was? Would he recover enough to tell us? Then, why did Starr lie to his wife about where he'd been? Starr had told Heather he had been at the Tides with record executives from New York. That didn't sound like something to keep from his wife. Considering what had happened, I wondered if he'd even been at the hotel.

I didn't think I had, yet apparently, I'd fallen asleep somewhere in my thought process. Otherwise the loud ringtone from my phone wouldn't be waking me up. The green digital numbers I had stared at most of the night now indicated it was seven thirty.

"Let's take a meeting with Cindy," Charles said. He sounded more enthusiastic than he had in days.

"Huh?" I said, with less enthusiasm.

"Sorry. You're not in the music business. That means let's give a holler out to Cindy and see if she can jabber with us."

Cindy LaMond was Folly's director of public safety, police chief to most everyone else, and top cop to the more verbally challenged. She was also a good friend, married to another friend, Larry LaMond, the owner of Pewter Hardware, Folly's pint-sized hardware store.

"I know what take a meeting means. The *huh* was for why?"

"I was sitting in the living room in the middle of the night and thinking about slime ball Starr and him fibbin' to his wife about being here."

"Not only do great minds think alike, so do mediocre ones."

"Whatever." He continued like I hadn't spoken. "We need to fill her in on what's going on. We need her coppy skills. We've got to get Heather out of that horrid place."

"I was already thinking about calling the chief. Maybe she can learn if Starr was staying at the Tides and who he was meeting. She—"

"So why are you wasting time talking? Call her."

It would have been pointless to tell him it wasn't yet eight o'clock and I would wait until there was a better chance of not getting cussed out by calling so early. I told him I'd let him know as soon as I talked to her.

I reluctantly selected Chief LaMond's number from my contacts list.

"Well, if it isn't trouble's lightning rod," came the chief's way too cheery voice.

I hated caller ID. "Good morning, Chief."

"Don't get all mushy with me. I'm sitting here at my super-duper, big-girl police chief's desk reading a report my officers filed last night. And whose name should appear in big almost illegible print right on this here piece of paper?" I heard paper crinkling in the background. "What in the big pile of pachyderm poop have you stepped in now? Whoa, don't answer. How's Cal?"

Cindy took a breath and I took the gap in her tirade to give her Cal's condition and said I would tell her all about the pile of poop if she'd meet Charles and me at the Dog. She said that's what she lived for and meeting with the two of us was right up there with spending a month in Paris with her hubby. The only Paris she'd ever seen was in her home state of Tennessee. I thanked her for the totally-insincere compliment and we agreed to meet in a half hour.

I called Charles and told him the plan. He told me he'd already figured that out and was on his way to the Dog. I had no desire to get in a car, so I walked the few blocks to the restaurant. It was already hot, and the humidity lingered in the air like smoke from a campfire. I dreaded the walk home. Charles was already there and sitting in my favorite booth in back, and was wearing a black, long-sleeve T-shirt with NYPD in large block letters on the front. It was one of the few T-shirts he owned that didn't have a college name or mascot on the front. He wore the NYPD shirt when he was meeting with the police.

Charles looked at his imaginary watch. "She's not here yet."

Empty seats had already given that away and I reminded my pre-prompt friend it wasn't time.

Charles said, "So?"

Cindy arrived before we had time to debate the merits of being early. The chief was in her early fifties, five-foot-three, with curly dark hair and most often a smile. Her smile was missing this morning. She rolled her eyes and gave a slight shake of the head as she lowered herself in the chair beside Charles.

"Welcome back, stranger," she said and pinched Charles's arm.

He smiled. "Thanks."

Cindy turned to me. "If it weren't for you two, I could lay-off half of my force and save the penny-pinching taxpayers a bundle." My several-year-long crusade to reintroduce civility to personal greetings and introductions continued to fail. "You're going to kill me with all the trouble you trip over. This bod's not meant to work this hard."

Charles patted her on the hand. "Ronnie Reagan said, 'It's true that hard work never killed anyone, but I figure, why take the chance?'"

She shook her head, this time with much more determination. "My crapometer says you and your quotes are full of it."

Charles held his hands out, palms facing Cindy. "Look them up."

"Like I have time, or care. Any news on Cal?"

I told her she knew everything we knew.

She nodded and turned to Charles. "How's Heather?"

Charles gave a brief, canned answer. He didn't delve into how she was adjusting to jail life.

"So, what's so all-fired important that you're going to buy me breakfast?"

Amber arrived at the table with coffee for the chief.

"Don't I get any?" I asked.

She patted my arm like she would a puppy. "Top cop first. You'll get yours soon enough." She leaned over and gave Charles an awkward hug. "Good to see you; sorry about Heather. You okay?"

"Not really."

"Poor baby."

The perceptive server saw Charles wasn't going to say anything else. "I'll get your coffee."

Cindy put her hands around the mug but left it on the table. "What questionable deed are you two hankering for?"

Charles and I tag-teamed her with details of the search of the apartment and car, the police finding the murder weapon in Charles's car, the other clients of Starr who would have had just as strong a motive to kill him, and the couple at the studio where Starr owed a boat-load of money, and details of how Heather had met Starr. We told her about talking with Starr's wife and how she said he'd never been to Folly Beach. And finished with what Cal had said about learning something about Starr being here.

Cindy finally sipped her coffee. "You think it had something to do with his mugging?"

I said, "It may have been robbery. My gut tells me it was something else. Add to that what Starr's wife had said about him not being here, and it seems to me there are too many coincidences."

"Ah, this is where you drag me into your little drama?"

"No wonder you're chief," Charles said. "Brilliant, beautiful, and willing to help citizens in need."

Cindy rolled her eyes. "Charles, now you've gone and blown the top off my crapometer." She turned to me. "What do you need?"

"Check with the Tides and see if Kevin Starr stayed there. Your clout as chief can get information from the hotel that we can't. If he was there, for how long; if he was alone, see if there were guests from New York at the same time, and if so, their names. If someone there remembers him, ask if they remember anything about his stay."

"Like who he was having an affair with?" she added.

Charles said, "Knew we could count on you."

"While I'm at it, why don't I see if Starr's little floozy told anyone at the hotel she planned to steal Heather's gun and kill him with it?"

Charles said, "Your thinking's getting gooder and gooder."

Cindy rolled her eyes. "I'll see what I can do."

Charles pointed his cane toward the exit. "Now?"

"No way. I was promised breakfast."

I gave her the approximate dates Starr had been here and she waved for Amber and ordered the most expensive item on the menu. Charles and I ordered the lowest priced meal. For the next forty-five minutes, we ate, Charles relaxed and talked about how Heather was, and told Cindy about Heather's appearances at the Bluebird. Cindy said growing up in East Tennessee her dream was to be a country singer at Dollywood in Pigeon Forge. She said the only thing that held her back was she couldn't sing "worth a bent toothpick."

I thought, but of course didn't say, it hadn't stopped Heather.

Amber slid the check to my side of the table. Charles grabbed it and mumbled, "You're the greatest friend anyone could ever have. I owe you big time."

Cindy grabbed her cell phone and took a photo of Charles and turned to me, "Chris, got the number of the *National Enquirer*? Aliens have done taken over Charles's body."

Charles said, "Ha, ha."

I smiled, and Cindy headed out to make our six-mile-long, half-mile-wide slice of heaven safer.

CHAPTER TWENTY-ONE

It hadn't been the twenty-four hours the doc said Cal needed to rest. It didn't stop Charles from insisting we stand outside his hospital room until he *comes to his senses* and tells what he had learned about Starr's murder. The nurse said Cal had improved, was alert, yet he was still vague about recent events. She said the doc allowed two detectives to interview him earlier, and since we were already here, we could see him. She tapped her watch and said we could only stay a few minutes.

"See," Charles said on our way to Cal's door. "Told you he was okay."

I followed Charles into the room. The head of Cal's bed was elevated and he was watching television. His head was wrapped in gauze from his eyebrows up. I didn't need to see that to know he wasn't well. He was watching *HGTV*, which was akin to me watching the *Food Channel*. That was proof his mind wasn't functioning properly.

He glanced away from an "incredible" bathroom makeover and

grinned. "Hear you two rustled me up and herded me toward this bunk. My hat's off to you if I can remember where I left it."

Smashed and along the side of the road, as I recall.

Charles asked, "How're you feeling?"

He touched his gauze-covered skull. "Like the bull flung me off and stomped on my head."

I said, "You were lucky."

"You wouldn't say that if you were livin' inside this pounding head."

"Lucky to still be with us," I corrected.

He nodded and winced. "Remind me not to move so fast."

I sat in the chair near the bed and Charles stood behind me.

"What happened?" I asked.

"That's the same question the cops asked." He ever so slowly shook his head. "I'll give you the same answer I gave them. I don't have a gnat-turd-sized clue."

"Remember anything?" I asked.

"Opened the bar. Sold some beer and think I ran out of Bud Light. Remember two grumpy cops trying to get me to say things I don't remember. That brings me up to now. How am I doing?"

I rested my hand on his shoulder. "You're doing fine, Cal. Take your time."

Charles started to speak. Instead, he closed his mouth. Maybe maturity was growing on him.

Cal closed his eyes and I leaned closer. "Remember us coming in last night when we got back from Nashville?"

"Nope, but the cops said you found me."

"You don't remember seeing us?" Charles asked like if he changed the words around he'd get a different answer.

He looked at Charles and at me. "Were you in the bar? Thought you found me on the street."

I explained how we were there and how he'd said he left his

phone in the car. We were worried when he didn't come back, and came to find him. He thanked us again.

"Do you remember calling us in Nashville and saying you had learned something about why Starr was in Folly?"

Cal closed his eyes, opened them, and looked at me. Nothing.

Charles's head dropped and he sighed.

"When did I do that?"

"Day before yesterday," I said. "You called from the bar. It was loud and you said you knew something about Starr's trip."

"If you say so." He looked around the room. "You know where my hat is? Feel naked without it."

I told him we'd find it for him.

"Much obliged." He closed his eyes.

The nurse stuck her head in the door and motioned us out.

I squeezed Cal's hand. He thanked us for coming and said he thought a nap would work wonders, and we headed to the door. To say I was depressed, bewildered, and worried would have been like calling the Grand Canyon a big ditch. I was also confused, although nothing compared to Cal.

We passed the nurse in the corridor. "Did he recognize you?"

"Yes," Charles said.

"That's good. He'll come around."

Charles said, "When?"

"If only we could tell. Could be hours, days, or—never mind. That's for the doctor to say."

Charles stopped in mid stride and looked around. "Miss Nurse, I ain't seeing no docs around. What's your guess?"

"I wouldn't venture a guess. I've seen it last months or longer. We just don't know."

I left Charles at his old apartment after we'd discussed going to the bar later to help Preacher Burl. It was open-mic night and this time of year Cal's was often full with singing wannabes, their dutiful family and friends, regulars who were there each night, and the few who felt it was their calling to make fun of aspiring, albeit untalented musicians. Charles wasn't enthused about helping Burl. A few years back, Cal had asked him to "go undercover" as a bartender and use his self-anointed private detective skills. Cal was new to the bar business at the time and had suspected someone was stealing from him. The plan would have been perfect if Charles could bartend, which he couldn't, and if he could detect, which he was inept at. Through the grace of God, a once-in-a-lifetime alignment of the stars, and pure luck, Charles, with the help of yours truly, had caught the culprit—sort of. That's a story for another time.

Cal's would be open beyond my senior-citizen, normal bedtime, and I was taking a nap when Cindy called.

"No one using the name Kevin Starr checked into the Tides on or before the dates you gave me."

"How about Starr Management?" I said, task focused.

"Gee, Chris. Why didn't I think of asking that?" She sighed. "Oh wait, I did. I'm not chief just because of my pretty face. Got the same answer."

"Did you happen to use your amazing police-chief skills and pretty face to ask if there was a group from New York staying around that time?"

"Yes and no."

I waited for more and finally said, "Yes you asked and no you didn't ask, or yes you asked and the answer was no."

"You've got it." Cindy chuckled.

"No New Yorkers."

"Two couples of geezers from Yonkers. That was it. Doubt they were on a music retreat or were singers meeting with an agent. Thickens your plot, don't it?"

"Not only was he lying to his wife, he misled Heather about where and why he was here."

"Sounds like it. Because he didn't check in under his name, doesn't mean he didn't stay there. Yell if I can break any more laws for you."

The Tides may not have had anyone named Starr as a registered guest, yet there was one person who would remember if he'd met the agent. Jay Vaughn was a friend and had worked at the Tides for years. No one seemed to know his official title, although everyone who had stayed at the hotel knew Jay, and he knew them. He was bellhop, unofficial greeter, provider of security, and information about everything Folly and most everything Charleston.

He was off Tuesdays, but I walked through the hotel's lobby on my indirect route from home to Cal's to see if other employees I knew might have remembered the agent. I was surprised to see Jay talking to two ladies dressed for a formal event in Charleston—or I hoped so, because if they went to any of Folly's restaurants dressed that way, they would have been as out of place as a cheeseburger at a vegan convention.

"Hey, Chris," Jay said when he saw me standing behind the women, "let me introduce you to two guests."

He proceeded to tell me who the ladies were, that they were on Folly to attend a high-school reunion, and introduced me to the women. I detected a slight *who cares* look in their eyes. It didn't stop Jay. They said they had to get to Charleston for the reunion and said it was nice meeting me and excused themselves.

Jay shook my hand and said he had heard about Heather and asked how she was doing. I wasn't surprised he knew since there wasn't much that happened in Folly that he didn't know. I told him she was doing the best that could be expected. He asked how Charles was taking it. I said he could be doing better and he asked me to give him his best then asked what brought me to the hotel. I told him he was the person I wanted to see, and I knew it was his day off, so I was looking for anyone who could answer a question. He was there because two employees called in sick, and asked what I needed.

"It has to do with Heather."

"I hope I can help."

I told him a little about Kevin Starr and how Starr said he was staying at the Tides the night he first met Heather.

Jay tilted his head and asked when that was. I gave him the date and he shook his head.

"I'm not great on dates," he said, "but I do remember that one because I had to take my car to the shop to have some work redone. To be honest, I was perturbed with the mechanic. Anyway, I don't recall anyone named Kevin staying here that night. Did he say how long he had been here?"

I told Jay I wasn't sure. From what he'd said, it could have been several nights.

"No, don't believe he was here."

"How about people from New York? I heard they were in the music industry and on a retreat that Starr was here for."

"New York," said Jay as he rubbed his chin. "The Lawrences, John and Louise, and a couple Carl and Missy, the Mosers, stayed three nights and were from somewhere near New York City. They're in their eighties and said they were on vacation. Doubt they're who you're looking for."

I agreed and seeing how much he had remembered about them, I was more sure that Kevin Starr wasn't a guest, or if he was, he didn't go by Kevin. I thanked Jay and he said if there was anything he could do to help Heather or Charles to let him know.

CHAPTER TWENTY-TWO

Cal's was packed. I was glad I wasn't there to sit and drink since all the tables were occupied. There was a smattering of guitar cases beside several of the tables. I noticed a few familiar faces, a couple of regular open-mic performers, and several customers I didn't recognize. Burl was behind the bar. His rotund body squeezed in a space made for someone several belt sizes smaller, as he tried to gather drinks for six men who were waiting. Charles was at the far end of the bar restocking the beer cooler. Kristin, a part-time waitress who had worked at Cal's since her junior year at the College of Charleston five years ago, was making her way among the tables trying to keep up with the demands of thirsty customers. She was falling behind because of the bottleneck caused by two amateur bartenders.

It was a half hour past the time open-mic was scheduled to start and two musicians were getting antsy and glaring at Burl. Kristin saw me, smiled, and shrugged her shoulders. I motioned to the bar so she'd know I wasn't looking for a table.

"Brother Chris," Burl said, "my prayers are answered. Please lend a hand. I have to get the show on the road."

I knew as much about bartending as I knew about skinning a porcupine, but figured I could move beer from the cooler to the bar or help Kristin clear empties off the tables. I waited for Burl to squeeze out from behind the bar before I took his place. Charles nodded and said he would tend bar if I could keep him supplied.

Other than grumbling voices coming from the guys standing in line to get drinks, the next sound I heard was Burl tapping on the antique mic on the stage sandwiched between the restrooms at the far end of the room.

"Hello, hello! Howdee." He sounded more like Minnie Pearl than a host. "Welcome to open-mic night at Cal's. I'm Preacher Burl…umm, just Burl, filling in for Cal. Some of you know he's over in the hospital in Charleston recovering from a blow to the head. Let's have a moment of silence for our dear friend Brother… umm, Country Cal."

The moment of silence was interrupted by clanking beer bottles and one patron yelling "What'd he say?" Silence wasn't silent, nor was it golden.

"Now," Burl said, "please silence thy communication devices."

I put my hand over my eyes. That was Burl's weekly opening to get his congregation to turn off cell phones during his Sunday services. I prayed he didn't expect the first musician to open with "Amazing Grace."

I was relieved when the next thing he said was: "Now we've got a bunch of singers tonight, so let's hold it to two songs each. Okay, let's make welcome our first entertainer, the young lady standing over there." Burl pointed to a mid-twenties woman dressed in a striped shirt and torn jeans. "Kera," she stage-whispered. "Kera," Burl said to the microphone.

Kera was well into Kacey Musgraves's hit "Follow Your Arrow" when Burl made his way back to the bar.

Charles patted him on the back. "Fine job."

Charles has a knack for saying what needs to be said, and Burl needed positive reinforcement for his MC duties. Despite his shortcomings, Charles had been better, or quicker, at selling beer and the line was down to two people. I offered to help Kristin clear tables.

She smiled. "You aren't going to hog into my tips, are you?"

I shook my head.

"Clear away."

And I did. Two more entertainers were standing beside the stage. Burl wasn't a great moderator, though he had learned to ask the singer's name before going to the microphone, and refrained from reading Bible verses between songs.

The next vocalist, a man in his forties, opened with a poor imitation of Darius Rucker's "Wagon Wheel," followed by an even poorer imitation of the classic "Kiss an Angel Good Morning."

I was facing the exit when Burl introduced the next singer, Edwina, who said she'd like to go back a few years for her song, Tammy Wynette's "Stand by Your Man."

I remembered her from her appearance during the earlier open-mic night I'd attended with Barb. The name also sounded familiar from something else but I couldn't remember where I'd heard it. I took a handful of empty bottles to the trash behind Charles and asked, "She a regular?"

Charles looked up from the cash register, and squinted toward the stage. "Looks familiar. Could be, not every week." He was distracted and grumbled about losing track of the money, so I didn't pursue it. If Cal had been here, he would have been quick with an answer.

Kristin leaned over the bar, and tapped me on the arm. At five-foot-one she struggled to reach me. "Chris, could I borrow you? Bottles are piling up."

By the time I had cleared two tables, Edwina had begun covering Dolly Parton's "Coat of Many Colors," and the crowd began tapping their feet to the classic. Edwina, in ample proportions or melodious voice, was no Dolly, although she performed an admirable rendition, and was better than most of Cal's regulars.

"I think I might remember where I saw her," Charles said as I dumped the empties in the trash behind him.

I wiped my hands on a bar towel and held them out for him to continue.

"Remember when we were standing in line at the Bluebird and Heather sneaked off to the bathroom at McDonalds?"

"Yes."

"I thought I saw Heather coming back." Charles looked at Edwina on stage. "The gal had on a yellow blouse like Heather's and her hair looked the same, but when she turned around it wasn't Heather." He paused and pointed to the stage. "I think it was her."

"Bro...umm, Charles," interrupted Burl, "More Buds."

I turned toward the stage but couldn't picture her from Nashville, but remembered why her name sounded familiar. The woman Caldwell was working with to change SHADES from rock to country had mentioned that one of the regulars was pushing her to offer open-mic nights. Wasn't her name Edwina? Olivia had said Edwina had performed at several other open-mic nights. It seemed likely it was the same Edwina, after all, how many Edwina's could there be who were performing at open-mic nights? Was Charles right about her being in Nashville?

How do I find out without arousing suspicion? I gave it some thought as Edwina was leaving the stage and Burl was preparing to introduce the next singer. Instead of introducing the singer, Burl was doing a thirty-second commercial for First Light Church, giving his confused beer-drinking audience the when and where of his Sunday service. If Cal had known what Burl was doing, he would have disconnected himself from the medical paraphernalia, hijacked a car, and charged in here to give Burl the boot, figuratively and literally. Cal had no idea and Burl had now slipped out of preacher, pitch-man mode and introduced the next singer.

Edwina was by herself. She latched her guitar case, waved at a couple of women who had applauded the loudest at the end of her set, and headed to the exit. I opened the door for her and followed her to the sidewalk. She thanked me, and I said, "Edwina, that's a nice name."

She glanced at me. It wasn't a hostile look but more a *who's hitting on me now* gaze. I didn't blame her. I held out my hand. "I'm Chris Landrum, a good friend of Cal's."

I thought she was going to ignore me, when she reached for my hand. Hers was damp and warm. "Hi. Nice to meet you." She smiled and started to walk away.

The smell of cigarette smoke mixed with the hot, humid air in front of the bar. A trickle of perspiration ran down my cheek yet Edwina looked as fresh as she had when she had taken the stage.

"A few days ago, I was with Cal and another friend, Caldwell Ramsey, at SHADES, and we were talking with the owner. She mentioned one of her regular performers was named Edwina. I was wondering if it was you."

She looked at her guitar case and at me. "Yes. Olivia's been good to me over the years. She lets me fill in when some of her scheduled performers cancel."

I didn't know where to go with the conversation, so I said, "Small world, isn't it?"

She stared at me like it was a trick question. "Sure is."

That didn't help.

"You play here often?"

"A few times. I try to go to as many open-mic nights as I can." She grinned. "Getting discovered is hard work."

"You must know Heather Lee. She played here most every week until she moved to Nashville."

"I see a lot of folks at these things. I might if I saw her."

How do I keep her talking without becoming suspicious?

"I think Olivia said you play out of state occasionally."

"Some."

"Ever played Nashville?"

"Been there a time or two."

"Heather plays the Bluebird."

"Good venue. Gotta be going, nice to meet you."

I ignored her dismissal. "You ever play there?"

"Tell Cal I hope he gets feeling better. That preacher guy's okay," She shook her head. "He's no Country Cal." She waved bye over her shoulder as she climbed in a black Mercedes SLK 350 hardtop convertible that looked more like it should be in a sci-fi movie rather than on the streets of Folly. It didn't look like Edwina needed to be discovered to get by.

The crowd was thinning as I returned to clear tables. There were only two other singers who had attempted to wow the audience. Both had failed. The good news was that the master of ceremonies had survived open-mic night. He had performed better than most of the aspiring singers. Charles, as he does with most things he attempts, had muddled through tending bar. And I was exhausted. Only Kristin appeared in good spirits and full of energy at closing and asked if we wanted to hit some of Folly's other bars before they closed. Charles, Burl, and I responded in three-part harmony: "No ma'am."

CHAPTER TWENTY-THREE

I didn't wake up until eight-thirty the next morning, late for me. I would have slept longer if the phone hadn't jarred me awake.

"Hey, pard," Cal said in his strong Texas accent. "You awake?"

I said I was now and asked how he was feeling. I wanted to ask why he was waking me up.

"The cute nurse who was holding my hand and taking my blood pressure a few minutes ago said my hard head was healing good."

"Great. How's your memory?"

"Ain't made it back yet. Still don't remember what happened that night and my last couple of weeks seem to be all twisted around. I do remember why I'm calling. Peppi, that's the cute nurse's name, she said it's French, anyway, she told me today's Wednesday and even as confused as I am, I know it meant yesterday was Tuesday, a big night at the bar. Was Burl there and did he handle the singers okay? They're a fickle lot, you know."

I told him everything was fine and Burl, with a little help from

Charles, was great and to not worry about anything other than getting well and getting out of the hospital.

"Be sure and thank the preacher man for me."

I told him I would.

"Oh yeah," he said. "Nearly forgot. When I was drifting off last night, my buddy Johnny R called. The old, cranky nurse that ain't French heard the phone on the table over there ring and gave me a scolding look. Anyway, we went to see Johnny R when we were in Nashville, didn't we?"

"Yes."

"Good, I'm glad that part ain't gone from my head. Last night he called and said he had a little something to tell me about the scoundrel Starr. I told him I was in the hospital and my memory was going through a fuzzy spell and I'd have you give him a call to see what he knew."

"Did he give a hint?"

"Don't think so. Nurse Ratched made me hang up, turn the ringer off, and go to sleep. Didn't get Johnny R's number, but he's in that home. I said you'd call him. Did I already tell you that?"

I said I'd give his friend a call.

"Well I'll be branded. Guess who just came a callin'?"

From the way he'd said it, I assumed it wasn't Nurse Ratched. "Who?"

"My favorite bartending preacher. Better go and be nice to him. God may've followed him in the door. You'll call Johnny R?"

I said I would and to say hi to Burl. I'm not sure he heard all of that since he'd already hung up.

I waited another hour to call since Nashville was an hour behind us, and spent most of the time wondering what Cal's friend could have learned about the agent who was fifty years his junior. I also wondered when, or if, Cal would remember what he thought he had learned about Starr being in South Carolina.

After several rings, I was about to hang up when a pleasant,

Hispanic sounding, female said, "Oak View, this is Sena, may I help you?"

I told her she may if she could connect me to Johnny R's room. She asked my name. I told her, and shared I had visited a few days ago and was calling for my friend Cal Ballew. Sena giggled. "Give me a minute. I will check and see if he is receiving calls, and if he is in the kind of mood in which you would want to talk to him."

I heard muted voices in the background and a mattress store commercial on a nearby television. It was closer to ten minutes before Sena returned and told me Johnny R told her any friend of Cal's was a sorry so-and-so. He didn't say so-and-so. He said that he could find a few minutes in his busy schedule to talk to you." She chuckled. "That means that his favorite soap-opera is not on yet. I will connect you."

Good to her word, the next voice I heard said, "You the boring looking one or the ragged dude in the long-sleeve T-shirt in two-hundred-degree weather?"

"Boring one."

Johnny coughed and said, "Like to picture who I'm talking to. Now, what in hell happened to my bud Cal? He said something about getting run over by a concrete mixin' truck before he got rolled over by a freight train." He coughed and caught his breath. "The old boy tends to push the truth, so I figured if all that happened to him, I wouldn't be sharing a conversation with him until after I bite the dust."

I gave him a shortened version of what had happened and didn't stray from the mugging theory.

"Good—glad he's going to make it. Not good he got smacked upside his thick skull." He coughed up a chuckle. "Bet his head busted whatever hit it."

I needed to move him along before he choked to death. "Cal told me you had information on Kevin Starr."

"Yep," he said, and gave another wheezing cough. "This old

bird's still got a few connections in the business. Only a few. Most of my best friends, and even most of my enemies are already sitting around the campfire and trading tunes with Jimmy Rogers and Hank Sr." He paused again. "I got ahold of an old flame. Can't be much more than a flicker left now. I'm sure you're not interested in my prehistoric sex life."

I'm not, and imagined how many questions Charles would have had. "Starr?" I said, to get him back on track.

"Damn, you're impatient." He wheezed.

I couldn't think of an appropriate response.

"Okay. According to my gal friend you don't want to hear about, Kevin Starr is new on the block. He's big on ideas and piss-poor short on the bucks needed to make his ideas come to life. He thinks if he played the odds and signed every Tom, Dick, and Harriet one of them would strike it big and bring him enough money to sign folks with more than a dream of talent. Crappy singing by a bunch of suckers is still crappy singing. The boy's master plan's doomed from freakin' day one."

So far, there were no surprises and I hoped that wasn't all Johnny R had called to tell Cal.

"Anything else?"

He wheezed. "Young man, anybody told you lately you're impatient?"

"You."

He laughed. "Good memory. There's more. Give me time to get there. I don't get a chance to talk to many folks who're still haulin' their mind around with them."

"I appreciate your time."

"Damn better, it's valuable. Crap, I could be playing nurse with the nurses, but no, I'm wasting my time with the boring friend of my buddy Cal. You sure he's going to be okay?"

I told him I was and apologized for keeping him away from the nurses.

He laughed again. "I heard your buddy Starr's sinking in debt and the hole in his boat's getting larger, until." He wheezed and coughed, and then silence.

"Until what?"

"Until he found himself a backer, a moneybags, a sucker with deep pockets. The person either is going to, or had already pulled his wallet out of the fire. Rumor is the 'backer' just might be a gal friend."

"Did your source learn who the backer is?"

"No, she said she don't think anyone over here knows. There was a rumor the mystery person got turned sideways with him, royally pissed. It was only a rumor."

"Any idea why?"

"No." His hacking cough returned. "Think I've had all the talking fun I can take this morning. You tell Cal he better get himself well or I'll tell everything I know about him to one of those tell-all TV shows. That'll get their ratings up."

I told him I would and thanked him for talking to me.

He coughed one more time. "Oh yeah, I almost forgot. You're in South Carolina, aren't you?"

I told him, "Near Charleston."

"Thought so. My old flame said Starr's money-chick was from your neck of the woods.

CHAPTER TWENTY-FOUR

Two things became clear. First, Johnny R didn't know that Starr was no longer among the living. And second, if Johnny R's friend was right, there was finally a connection between Starr and South Carolina that went beyond his being in Folly for a retreat and a connection where someone was "royally pissed." Was the person angry enough to kill? And a more important question, how do I find out who? Edwina Robinson came to mind. From the car she drove, she appeared to have money. Would she have had enough money and motivation to kill the agent? According to Olivia Anderson, Edwina was a regular at several open-mic nights, and had evaded my question about singing at the Bluebird. She and Starr were about the same age, had made music their life's focus, and she was attractive and talented enough to have gotten Starr's attention, although talent didn't seem to be a criterion. That was all I knew about her.

Caldwell may shed more light on Edwina, so I took the chance and gave him a call.

"Hi, Chris, nice to hear from you," Caldwell said in his well-modulated, calm voice.

Caller ID strikes again. Out of habit, I told him who I was and asked how he was. I heard music in the background as he said he was fine. I asked if he had a few minutes. He said he was leaving a meeting with a client and to give him a second to get outside where he could talk.

The background music subsided. "How's Cal?"

I updated him and he asked me to tell Cal he was praying for him. I told him I would.

"So, what did I do to have the honor of this call?"

I asked if he knew a singer named Edwina Robinson. He said the name sounded familiar, although he wasn't sure from where. I reminded him her name was mentioned when we were meeting with Olivia Anderson.

"Oh, yeah, that's the singer who's pushing Olivia to switch to country."

"Do you know her?"

"No, why?"

I shared what I knew and how it could possibly be tied to the murder in Nashville. Caldwell didn't respond at first, and finally said, "That's quite a stretch."

I said it was. It was all I had.

"Tell you what, I'm meeting with Olivia in the morning. If you don't mind some tedious financial talk about business, you can tag along. You can ask her about Edwina."

I told him it would be great and asked if I could bring Charles with me. Caldwell laughed. "Couldn't stop him, could you?"

Thunderstorms rolled through Lowcountry early Thursday morning and took some of the sweltering humidity with them as they had moved out to sea. It looked like it was going to be a gorgeous day; a day I would rather walk along the beach or take a photo-stroll along the historic Battery in Charleston, more than *take* a meeting in a bar. I called Charles to invite him, and was again reminded the second he got in the car we had to do something to "spring Heather." Talking to Olivia was the best I could come up with. A walk on the beach or around Charleston would have to wait.

Caldwell and Mel lived near downtown Charleston so Charles and I met the music promoter in the bar's parking lot. Charles, to look more professional, wore a muted-yellow, long-sleeve T-shirt with a University of Tulsa logo on the breast pocket.

Caldwell said, "She doesn't know you're coming, so follow my lead."

Charles pointed his cane at the door. "Of course."

Right, I thought.

It was several hours before SHADES was to open, and the only vehicle in the lot was a red metallic Porsche Panamera that probably cost more than Charles's, Caldwell's, and my vehicle combined. Charles, the budding detective, detected the red mass of fine German ostentatiousness belonged to the bar's owner; a deduction that was verified moments later when Olivia opened the side door and invited us in. If she was surprised to see Charles and me, it didn't show. She smiled and shook our hands as Caldwell introduced Charles and reintroduced me. Today, she wore a navy suit with light gray blouse. Instead of the dress shoes she had on the last time we met, she wore a pair of black, Nike running shoes.

She caught Charles looking at her shoes and chuckled. "The shoes I wear when we're open kill these aging feet."

Charles smiled. "I was thinking how great those look. Hate dress shoes, as you can tell."

Charles pointed his cane at his torn, mud-stained, generic tennis shoes. Olivia smiled, not knowing how else to react.

Her gold bracelets clinked against each other as she motioned us toward her office.

"Hope you don't mind Charles and Chris tagging along," Caldwell said. "They had a couple of questions and I thought this would be a good opportunity."

"Not at all. If they don't mind a boring meeting with our discussing budgets and your recommendations on how we start the rebirth."

Charles leaned forward and said, "President G. W. Bush said, 'It's clearly a budget. It's got lots of numbers in it.'"

Olivia tilted her head and looked at Charles like she was studying an aardvark in the zoo. I suspected she was reevaluating her response to Caldwell's comment about our being here.

Caldwell said, "Charles is big on quoting presidents."

Olivia chuckled. "Well he's right about what the president said. My dearly-departed husband was the financial whiz. To me, budgets are as Bush said, *lots of numbers*."

Charles sat back in the chair and grinned.

Olivia turned to me. "Questions?"

This was where it would get tricky. How do I ask what she knows about Edwina without arousing suspicion? I didn't know how well they knew each other or how much Olivia would tell Edwina about my curiosity.

"A couple of nights ago I was in Cal's bar in Folly and heard Edwina Robinson sing. She was good. We talked a little after her set before she had to leave. She told me she'd performed in Nashville." I tilted my head toward Charles, "Charles lives in Nashville and his fiancée Heather is a singer. Since Edwina was so good, I wanted to ask if she had an agent, or if she would have some tips I could give Heather."

"Glad you mentioned Cal," Olivia said, "I meant to ask, how come he didn't come with you? I like the old-timer. Makes me wish I had been in the business in the good old days."

Charles said, "He's a little under the weather."

"Sorry to hear it. Hope he gets well soon." She slowly shook her head. "Back to Edwina. She had an agent. His last name was Starr. Since you were talking about Nashville, that's where he had his agency."

"Was?" I said, after she had said it twice.

Olivia bowed her head. "Tragic. He was killed a while back. The story going around is one of the people he represented shot him. Edwina's torn up about it. She didn't tell me. I heard it from another singer that Edwina had given him a lot of money to advance her career. The kid's had a hard life. She inherited a fortune from her parents who were killed when she was in her teens."

Charles leaned forward. "What happened?"

I cringed. Let her talk.

Olivia looked at her hand and at Charles. "They were coming home from a Christmas Party. Tipsy, I gathered. They ran a red light and were broadsided by a semi. Killed instantly. Thank God, Edwina wasn't with them. Don't know much else."

"I'm sorry," Charles said.

"Anyway, Edwina's got a lot of talent, but not much business sense. She spends her money like she's got an unlimited pot of it. I don't see her outside here." She waved her hand around the room. "She's always talking about her cars, boats, a big, upscale condo overlooking the City Market, singing lessons, and paying her agent whatever he said he needed to make her famous." She shook her head. "I love her to death. You know what, I'd like to shake some sense into her."

Charles asked, "Did she ever talk about meeting with this Starr fellow over here?"

"She did. She told me—I think I have this right—he heard her sing, over by the ocean, I believe. He was impressed and asked to represent her. Think he's been back a few times since then and I know Edwina's been to Nashville." She looked at the huge diamond on her left hand and at Charles. "She's devastated about his death."

"That's too bad," I said. "I hope she got whatever she paid him for."

Olivia frowned. "I think the bundle she gave died with him. She doesn't talk about it. I've been around her in here long enough to know she's more upset than she lets on."

I glanced at Charles, then at Olivia. "When I was talking to her, she had to leave before I could get her contact information. Do you have her phone number or e-mail address?"

She flipped through some papers on an expensive, black leather blotter on her polished mahogany desk, jotted down a phone number, and handed it to me.

Caldwell looked at his watch and glanced at me.

I took the hint. "Don't let Charles and me keep you from your meeting. Charles, let's take a walk and let these two get on with their work. It's a perfect day."

Curiosity may kill the cat, yet Charles was ready to kill me for suggesting we miss anything Caldwell and Olivia would say. No feline alive could compete with Charles when it came to curiosity—nosiness.

Charles groused as soon as we were outside. "Why leave?"

"I don't want Olivia thinking more about Starr's death. If she's been following it, she may have heard the name of the person who'd been arrested. I shouldn't have mentioned Heather's name. If Olivia puts two and two together she'll realize why Heather sounded familiar. I'm afraid she'll tell Edwina. Talking shop with Caldwell without us around may distract her enough to keep her mind off it."

"Wise," Charles said, somewhat mollified.

Forty-five minutes later, Caldwell called to say the meeting was over. Olivia had walked him to his car where Charles and I were waiting. We said our goodbyes and Caldwell asked us if we got what we were looking for.

I said yes. At the same time, I wondered what it meant.

CHAPTER TWENTY-FIVE

Charles called Heather's lawyer while we were on the way back to the beach. The receptionist said the attorney wasn't in, and that if Charles called, to tell him there was nothing new to report. He slammed his phone on the console, and I spent the last few miles reassuring him the attorney was doing all he could. Charles said he knew it and it still didn't make him more patient. He suggested I could be more successful calling Edwina.

"What do you propose I say?"

"You're the smart one, figure it out."

"That helps."

"Say the same stuff you lied to Olivia about. Tell her how great she is. Ask about her agent. Ask if she has any tips she could offer Heather. Ask if she killed Starr."

I looked at Charles. "That's the kind of question only you could get away with."

Charles rubbed his chin. "Okay, leave out the last part. We can't learn anything if you don't call."

Except for asking if she killed Starr, his ideas weren't horrible and I didn't have a better plan. I motioned for him to punch in her number. He did and hit the speakerphone icon and handed the device to me.

Instead of a live voice, I received a recording that said, "You have reached the voice-mail of recording artist Edwina Robinson. Please leave a message at the tone."

I tapped *End Call.*

Charles leaned forward. "Recording artist?"

I nodded. "She recorded a demo."

"So did Heather. She could add that to her message." He hesitated and looked out the window. "When she gets out." He jerked his head in my direction. "Why didn't you leave a message?"

I explained I was afraid she wouldn't return my call. I'd rather catch her by surprise and play the conversation by ear. Charles agreed it was a decent idea—this time he didn't go as far as saying it was wise.

I had to promise I would continue calling until I reached the recording artist before he would get out at his near-empty apartment. We decided the best way for me to approach her would be to say she was so good I wanted to hear her sing and ask about her next gig. Maybe it would be soon, and nearby.

I reached Edwina on the third try. At first, she was reticent to talk; after all, I was a near stranger. When I told her how much I enjoyed her set at Cal's, she turned more friendly. She told me when and where she would be performing. My enthusiasm increased when she said it would be tomorrow night at one of the restaurants beside Charleston's historic market. I said I'd try to make it. She said wonderful, the same word Charles used when I called and told him about it. She said she'd look forward to seeing me again. Charles said, "What time are you picking me up?"

I had asked Barb to supper, and met her at her condo where we could walk to the restaurant. She met me at the door, again wearing one of her trademark red blouses, and white, linen slacks. The temperature was still in the upper eighties so I suggested we go next door to Blu, the upscale restaurant in the Tides Hotel. She agreed and once we reached the hotel also agreed we should eat in air-conditioned comfort and not on the patio. We got the best of both worlds when the hostess seated us at a table beside the window overlooking the beach.

I hadn't seen Barb for a few days and asked if she'd heard about Cal.

"What about him?"

I told her about his encounter with a blunt object and where he was recuperating.

"That's terrible. I overheard some women talking about someone getting mugged. I didn't hear who it was. Who would do that to such a dear sweet old man?"

Cal would have liked her sentiment until she got to *old man*.

I told her the police didn't know but suspected robbery.

The waitress arrived and took our drink order. Barb watched her head to the bar. "Do you think it had to do with Heather?"

"Yes, he called me the day before. I was in Nashville and he said he knew something about why Starr was in Folly and wanted to know when I was getting back. I told him the next day and he wanted to tell me in person. He didn't get a chance."

"How would whoever hit him know he was going to tell you something?"

I sighed. "No clue."

"So, what did he know?"

"Don't know. Cal can't remember anything about the attack or what he was going to say. The doc thinks his memory will be back. The problem is no one knows when."

Our drinks arrived. We took a sip and gazed at the ocean as the shadows of the setting sun reflected off the rolling waves as they approached shore. There were still several people lounging on the beach and a couple of joggers weaved their way past the loungers.

"Let me bounce something off you." I began telling her about Edwina Robinson.

Barb leaned forward and interrupted. "Is that the gal we heard sing at Cal's?"

"Yes. I'm impressed you remember."

"Don't be impressed, it's not often I hear the name Edwina."

I told Barb that Starr was Edwina's agent, she had given him a substantial amount of money, and had gone to Nashville several times.

Barb listened and didn't interrupt which was one of her more endearing traits and unique among my gaggle of friends. She took a sip. "Any evidence she had something to do with Starr's death or Cal's run in with a blunt object?"

"No."

The server returned and took our order. Barb chose soup and asparagus salad, and I went with the pork chop, another reason she was thin and I was, well, not.

"Okay," she continued, not distracted by the interruption. "Did Edwina know Heather?"

"I don't know. She told me that she might remember her if she saw her."

"So, all you know from the woman in Charleston is Edwina's another wannabe singer pissed-off at Starr."

I nodded. "And she gave him a lot of money. Olivia didn't say how much although it sounded like more than it would take to cut a demo and to use his marketing services."

Barb said, "There's no telling how many other aspiring singers have done the same thing."

"True. I doubt there were many from here. And remember, Cal said he knew something about Starr being in Folly."

Barb paused, glanced at the ocean, and turned to me. "Not necessarily that it had anything to do with Edwina or the murder. I hate to say this since I know you're close, but Edwina's not the only wannabe from here who's in Nashville."

"I know. Heather had the same motives as Edwina."

"Motive, no alibi, and it was her gun. Do you even know if Edwina was in Tennessee when Starr was killed?"

"Good question."

Our food arrived and we ate in silence as I thought about the facts Barb had so lawyerly pointed out. She, of course, was right, yet I still couldn't picture Heather killing anyone. Sure, she had changed since moving to Nashville. Had it been enough to lead her to murder? Were my views clouded, as Barb had said, by my knowing Heather and her relationship with Charles? Could be. The police had a circumstantial case, a strong one, but circumstantial nonetheless.

Barb broke the silence. "I don't know Heather, and little about Charles, other than he has read most every book written since Gutenberg. I couldn't speculate on what may have happened, but if I were the cops, I'd feel pretty good about my case."

"She—"

Barb waved her fork in front of my face. "If I were her attorney, I would keep pounding the jury with the fact the police have no proof. I would parade all the other singers who felt ripped off in front of the jury, and I would call his wife to the stand and keep hitting her about how angry she must have been about his lying to her about where he had been, and imply it happened all the time, not only when he was in South Carolina. I would plant in the jury's head that the wife could've killed him, any of the many aspiring singers could have pulled the trigger, the people with the recording studio had a reason to kill him, and he was a stealing liar with people lined up around the block to have a figurative and literal shot at him."

"Would it get her off?"

She shook her head. "Fifty, fifty. The gun's the problem."

"I know."

Barb looked at her fingertips. "Were Heather's prints on the gun when the police found it?"

"No."

"That's something else a good defense attorney would pounce on. If she were going to get rid of the gun, it would make sense to wipe it clean. Why would she do that if she was leaving it in her car?"

"The car's lock was broken so anyone could have taken it."

"Yes. Who knew she had it, where it was, and that the lock was broken?"

"I don't know."

She grinned. "You're going to find out, aren't you?"

I sat up straight and nearly strangled my fork. "My best friend's girlfriend is sitting in jail in Nashville. My good friend Cal is downtown in the hospital. Charles is devastated. And the police are convinced the case is solved. You bet I am."

She set her fork on her empty plate and stared at me. "How?"

Our server returned and asked if we wanted dessert before I could tell Barb I was clueless about how. We said no, and I asked Barb if she wanted to get another drink at the outside bar. She said no, smiled, and said we could have one on her patio.

It was comfortable with a steady breeze coming off the ocean. Barb poured each of us a glass of white wine and said for me to go on the patio while she changed into cooler clothes. Ten minutes later, she'd substituted white shorts for her slacks, and had put on a red T-shirt. I noticed red polish on her toes. Red was beginning to grow on me.

Barb lowered herself in the chair and looked at the Folly Pier. "It's a beautiful sight."

I nodded.

Evenly-spaced lights illuminated the pier and I could see the silhouettes of people strolling to the end and back of the thousand-foot-long structure. The sound of waves slapping the shore provided a soothing background melody, broken occasionally by the engine of a vehicle on the street behind us.

"What's next? How are you going to do what the police can't?"

I told her Charles and I were going to hear Edwina perform tomorrow night. She asked what we planned to learn, and I told her I didn't know. I was going to play it by ear, and hoped Edwina would say something that would help.

"Sounds like a feeble plan."

"I agree."

"Want me to go?"

I was surprised. "Thanks. It may be best if just Charles and I were there. I wouldn't want her to think we were ganging up on her."

She looked out at the waves illuminated by lights from the pier breaking on shore and turned to me. "Here's a thought. It would appear more natural if you had a woman with you. Tell her I was your date. That might put her at ease."

It made sense. "You've got a date."

She smiled. "Have you asked Chief LaMond to check into Edwina? You and Cindy are good friends and she has access to more databases than you have. Edwina might have a record, and all the information you can gather the better."

I said I'd call Cindy tomorrow and tonight was a good time to simply enjoy the view and the company. After enjoying both for another half-hour, I took Barb's yawns as a hint, thanked her for a nice evening, and said I'd better be going.

She grinned. "If you must."

I didn't know about *must*. I told her it was late and she needed her sleep. She said something about a rain check, walked me to the door, gave me a hug, followed by a lingering kiss.

CHAPTER TWENTY-SIX

I caught the chief on her way to the office.

"You want me to do what?" Cindy shouted. "I just spent an un-fun filled breakfast with Council member Houston listening to him bitch and moan about what he called 'middle-of-the-freakin'-night hoodlums' disturbing the sleep of his dear sister who happens to live fifty yards from one of our fine imbibing establishments and thinks retired librarians should be patrolling the streets in front of her house to *shhh* everyone walking home."

"Life of a police chief. Ain't it grand?"

Cindy ignored me and continued to rant. "I suggested to our illustrious member of the city council I could post some of my officers in his sister's front yard so they could shoot everyone who passed by who made noises louder than a giraffe. I was teasing, by the way."

"Of course."

"And you know what the knucklehead said?"

"Tell me."

"He said the gunshots would make too much noise for his *stupid to buy a house by a bar* sister."

I stifled a laugh, and chuckled. "Wow, Chief, my simple request for you to run Edwina Robinson through your databases will be a snap compared to Houston's sister's horrific situation."

Cindy exhaled. "Chris, if you weren't such an endearing creature, and not such a good friend of my hubby, and I suppose a friend of mine, I'd have one of my guys save one of his bullets after shooting the noisemakers, and put it in your troublemaking brain."

"So, when will you get back to me with the information?"

"And I thought Charles was the biggest pest I knew. If I don't have to deal with any *real* police business when I get to the office, I'll let my fingers do the walking on my keyboard. I'll call you."

"You're an angel."

"Tell that to Councilmember Houston."

I hadn't heard from Cindy when I picked up Barb at her condo and Charles at his apartment. Barb, to no surprise, had on a short-sleeve red blouse, but had switched from white linen slacks to tan chinos. Charles, also no surprise, had on a long-sleeve black T-shirt with Belmont Bruins in red on the front. Charles said since Belmont University was in Nashville it would get Edwina talking about her visits to Music City.

He leaned back in the back seat and confidently said, "It'll make Edwina cough up a big-ass clue."

Barb glanced at me from the passenger seat and raised her eyebrows.

"Yes," I said. "He's always like this."

She whispered, "Wow."

Charles said, "What?"

And I thought regardless how strange and desperate the situation was, I truly missed his being here and, well, being Charles.

Rubino's was a block off King Street near the College of Charleston. The Italian restaurant with its nondescript front, was known by the college community as well as young professionals in search of reasonably-priced pizzas and eclectic music. Because of its popularity and small size, we were told we'd have a thirty-minute wait. That was fine since the postage-stamp sized, raised stage was occupied by an empty bar-stool. Edwina hadn't arrived.

There was one vacant stool at the bar and Charles nudged a boisterous twenty-something year old man wearing a College of Charleston T-shirt aside and motioned for Barb to be seated. A harried bartender, with sweat running down his cheeks, was quick to Barb who ordered Chianti and pointed to me. I asked for a glass of pinot grigio, and Charles bypassed the Italian drink options, and said *birra*.

The server looked at Charles like he was a termite. "Huh?"

"Beer, *birra*."

The server rolled his eyes. I didn't blame him, though I was impressed with Charles's Italian.

We were halfway through our drinks when Edwina pushed the door open with her shoulder and lugged a black box the size of a carry-on suitcase around the crowded tables to the stage. She was dressed in black. If she had worn a straw hat and yellow blouse, she would pass for a younger version of Heather. She set the box on the stage and headed back outside.

A few minutes later, she returned carrying a guitar case with Edwina written in script on the side and a three-foot long narrow container, and a portable mic stand. A male student standing near the door took two of the cases out of her hand and helped get them to the stage. She rewarded him with a grin and started assembling the contents of the cases.

Ten minutes later, the portable Bose sound system was operational, Edwina was tuning her Martin guitar, and my phone rang. The screen said *Cindy*. I answered and asked her to hold a second while I walked outside where I could hear without having to strain my ears over the loud din inside the restaurant.

"Where are you, at a circus?"

I gave her a brief explanation of where we were and asked what she'd found on Edwina.

"Your gal must have some bucks. She lives in a ritzy condo overlooking the Market, not far from where you are now. She ain't a serial killer or terrorist, but she ain't Mother Teresa's good twin. Three years ago, she took a knife to a food fight, and not to butter the croissants or whatever you do to those flaky things. She was living with a guy who owned a hole-in-the-wall hamburger joint and learned he was Frenching more than fries with one of his cook-chicks. Sweet, two-timed Edwina took a hankering to slice-and-dice the cook-chick. Thirty-five stitches and a successful workers-comp claim later, the cook-chick was in court pointing her bandaged finger at Edwina, who was assigned to the local jail for a day short of a year. The prosecutor tried to get more temper-tantrum crimes admitted as evidence but the wise old judge said they were too far in the past to reflect on current events, or some such judgy proclamation."

"That it?"

"Isn't that enough? Oh yeah, there's one more thing you might find interesting."

The restaurant's door opened and three coeds came out, all talking at the same time, two of them on phones and the third either talking to herself or to someone through an earpiece. Edwina's powerful voice singing a Martina McBride hit echoed onto the sidewalk, and I couldn't hear Cindy.

"Say it again. It's loud here."

"Your old ears are giving out. Okay, remember the day you said the cops first interviewed Heather?"

"Hard to forget."

"Miss Edwina Robinson was pulled over on I-40 near Crossville by the serve-and-protect Tennessee State Police. Seems she was tooling along just shy of the speed of sound."

"Heading toward or from Nashville?"

"Excellent question. Miss Edwina had her Mercedes SLK 350 pointed toward London, England, with an intermediary stop in South Carolina."

"She could have been in Nashville when Starr was killed."

"Yeah, but she could've been coming from anywhere west of where she was stopped."

"I'd put my money on Nashville."

"Me too. I don't have anything to prove it."

"What happened?"

"Nothing," said Cindy. "She charmed the cop into giving her a ticket rather than giving her a lift to the pokey. Listen, Chris, and I know this is going to fall on deaf ears, leave it alone. If Edwina had anything to do with Starr's death, she's trouble. And she knows her way around a gun and a knife. I'll do more digging. Remember: Me, cop. You, retired geezer."

I thanked her for the information and for reminding me of my status in the universe. What I didn't say was that I'd leave it alone.

I rejoined Charles and Barb who had been seated at a table in the middle of the room. Edwina was sitting on the tall bar stool on the stage, playing guitar and singing "Tennessee Waltz."

Barb said "Welcome back," and Charles grabbed my arm and said, "What'd she say?" He nodded toward the stage, "Did she kill Starr?"

Edwina picked up the tempo and dove into Jeannie C. Riley's "Harper Valley PTA." I pulled Barb and Charles closer and shared what Cindy had learned.

"See," Charles said. "She did it."

Barb leaned even closer. "Allow me to put on my attorney's hat.

I didn't hear anything that would convince a jury to convict her. Sorry, Charles."

"Her quick temper," Charles said. "Willing to poke a knife in someone. Coming from Nashville. Represented by Starr. And…and, Heather didn't do it, damn it."

I sympathized with him, but agreed with Barb. I was also pleased Charles was more optimistic about Heather's innocence.

Edwina had finished Mary Chapin Carpenter's "Passionate Kisses," and was telling the few people in the room who were listening she was taking a break. We, for reasons Edwina would not approve of, were among those who were paying attention.

Charles said, "Let's grab her."

Barb put her hand on Charles's shoulder and watched Edwina put her guitar in its case. "Give me a few minutes and I'll see if I can get her over. It'll look more spontaneous."

Charles started to protest, sighed, and nodded at Barb. His approach would have been to go to the stage and drag her to the table, while slathering words of praise along the way.

Barb met Edwina by the stage. She shook her hand and leaned close and said something. Barb pointed to our table and said something else to Edwina, who looked at us and gave a weak smile.

Barb retuned and Edwina headed to the restroom.

"What'd you say?" Charles asked. "Where's she going? Is she skipping out on us?"

Barb looked at Charles and at the restroom. "Unless she's going to climb out the bathroom window, she'll be here. I told her my date remembered her from Cal's and was too shy to ask her over. I asked if we could buy her a beer. She looked over here and said she sort of remembered Chris, and asked who the straggly, street person was."

"The what?" Charles said.

Barb grinned. "Kidding."

My admiration for Barb soared.

"Hmm," Charles said. "So, she's coming over?"

Barb nodded, although she didn't have to since Edwina was standing behind her and pointing at the empty chair. Barb told her to have a seat.

She did and pointed at Charles. "I remember you now. You're Cal's bartender."

"I was only filling—"

Edwina interrupted and nodded to me.

I said, "You talked to me outside Cal's, and when I called yesterday."

"That's us," Charles said. "We really enjoyed your singing and wanted to hear you again."

Edwina squinted and said with little enthusiasm, "It's kind of you."

Our act was clearly not being bought when Barb said, "Chris has been telling me how good you are and he may have seen you in Nashville at the Bluebird. I hear it's the place to be. Congratulations."

She smiled. "Thanks. I love playing there. We get over every opportunity."

Edwina's ego was greater than her skepticism, and confirmed she had played there. It was a fact she danced around when I'd asked her the same question at Cal's.

"My fiancée plays there on open-mic night," Charles said. "You probably know her. Name's Heather Lee."

Edwina looked toward the stage, and the server returned with her beer. I thought she was going to jump up and run. She surprised me when she said, "Yeah, I like her. Terrible that they arrested her, terrible. I knew her from the Bluebird, and we had coffee a couple of times at a place downtown near her apartment."

I wondered if she remembered telling me outside Cal's she wasn't sure if she knew Heather and she might recognize her if she saw her. Not only does she know her, but knows Heather is accused of killing Starr, and she and Heather had coffee together.

"Did you know—what's his name, Chris? The guy who was killed?" Barb asked.

"Kevin Starr."

"That's it," Barb said. "Did you know him?"

"He was my agent and a nice guy. Such a tragedy."

The server returned to the table carrying a large pizza Charles and Barb had ordered while I was talking to Cindy.

Edwina said, "Smells good."

Barb slid the pizza toward Edwina. "Have a slice."

"How long had he been your agent?" Charles asked. No way he was going to let Edwina get off topic.

She grabbed one of the plates and slid a slice of pizza on it. "Less than a year. Why?"

Charles took a slice of pizza. "Just wondering. He'd been Heather's agent for four months."

"Heather met him at Cal's," I said. "Did you meet him in Nashville?"

"No," Edwina said between bites. "He caught my set in Charleston. Said he was in the area meeting with music bigwigs."

Sounds familiar, I thought. "That's great. Did he get you any jobs?"

She took another bite and shook her head. "Not enough for the money I gave him. He got me a couple of gigs in Music Row bars and one on lower Broadway. Didn't get paid, but got all the drinks I could put away." She paused, looked around the room, leaned closer to the table, and whispered, "Don't blame Heather for shooting him. He sold a bigger bill of goods than he could deliver. He screwed a lot of people."

Charles jerked his head closer to Edwina. "Heather didn't kill him."

Edwina slowly shook her head. "Hope you're right. I like her. From what I hear, it looks bad. Wasn't it her gun?"

Barb gave Edwina a motherly pat on the forearm. "For the sake of argument, let's say Heather didn't do it. Do you know anyone who might have been angry enough to want him dead?"

Edwina smiled. "Me, for one. And I could name four or five others I know personally. No telling how many more there could've been."

"You didn't do it, did you?" Barb chuckled. "Just kidding."

Edwina started to say something, hesitated, and smiled. "Should have."

I asked, "Were the other people you thought were angry enough to shoot him in Nashville?"

"Some of them. Look, I need to get back to work. Good talking to you, and Charles, if you see Heather, tell her I said hey and hope everything works out."

Barb touched Edwina's arm. "Even if a bunch of you were angry with him, it had to be terrible learning he was killed. Were you in Nashville when it happened?"

Edwina cocked her head in Barb's direction. "Nah, I was taking some time to clear my head. I was surfing over in Folly. That's how I get away from worrying about things."

"Sounds like fun," Charles said, the person I'd never known to wade into the ocean, much less surf.

"Yeah, it is. Thanks for coming." She took another bite, guzzled the last of her beer, and returned to the stage.

Edwina opened her set with Tanya Tucker's "Delta Dawn," we finished our pizza and drinks, and Barb said we needed to head out as well, since she was the only one in the group who had to go to work tomorrow. I agreed since it was already past my bedtime.

We spent most of the ride home in silence. Charles finally said, "Well, she didn't feed us a pack of lies, but there was one whopper, wasn't there?"

"That she was here when Starr was killed?" I said.

"Yep."

"She also told me a pretty big one when I was talking to her at Cal's the other night," I said.

"That she didn't think she knew Heather?"

"Tonight, you'd think they were best buds. Sounds like she knew her well enough to frame her."

Barb said, "Lies aren't proof."

Charles said, "Thank you, Miss Defense Attorney."

"They're enough for me to tell Cindy," I added. "She'll find it interesting."

"Interesting enough to share with the police in Nashville or enough to talk to Edwina?" Barb said.

"Hope so," Charles said.

CHAPTER TWENTY-SEVEN

I called Cindy before I headed to the hospital to spring Cal. She was in a meeting with the mayor and said she'd call as soon as she "agreed with everything His Honor said and followed all of his wise and perceptive wishes and commands."

"Brian's listening, isn't he?"

Cindy giggled. "Yes, Mayor Newman is finding this conversation both stimulating and interfering with his meeting with the best police chief that has ever been under his command."

"You mean *only* chief."

"I'll call."

Cal was in an equally good mood, as I would have been if I were escaping from the hospital. He said the doctor had been in and told him he could leave as soon as someone showed up to collect him. I commandeered a wheelchair parked by the nurse's station and had Cal in it and headed to the exit before anyone saw us. We had almost made it to the door when two nurses spotted us and rushed over. I was afraid they were going to herd Cal back to his room. Instead, they hugged him, said he was a delight to take care of, and wished him and his injured Stetson complete recoveries.

Cal patted his back pocket and looked from one nurse to the other. "Got your numbers. I'll be a callin' as soon as I'm back to full strength so we can get together."

The health-care providers smiled. I wondered if Cal was serious. I suspected he was.

We sat at a stoplight a block from the hospital. Cal gazed out the windshield. "More's coming back to me."

Traffic, like most mornings in the hospital district, was terrible and we spent more time stopped than moving.

"You remember what you figured out about Starr?"

"Not at all. Still don't remember anything about getting conked, but think I remember that gal singer Edwina, umm, Robinson in the bar a couple of days earlier, or maybe it was weeks, little vague on that. She could've been talking about Starr."

"Who was she talking to?"

"Some younger gal, don't recall seeing her before, but with my memory cells dying off, I could have. They were sitting at the bar so I was close enough to hear some of their yacking."

"What do you remember?"

"The young chick was POed about something. I didn't hear what. From what Edwina was saying, I figured it was about Starr. Something about taking a bunch of money, and Edwina said, and I do remember this, that the young chick didn't lose nearly as much to the conniving shyster as she lost, and she knew others who were suckered out of their hard-earned cash."

"Did she say how much or why?"

"May have, I didn't hear. Now here's the interesting part. She didn't use these words, but I had the impression Starr and Edwina may have been close, if you get my drift."

I did. "What makes you think that?"

Cal touched the bandage on his head, and turned to me. "I've been hanging out in bars since Noah parked the Ark. Been singing most of that time, drinking a few decades' worth of hours, and watching humans and their nature all my life. I've known more drunks than show up at an AA convention. Cheating and affair talk has its own ring to it, and it ain't a wedding ring. I know it when I hear it."

Clearly, I hadn't been around nearly as many bars as Cal, so I tried again. "Do you remember what was said to make you believe Edwina and Starr were lovers?"

"Not all of it. I recall her saying the other woman kept getting in the way. That's the problem with affairs; pesky wives complicate sinning."

All Cal could add before I left him at his apartment was his head hurt and he needed to "rest a spell" before relieving Burl at the bar. I said he should stay in bed and let Burl tend bar until Cal had regained his strength. He waved me off and said he needed to get back before the good Preacher turned the place into a branch of First Light Church and the only wine to be found was at communion.

"Whatever."

Cal turned and looked in the back seat like he'd just remembered it was there. "Where's my hat? You did pick it up from where I got smacked?"

I told him it was pretty mushed up and had saved his life.

"Knew I could count on it. Where's it recuperating?"

I told him it was at my house.

"That old thing's been with me through thick, thin, and thinner. I'd hate to part company with it now."

"I'll bring it by."

He tipped an imaginary Stetson. "Thanks, pard."

~

On Cindy's way to following Mayor Newman's wishes and commands, she called and asked if I was buying her breakfast at Black Magic Cafe. I asked if breakfast was enough to get her to do a favor for me. She said, "Yes, if the favor doesn't involve taking time, energy, money, or breaking any laws."

I agreed even though I knew what I wanted would infringe on one or more of those things.

The Black Magic Cafe was less than a block off Center Street, located near the Folly's retail area, and three blocks from the ocean. It was closer than that to my house, so I walked. Cindy's unmarked GMC Yukon was parked in front of the restaurant and she was waiting for me near the entry at a table beside a large potted plant. She was gripping a yellow Black Magic mug.

She held the mug up. "I couldn't wait. Meetings put me to sleep and your duly-elected mayor didn't offer caffeine. They're fixing my breakfast. Told them you'd be in soon to pick it up and pay. You can get yourself something if you want."

Cindy, like Charles, was generous when it came to allowing me to pick up the tab. Meetings with the mayor not only had put the chief to sleep, they whetted her appetite. She had ordered the chicken and waffles with a side of hominy grits and orange juice. I grabbed a cheese Danish and coffee and joined her on the deck.

"How's hardheaded Cal?"

I told her.

"How's Heather?"

I told her I hadn't heard anything in the last few days.

"How's Charles?"

I said he wasn't doing well, but was hiding it.

Cindy cut into her waffle, and to the chase. "What do you need?"

"Edwina Robinson," I said and sipped my coffee.

"Her again."

I spent fifteen minutes telling Cindy what I knew, much of what

I speculated, and everything I hoped about Edwina. To my surprise, the chief took notes and only interrupted twice. She had already heard some of it, and still listened as I repeated my thoughts.

"Is that all?"

I said it was.

She closed her notebook and stared at me. "Let me get this straight. You want me to traipse over to her fancy-dancy downtown condo, lock her in a windowless room, and browbeat a confession out of her?"

"Of course not." I smiled. "The room doesn't have to be windowless."

"Funny," she said, slobbering sarcasm.

"I don't know what you can do, Cindy. I know she lied about knowing Heather. According to what you told me, she lied about where she was when Starr was killed. She could've known about Heather's gun, and it's clear she was angry with the agent about taking her money. From her previous encounter with the law, she's capable of violence."

"Chris," Cindy pointed toward Folly's main street. "I'm one insignificant police chief on one tiny island. I have no jurisdiction outside Folly Beach. What do you think I can do?"

"Talk to her. Apply some of your endearing pressure. She doesn't know what authority you have. Give it a try."

She pointed a fork at her half-empty plate. "If you think you're getting by with this itty-bitty bribe, you're dumber than an earthworm with a lobotomy. I'll give it my best shot, although I won't be able to do it for a few days. I promised Larry I'd go with him to Charlotte for a hardware store trade show. We're leaving in a couple of hours. He says next to the latest innovations in power drills, I'll be the most exciting thing there."

I smiled. "Such a romantic."

"He's a charmer. I used to be offended. Now I know how much he loves power drills, so I figure I'm swell. Anyway, it'll be a few days, and when I do talk to her, don't expect her to hand me a written confession."

"All I ask is that you talk to her."

I spent the rest of the day doing what I often spent mindless hours doing: catching up on my bills, housecleaning, and rationalizing that my aching back, arthritic hands, and pain in my knees were caused by healthy, strenuous exercise rather than old age. I spent less time on the routine rationalization than usual and devoted more time to trying to figure out if there was anything I had learned that would get Heather off the hook.

The longer I thought, I realized I had moved past the belief she had murdered Starr and was convinced Edwina was the killer. So, how did she know about Heather's gun and where it was hidden? When did she take it, and return it? If she hit Cal, did anyone see her that night in the bar or the night when she could have overheard Cal telling me he knew something? Should I have taken my suspicions to the cops in Nashville rather than sharing them with Cindy who couldn't investigate in Tennessee? And, was I focusing on Edwina because she was one of Starr's clients and she had told us a couple of lies? I wanted to call Charles but figured he needed a day of rest and if he needed anything he knew how to get me.

Something had to be done and I didn't want to wait for Cindy to get back in town to talk to Edwina. I could stop by her condo. Other than looking like a stalker, what would I accomplish? I could call her again, and say what? Cindy had already culled whatever was available on the Internet and from police databases, so there wasn't any reason to try to go down that road.

I fixed a well-rounded supper of Velveeta cheese on rye and kettle chips, washed it down with a Diet Pepsi, and decided to walk to Cal's to see if the owner was there. I grabbed his sad-looking, mashed Stetson, tried to shape it to look more like a hat, was halfway successful, and headed to the bar.

It was early and there were only a handful of customers spread around the room. Burl was in deep discussion with Cal who saw me—saw his Stetson—and his face wrinkled into a frown. I thought he was going to cry. He stepped from behind the bar and took the hat in his hands like he was lifting a baby bird with a broken wing. He flipped the hat over and looked inside the crown, and up at me and thanked me for returning it. I asked how he was feeling.

"Was feeling like a hundred-fifty-three bucks until I got here and that preaching dictator told me I should go home." He looked back down at his hat, and sighed. "I told him the joint's name was Cal's and not Burl's Bible Bar and I appreciated everything he'd done. I was just fine, thank you."

"What'd he say?"

"He'd pray for me to get better and if I kicked the bucket because I didn't take his advice, he'd preach my funeral. I thanked him and said that's what preacher friends are for."

If there'd been a bigger crowd, Burl would have been right, but the preaching bartender and I managed to get Cal to park his weak, thinner-than-usual body at a table near the door and serve as greeter while Burl and I handled the beer distribution. His part-time cook fried a burger or two for the few hungry patrons. Every so often, Cal sauntered to the jukebox at the corner of the bandstand and punched in some country classics. His halted movement and forced smile revealed he was more comfortable at the table than he wanted us to know. It was still good seeing him back and getting better.

Burl wanted to talk about two members of his flock and their earthly trials and tribulations, and I was happy to listen, since I didn't know what to say about Heather and Starr's murder. I wondered when Cindy would have a chance to talk to Edwina and what, if anything, she could learn that could help Charles's fiancée. More than anything, I was frustrated.

Fortunately for Cal, Burl, and me, we closed the bar around ten after the last two customers drifted off. Sleep came slowly as I kept thinking there must be something I could do to help Heather, and wondering if there was something I already knew that could tie Edwina to the murder.

Short hours later, I was awakened by the shrill sounds of my phone. I opened one eye and glanced at the clock that told me it was only five thirty-five. I shook the cobwebs out of my head, picked up the phone.

I heard sobbing and realized it was Charles. "She tried to kill herself. Gotta go back. Can…can I borrow your car?"

He was gasping for breath and I couldn't understand what he was saying. "Slow down, are you talking about Heather?"

"Yes. Gotta go back now…now!"

It wouldn't do any good to try to ask for details. "I'll drive. When do you want me to get you?"

"Now, Chris. She may be dead."

"I'm on my way."

CHAPTER TWENTY-EIGHT

Charles was pacing the gravel and shell parking area in front of his apartment when I pulled in. He wore a plain white T-shirt without any logos, so I knew he was traumatized. He slid in the passenger seat before I got out of the car. His eyes were bloodshot from being up all night or from crying. His hand shook as he threw his cane and clothes bag in the back seat.

All he said was, "Go."

He wasn't ready to talk and I didn't push. I had driven off the island and was in Charleston on the way to the Interstate before he spoke.

He stared out his side window. "Her attorney called at one-thirty." He hesitated and sniffled. I didn't think he was going to say anything else, until he added, "He didn't know anything—wasn't certain if she was alive. Chris, what will I do if she's…you know?"

"What did he say?"

"She wasn't adjusting to being in there. They wouldn't let me to talk to her much. Each time I did she seemed so … depressed. She wouldn't say anything. I just don't know."

That didn't answer my question. We'd be in the car for many hours and he would talk when ready. Before today he'd confided that she seemed down when he had talked to her. He hadn't hinted it was more than what anyone would experience if locked up.

Thirty more miles of silence and I started telling him about last night at Cal's and asking Cindy to try to talk to Edwina.

He turned from staring out the window. "Too little, too late," he interrupted before I told him my suspicions.

"We don't know."

He took the phone from his pocket and set it on the console. "Edelen's supposed to call when he learns something." He looked at the phone like it would ring if he stared at it. "They called him around one this morning. The person he talked to knew she had been taken to the hospital. Said it was serious and that was it." He smacked his hand on the dash. "I was numb. I wanted to call you and go then. I was shaking so bad I couldn't hit the right numbers on the phone. What's going to happen?"

I put my hand on his shoulder. "I don't know. Let's wait and see."

An hour later, the phone jolted Charles out of his funk. He stared at it like it was a poisonous snake and nothing bad could happen if he pulled away from it. Curiosity got the better of him and he grabbed it and cringed. "Hello."

I heard a muted voice on the other end and Charles said, "Yes."

The low hum of the tires on the Interstate kept me from hearing much. Charles finally said, "When will they know?" More silence. "What happened?" He moved the phone to his other ear and tapped on the armrest with his other hand. Finally, he said, "How could that happen?" His pause wasn't as long this time. "Yes, as soon as ... okay, yes." He hit *End Call* and closed his eyes.

I returned my hand to his shoulder. He looked at it. "She's alive, but ..."

I waited. He didn't say anything. "What?"

He looked over like he just noticed me in the car. "They don't know if she'll make it."

"What happened?"

"He didn't know much. He thinks she sneaked a plastic water cup from dinner to her cell. She broke it in pieces and slashed her wrist with a sharp edge. They didn't find her for a long time and she lost so much blood that she was almost…you know." He paused and wiped a tear from his cheek. "They got her to the hospital …"

"She's alive."

"Yeah. Edelen promised to call when he knows more."

It took passing three exits before I convinced him he needed to eat. He kept saying he wasn't hungry. He had to be and I said I needed food and while we were at the Interstate McDonald's he should order something. He huffed then ordered two cheeseburgers and pushed me out of the restaurant so we could get on the road.

An hour later, he had chewed on the cheeseburgers and was fidgeting less. He said, "I knew she couldn't handle a cell. She told me years ago, she almost didn't rent her apartment because she was claustrophobic and thought it was too tiny. She didn't have enough money to get anything larger. Chris, she still had to leave the bedroom door open all the time so she could see sunlight from the windows." He paused. "Every time she came to my place she had to sit near the window. It bothered her."

"Did she say anything about the cell?"

"Only every time. She shouldn't have been in there—not one day, one hour, one minute." He shook his head. "What did she do to deserve that? All she wanted to do was become a singer. What, Chris? What?"

We had reached the outskirts of Nashville and the attorney hadn't called. Charles took the phone and hit redial. Edelen had called from his cell phone, so Charles didn't have to go through his office gatekeepers to reach him. Charles asked if there was an update and Edelen must have said no. Charles asked what hospital, paused for the attorney to respond, and said, "I'm going there anyway."

Charles slammed the phone down on the console. "Edelen didn't have anything and didn't think the hospital would let me see Heather." He hesitated, looked out the side window, and mumbled, "Let them try to stop me."

If the automatic front doors at the hospital hadn't opened as fast as they did, Charles would have knocked them out of their track when he barged through the entry. I thought the elderly woman sitting behind the information kiosk was going to fall out of her chair as he stormed up to her.

"Heather Lee. Room number?" he shouted at the startled woman, whose name was Hazel according to a name tag that also read *Volunteer*.

Hazel regained her balance and checked the computer.

"I'm sorry, sir. We don't have anyone by that name."

Charles stepped back like the woman had rammed her fist in his stomach. "Oh, my God. She's dead."

I moved beside Charles, looked at the volunteer, and gave my best calming smile. "Hazel, would you, by chance, have anyone registered under the name of the jail?"

She looked at me like I was getting ready to spring a prisoner. I didn't pull a gun or flourish an ID, so she tapped more computer keys, glanced at Charles who was still traumatized, and turned to me. "Sir, if you go to the fourth floor, there should be a police officer near the elevator. He may be of assistance."

I smiled, thanked Hazel, and led Charles to the bank of elevators. A uniformed officer greeted us as we arrived at the fourth floor. Hazel must have called while we were on the way up.

The officer smiled—the practiced smile he would use when

asking a speeding motorist for his license and proof of insurance—and pointed us to an empty waiting room. "I'm Officer Neil. May I be of assistance?"

Charles eyes darted around the corridor. "Is she alive?"

"Please be seated, sir."

Charles started to protest, and instead flopped down in the chair. I sat beside him.

"Sir," Neil said as he remained standing. "Are you referring to Ms. Lee?"

Charles hands balled into fists and he looked like he was going to pounce out of the chair. "Of course, I am."

"Sir, please dial it down. Are you related?"

Charles's fist tightened. I was afraid he was going to lash out against the man who was simply doing his job. Charles took a deep breath before saying, "She's my fiancée."

Neil must have decided that was close enough to a relative. "To answer your question, Ms. Lee is alive, but in critical condition. The doctor says it's touch-and-go. I wasn't here when they brought her in, but I've heard she'd lost a lot of blood. It was a long time before the jail's medical staff got to her."

Charles sighed, and yanked his head up and stared at Officer Neil. "Why in the hell did it take so long?"

"Again, sir. I wasn't there. No one can keep a constant eye on the prisoners. Your fiancée was in her cell several hours after supper between routine rounds. They don't know when she tried to…umm, when her injuries were sustained. I'm sorry, sir. It's all I know."

Charles said, "Can I see her?"

"I don't believe that will be possible, sir. Not for a few days."

"What—"

The officer stopped Charles. "Sir, her condition is critical, and even if she were able to have visitors, someone from the jail must authorize it. My suggestion is you work through her attorney. He or she will know the ropes and what you need to do."

Charles started to stand. "Is she on this floor?"

"Sir, I can't—"

I put my arm on Charles's shoulder and pushed him back down in the chair. "Charles, why don't we go to your apartment and call her attorney?"

Neil said, "That would be a good idea, sir."

CHAPTER TWENTY-NINE

I was afraid I was going to have to drag Charles out of the hospital until he turned to putty and I helped him to the car. I kept reminding him Heather was alive. By the time we reached his apartment, he'd regained some energy, yet relied on the handrail to support him up three flights of stairs.

I got him a beer as he moved to the couch. "Think it's too late to call her lawyer?" he said, before taking a sip.

It was eleven o'clock. I told him it would be okay. I didn't want to hear him mention it a hundred more times, and besides if he didn't call now, he would want to make the call before sunrise.

Edelen must keep the phone by his side. He answered on the second ring. Charles, as usual, dove into the middle of the conversation before the attorney had time to ask who was calling. Charles switched on the phone's speaker so I could hear. To the attorney's credit, he didn't hang up on Charles, was sympathetic, pleased his client was still among the living, and assured Charles he would contact the jail first thing in the morning and see if he could get approval for Charles to see Heather once she was out of immediate danger.

My friend was somewhat relieved and finished off his beer and hinted for me to get him another. I got him the second bottle without pointing out he was as close to the refrigerator as I was. He finished the second drink and I asked if he thought he could sleep. He said he doubted it and wanted to take a walk. I asked if he wanted me to come, and he said he needed to be alone. I was exhausted and didn't try to change his mind. Before falling asleep, I realized I hadn't finished telling Charles about Edwina's past and my increasing suspicion about her guilt. I also decided that since we were in Nashville, I should meet with the detectives and lay out my thoughts and what I'd learned. None of that would matter if Heather didn't make it through the night.

I heard car horns on the street below. I blinked a few times and glanced at the time on my phone. It was nearly nine in the morning. I padded to the kitchen and found Charles at the table staring in his coffee mug. His eyes were bloodshot, but alert. He wore a blue, long-sleeve University of New Haven Chargers T-shirt, tan shorts, and considering what he had been through, a close replica of a smile.

He held up his mug and tilted his head toward the Mr. Coffee machine. "Sleeping the day away?"

I fished through the cabinet and found a clean cup and filled it and refilled his mug. "Sleep any?"

"Not a wink."

I nodded toward his phone. "Any word?"

He shook his head. "Expect it to ring any second."

I wondered how many seconds he had been sitting here waiting for a call. "No news is good news," I said, and hoped it was true. Heather could have died, and I doubt anyone would have thought to contact Charles, and wouldn't have called her lawyer until a reasonable hour this morning.

"Please be right."

I didn't see anything good coming from my staring at Charles staring at the phone, so I began filling him in on what Cindy had found about Edwina and that the chief was going to interview her once she returned from the trade-show.

I had his attention. "We've got to tell the Nashville cops. They've got to start looking at Edwina. Chris, she's the killer."

He said it so quickly that I wondered how much coffee he'd already had. Before I could tell him that it didn't prove anything, the phone rang.

He hit the speaker icon and said hello. The first thing Heather's lawyer said he had just gotten off the phone with the hospital and she was alive.

"Thank God. When can I see her?"

"Not so quick, she's not out of the woods. It'll be tomorrow, maybe later, before anyone could get in. I'll have to coordinate your visit. Let me call you around nine in the morning."

Charles leaned toward the phone. "Tomorrow, no—"

"Mr. Fowler," Edelen interrupted. "That's all we can do. They promised to call if there's any change. I'll talk to you tomorrow."

Charles slumped in the chair. "Okay."

He stared at the phone, walked to the window, and returned to stare at the phone. I wanted to do something to help, if only I knew what it could be.

He saved me when he said, "Let's call the detectives and tell them about Edwina. The sooner they figure out she killed Starr the quicker Heather gets out."

Charles jumped up and went to the bedroom to find the detective's card, and had punched the number in his phone before he was back in the kitchen. I wasn't certain we had enough to talk to the police about, but it would get Charles's mind off Heather's condition. Detective Lawrence answered and Charles told him who he was. It took the detective a few seconds to remember Charles, who then said he had some information that would help the police catch the "real killer." A few seconds later, Charles said, "Great, we'll see you then," ended the call, and smiled for the second time in two days. "He's on his way."

The detective wasn't in as big a hurry to get to us as Charles thought he should be. It was an hour before he knocked on the door. Charles had it open before the detective had a chance to knock a second time. He stepped in. Charles held out his hand to shake. The detective ignored it, and glanced around the room. I gave a half-hearted nod to the visitor.

"So, what's so all-fired important?"

Charles looked behind the detective. "Where's your partner?"

"Not here."

I figured that out, and I'm not a detective.

Charles seemed disappointed he didn't have the full complement of detectives to share his wisdom with. He got over it quickly and motioned for Lawrence to follow him to the kitchen.

The detective sighed, and took one of the chairs. "I heard about your girlfriend trying to kill herself. Hope she's okay."

Charles scratched the side of his head. "They say she's going to make it."

"Good. What's so important?"

"Chris and I just got back from South Carolina." Charles pointed to me. "We've learned some stuff that'll put you on the right track to find the guy's killer." He abruptly turned to me. "Tell him, Chris."

Thanks, Charles. "It's about a woman named Edwina Robinson. She's a singer from Charleston and Starr was her agent." I proceeded to tell him about her contact with Starr and how he ripped her off; her relationship with others in the Charleston area; why we suspected she was in Nashville when he was killed; how she could have been mistaken for Heather in a poorly lit bar; and, how she could have killed Starr.

Lawrence had started taking notes, set his pen on the table, closed his notebook, and glared at me. "Is that what you took me away from my job for?"

I thought finding killers was his job. Instead of pointing that out, I told him it was.

He turned to Charles. "I don't blame you. If I were in your shoes and my girlfriend was in jail, I'd do anything to get her out. I'd look for anyone with the most tenuous connection to the dead guy." He put both palms down on the table and leaned to within a foot of Charles. "Let me tell you what I see."

Charles leaned closer to the detective and said, "You've got the wrong—"

"What I see is the person who killed Starr is cuffed to a hospital bed. She has motive. We have a witness who has no reason to lie. Her gun shot him. And, because she was overcome with guilt, she tried to kill herself. Case open and shut. Unless you have something that means something, I'm out of here."

Lawrence grabbed his pen and notebook, pushed away from the table, smoothed out his sports coat, and headed for door."

Charles was quick to follow. "Assho—"

Lawrence pivoted and glowered at Charles. "What?"

I stepped between them. "Detective, my friend's upset. We apologize for any inconvenience. We thought you should have the information about Ms. Robinson."

Both Charles and the detective glared at me.

"I'll give him a pass this time. I'm sorry about the suicide attempt. She's guilty. Period." He slammed the door on his way out.

Charles walked to the kitchen and back in the living room where I was standing. "Thanks a hell of a lot. Couldn't you have given me a tiny bit of support? He's convinced Heather killed the son of a bitch, and all you offer is 'my friend's upset.'"

I reached out to pat my friend's arm. He jerked back, went into his bedroom, and slammed the door shut. I lowered myself on the couch, lowered my head, and massaged my neck.

CHAPTER THIRTY

Twenty minutes later, another knock on the door disturbed my feeling sorry for Charles, Heather, and to be honest, myself. I wondered if Detective Lawrence had second thoughts about what we'd shared, or if he had returned to either arrest or berate Charles for his mini temper tantrum. What I didn't expect to see was Heather's friend Gwen.

"Oh, it's you." She looked past me into the living room.

Nothing like being welcomed. I invited her in and said I'd get Charles.

"Is the famous old guy here?"

"No, sorry."

"Me too. It's pretty thrilling to meet someone who was really, really big way back when."

I thought it was the same thing she could have said about a dinosaur, as I tapped on Charles's door.

"What?"

I opened the door a crack and told him Gwen was here. I closed the door and said he would be out and told her she could wait on the couch.

After a couple of minutes, I was afraid Charles wasn't coming out and I was running out of chitchat. He saved me when he opened his door. "Hi, Gwen."

"Sorry to drop in like this. I didn't have your phone number and was down the street, so I took a chance you'd be here."

"That's, umm, okay," Charles made the switch from anger to hospitable. "Thanks for stopping by."

"I was worried about my friend sitting in a jail cell and wondering how she was doing."

Gwen wouldn't have known about the suicide attempt. I waited to see how Charles handled it.

Charles shook his head. "She's not happy about being there. She's doing as good as anyone would."

That's one way of dealing with it.

"It sucks that she's locked up. She's such a sweet gal. What do you think the cops have on her?"

Charles tilted his head toward Gwen. "The gun."

"That's all?"

Charles shrugged.

I knew there was more. Charles didn't want to elaborate, so I jumped into the discussion. "Gwen, let me ask you something. Do you remember a singer named Edwina Robinson? She performed a few times at the Bluebird. You might have been there when she was."

She rubbed her chin and gave a slight nod. "Don't know for certain. There're a lot of singers every week and they start running together. I might know who you're talking about. I think the gal's name is Edwina. I don't know her last name. The reason I remember the name is because Heather said she'd been meeting her for coffee. Why?"

I wanted to say, how many Edwinas could there be at the Bluebird. Instead I said, "Remember if she ever had anyone with her?"

"You're asking some mighty hard questions, Mr. Landrum."

"Sorry, it's important."

"Most of the singers have someone with them." She grinned. "Somebody's got to clap after they sing."

"Yeah, but did she?" Charles asked. He had stayed out of the conversation too long for his liking.

"I don't remember. Not saying she didn't; just don't recall."

I nodded and smiled to indicate we understood. "You said Heather mentioned having coffee with Edwina. Did she say anything about it?"

"Why's this Edwina so important?"

"We think she knows something about Starr's death," Charles said. "The police want to talk to her."

Did he forget how he and Detective Lawrence had left their conversation?

"You know if there's anything I can do to help Heather I will. Do the cops have anything other than it being her gun? Think they're looking for other suspects?"

Charles sat straighter. "Nothing that proves she did it, because she didn't." He hesitated. "They're not looking for anyone else. They're convinced Heather's guilty."

"Her gun shot him," she repeated. "That's why she's in jail."

I wondered why she'd mentioned the gun a second time. I asked if she wanted a drink to keep her talking. I didn't know what she might know, but at this point, she was the only person we could learn from. She said she was fine.

I said, "Do you remember if Heather mentioned the gun to anyone?"

Gwen nodded. "Sure. She told her friends about it. I already knew since I sold it to her. She liked having it and wanted everyone to know."

"Where'd she keep it?"

"Most of the time in her purse. Wouldn't do her good if it was in here and she was out somewhere. When she was at the Bird she left it in the car because she didn't want it in her purse when she was on stage. Someone could steal it. She said even if the car didn't lock, it was safer there."

Charles said, "Who else knew that?"

"Where it was or that the car didn't lock?"

"Both," I said.

"Probably everybody who knew her. Wasn't a secret, you know?" She looked at her oversized, colorful watch. "Whoops, have to go. Nice talking to you. Don't forget to tell Heather I said hey."

She was at the door and turned to Charles. "Don't know if it means anything, but I do think I remember someone being with Edwina."

Charles took a giant step toward her. "Who?"

"I don't remember seeing anyone, but I recall one time she was talking about not performing because some guy with her needed to get to something on the other side of town."

"And you didn't catch a name or see the other person?"

"Nope."

Gwen left and Charles stayed in the living room rather than holing up in his bedroom. He was thawing. He asked what we'd learned from Gwen's visit. I told him I thought it strange for her to drop by. He said he thought it was sweet. I didn't disagree, although something kept nagging me about how helpful she appeared to want to be; and how she kept asking if the police had any other evidence and if they were looking for other suspects.

Charles began pacing, and I asked what he wanted to do. He started to say something about trying to find Heather's other friends and see if they knew anything about Edwina. I asked if he had any of their phone numbers, when my phone rang.

Cindy asked, "Where are you?"

"Nashville, in Charles's apartment. Are you taking a survey of all your residents?"

"No."

"You still in hardware heaven?"

"Screw you, or maybe that's auger you. This hardware stuff's confusing."

"You're calling to tell me that?"

"No, it's about Edwina," The chief switched out of teasing mode.

"Did you talk to her? What did she say?"

"No, I couldn't talk to her."

"What do you mean, couldn't?" I said it with more of an edge than I had intended. "I know you're in Charlotte. You could've called her."

"I couldn't because—"

My frustration from the last two days was overflowing. I interrupted, "She's Heather's only hope. Come on, Cindy, you've got to—"

"Stop!" Cindy blurted. "I can't talk to her because she's dead."

"She's what?"

"I said Edwina Robinson's dead. A guy and his Dalmatian were renting a house out past the Washout and found her body yesterday morning floating in knee-deep water. The dog was barking up a storm or the guy wouldn't have noticed her."

Charles was flinging his arms around and pointing to the phone. I took the hint and hit the speaker button.

"What happened?" I asked.

"They said she had on a bathing suit so it looks like she was swimming and got caught in a rip current."

I remembered Edwina had told me she liked to surf. "She was a surfer. Did they find a surfboard?"

"Not that I know of."

"When did it happen?"

"Best guess is she had been in the water for several hours, probably drowned day before yesterday, late afternoon."

"Why do they think it was an accident? That's a gigantic coincidence."

"First, there were no signs of foul play, and second, it's only a *gigantic coincidence* in your mind. You're the only person who thinks she was tied to Starr's murder."

"I do too," Charles cried. He leaned closer to the phone as if Cindy hadn't heard his outburst and repeated it.

"Hi, Charles. How's Heather holding up?"

Cindy hadn't heard about the suicide attempt. I didn't want to muddy whatever she had to say about Edwina with news about Heather. I put my forefinger to my lips and hoped Charles would take the hint and not mention Heather's current condition.

"She's doing the best she can."

I couldn't understand why Cindy didn't think Edwina's death was more than an accident. "What about Edwina's lies about knowing Heather, or what about her saying she wasn't in Nashville when he was killed? Or what—"

"Whoa. I'm not saying you're wrong. Just saying there's nothing concrete to follow up on. Sure, she lied. I'll tell you something I learned in cop world a long time ago. People lie all the time. It doesn't mean they're guilty of anything except skirting the truth."

I took a deep breath and rubbed my hand through my thinning hair. Charles stared at the phone and didn't say anything.

I leaned closer to the phone. "Cindy, you have good cop instincts. Anything suspicious strike you?"

"Not really. There were no obvious signs of foul play, no signs of a struggle. I'll call a little later and see if the autopsy showed anything out of the ordinary."

"What about no surfboard?" I was reaching. I couldn't get my mind around it being an accident.

"That might be strange if she'd been surfing. We don't know

she was. Even if she had a board, it wouldn't be unprecedented for someone to find it with no one around and *borrow* it, if you catch my wave."

Cindy was right. "Thanks for letting me know."

"Before you ask, I'll call as soon as I learn something about cause of death."

I thanked her, ended the call, looked at Charles, and said, "Now what?"

He looked at the silent phone and at me. "Even if Edwina's death was an accident, she could have killed Starr."

"Or, did someone kill Edwina? I can't believe she went and accidentally drowned when everything was starting to point to her."

Charles nodded. "If she was killed, was it because someone found out she killed the sleazy agent and was getting revenge?"

"Consider this," I said. "If Edwina didn't kill Starr, did someone murder her because she knew who had killed him?"

"Who?"

"Your guess is as good as mine. It could be Edwina had nothing to do with Starr's death, and drowned."

Charles shook his head. "No way. She was killed because she either killed Starr or knew who did."

I walked to the window and looked at Charles's car in the parking lot. Cindy said they hadn't found Edwina's surfboard; she didn't say if her car was nearby. I punched in Cindy's number and was sent to voicemail. I left a message asking about Edwina's car.

Then I remembered something Edwina had said. I had asked her if she ever played Nashville. She'd said *we've* been there a time or two. And, Gwen also said she thought Edwina had someone with her.

"Do you know where Heather's friend Jessica lives?" I asked.

"No, why?"

"How about her address?"

"Should be in Heather's book. Did you forget my question?"

"No. I wanted to drop in on her and see if she remembers Edwina and anyone she may have been with at the Bluebird. I'd rather see her reaction in person. If you don't have her address, a call will have to do."

Charles must have decided my answer was acceptable. He went to the bedroom to get Heather's book and returned without an address but with a number. I called and hung up when her machine kicked in.

I said, "Let's visit good ole Dale and Kelly Windsor."

"Same questions face-to face?" Charles said and looked at his imaginary watch.

"What else do we have to do?"

"Nothing. Just wondering when the lawyer's going to call." He grabbed his Tilley and cane, and headed to the door.

We got to DK Studio quicker than the last time and found a parking space in front of the building. It helped that I had learned the way and that it wasn't rush hour.

Charles looked at the studio. "So, are you going to first ask them if they killed Edwina or if they killed Starr and then Edwina?"

"Thought I'd start out more indirect and ask if Edwina had anyone with her when she cut her demo."

"Next, you can ask if they ever take vacations, like going to Charleston in the last few days. And, here's one, ask if when they were on vacation, if they happened to drown Edwina?"

"Did you forget the indirect part? Let me do the talking."

"Okay. I'll only butt in when you ask the wrong questions."

I rang the bell and smiled at the camera staring at me from near the ceiling. Our last visit ended on less than hospitable terms, and hoped Dale and Kelly would be more accommodating today.

I recognized Dale's voice from the speaker. "What now?"

"Hi, Ms. Windsor," I said in my cheeriest voice. "We'd like to ask a few questions about one of your customers."

"Who?" she said in less than a cheery voice.

I would rather have told her from the confines of the reception room. "Edwina Robinson. I believe she cut a demo here a few months back."

There was a long pause before she said, "I told you before we had no more to say to you or your friend there."

"We'd like to talk to you and your husband."

"Kelly's out of town and I've said all I'm going to."

"Yes, but Edwina—"

"Goodbye."

"That went well," Charles whispered as we headed back to the car. "They're back at the top of the suspect list."

"Don't jump to conclusions. Something has them agitated. Don't forget, they told us the last time we were here they didn't have anything more to say."

"Wonder why she asked who we wanted to know about before running us off?"

"Interesting."

"You're danged right it is. Did you catch that her hubby's out of town? Bet he's in Charleston. Let's go back and get her to let us in."

"I've got another idea." Anything to prevent him from storming the fort—or the recording studio. "Let's find out if the Windsors or Heather's other two friends were in Folly when Edwina *accidentally* drowned."

"So, your plan is to call each of them and ask if they've been in Folly lately. Oh, and if they had been, ask if they happened to drown Edwina while they were there?"

"Good idea, except I doubt it'll work. I'll call Cindy and have her check the Tides, and if she has time, a couple of the other nearby hotels. There are many places someone could have stayed in the area, so it's a long shot."

Charles stopped staring at DK Studios and hopped in the car. "Don't forget to add Kelly Windsor to the list. A long shot's better than no shot."

"Did a president say that?"

"Not that I know of, why?"

"Never mind." I punched Cindy's number.

"What?"

"And a pleasant hello to you, Chief LaMond. Are you still in Charlotte?"

"Bolts and a bunch of nuts running all over the place. What now?"

I shared our thoughts that some of the people we knew were angry with Starr and had killed Edwina. If so, he or she would have been in the Folly area at the time of the alleged accident.

"What am I supposed to do about that?"

I asked if she could check the local hotels. She huffed, mumbled a profanity, and asked for the names. I gave them to her and thanked her for considering it. Another profanity was uttered. I started to end the call.

"Hang on," the chief said. "I talked to the detective who's considering the drowning and told him your thought that it wasn't accidental. He asked if I agreed and I told him you were a prolific pain in the patoot, but were occasionally right. He said it looked like an accident. As a favor to me, he'll look at it again."

"Great," I said. "Did the detective find out if her car was nearby?"

"He's checking."

"Thanks."

"Once again, you owe me."

CHAPTER THIRTY-ONE

At seven the next morning, Charles was in the kitchen with both elbows resting on the table. He was staring at his phone. I resisted the urge to tell him a watched phone doesn't ring, and instead poured a mug of coffee.

"When's he going to call?" Charles asked as I joined him.

"It's early."

He turned away from the phone. "Abraham Lincoln said, 'If there is a worse place than hell, I am in it.'" He pounded his fist on the table. "It couldn't have been worse than waiting, wondering if she's alive, and if she is, getting convicted and spending the rest of her life in prison." Charles pushed away from the table and started pacing.

He wasn't helping himself, and I couldn't stand spending the day in here watching him suffer. "Let's walk."

"Nothing's open."

"Good, we won't spend much money. We could go to that coffee shop and get some breakfast. The alternative is for me to fix cereal with water since there's no milk."

Charles grabbed his phone, and started toward the door.

Combining a coffee shop breakfast, a brisk walk to the bank of the Cumberland River, sitting for an hour watching the meandering river and watching commuters cross the bridge to the city, and a slower walk seven blocks along Broadway, kept his mind off Heather's situation for three hours. Each time he started to bemoan the attorney not calling, I changed the subject. I avoided walking by the Top Ten Bar; he didn't need a visual reminder of why Heather wasn't with us.

I was as excited as Charles was when Darnell Edelen called. I could get away with distracting Charles only so long, and he was about to explode. I pointed for him to put the phone on speaker, as we moved off the sidewalk to a quieter spot in a drive between two commercial buildings.

"Have good and bad news, Mr. Fowler." I had never gotten used to hearing Charles referred to by his last name. "Ms. Lee's condition continues to improve."

"Thank God. Can I see her?"

"That's the bad news. The doctor told the officer who called he didn't want any distractions for his patient, and was prohibiting anyone visiting until tomorrow."

Charles gripped the phone so tight his knuckles turned white. He kicked the gravel drive. "If she's better, why not?"

"Mr. Fowler, I'm sharing what I was told."

"Then do something about it."

"Sir." Edelen's voice became louder and unsympathetic. "I will call you when I have been given authorization for you to see the prisoner—umm, Ms. Lee."

I leaned close to the phone and told the attorney who I was and thanked him for doing what he could for Heather.

"Please reiterate to Mr. Fowler that I will call tomorrow."

I did, and slid Charles's phone in my pocket and put my arm around him. "That's all the man can do."

"I know, dammit." Charles pushed my arm away and started toward the apartment.

He was several paces in front of me, when his phone rang again.

Charles stopped and pivoted. "That's him calling back. We can see her today."

In Charles's parallel universe, it was possible. In the real world, it had only been a minute since we had talked to the attorney. The phone's screen read *Cindy*.

"Why's she calling me?" he asked as I handed him his phone.

He answered and a few seconds passed. Finally, he said, "Umm, yeah, here he is." He thrust the phone in my hand.

"Why in the hell didn't you answer your phone?" the chief asked.

I patted my pocket. Empty. "Sorry, must've left it in the room."

"You're getting so big for your britches you have Charles play secretary?"

"Cindy, I forgot the phone. Give it a rest."

"It appears you've been smacked by a bad mood."

"It's been rough here. Please tell me you're calling with news someone on the list was in Folly when Edwina was killed."

"Sorry, the only good thing about all those calls was it gave me an excuse to stay in the room while Larry drools over new saw blade technology. I couldn't find anyone who had knowledge of any of them staying in the Folly area. You know that doesn't mean much; there are oodles of places to stay I couldn't check, even if I had time."

Charles knocked me off balance while leaning close to hear Cindy's side of the conversation. I caught myself before falling and then a tour bus lumbered by and blocked her words from both of us, and filled the air with the rancid smell of burnt diesel fuel.

"Why did you call?"

"To tell you I just got off the phone with the detective on the case. After my pestering, he said Edwina's death may be accidental, although there were some bruises on the body that were, per the ME, curious. Still there were no overt signs of violence, and her lungs had saltwater in them, meaning she was alive when she went under."

"What now?"

"He said he would check her phone records and search her condo to see if anything seems amiss."

Before Charles knocked me in the street trying to get closer, I hit speaker so he could hear. "What about her car?"

"They found it a quarter of a mile from where she washed up. The door was unlocked and her keys were under the floor mat. It's not unusual for surfers to leave them there."

"Surfboard?"

"Nope. But like I told you before, it doesn't mean anything."

"Still—"

"Listen Chris, I'm doing what I can."

I wondered if she had been taking lessons from Heather's attorney.

"What now?"

"I made the strongest case possible the death should be investigated as a homicide. The detective said he would follow up. That's it."

We didn't hear from anyone the rest of the day. No news could be good news. You couldn't prove it today. Charles continued to mope, wander around the apartment, and glance at his phone like he could make it ring. My only relief came when he decided he needed another walk and said he'd rather be alone. It was fine with me.

He didn't return until ten o'clock, which had given me several hours to go over everything I knew about Starr, his murder, Edwina, her alleged accidental drowning, and the hours I had spent with Heather over the years. The simplest explanation for everything was Heather, in a moment of anger, pulled the trigger. It would explain her gun being the murder weapon, her not having an alibi for the time of his death, and her attempted suicide.

After Charles returned, his conversation bounced from topic to topic. He avoided mentioning Heather. He shared trivia about the history of some of the lower Broadway bars, gushed about the singer in one of them, shared every detail about a conversation he had with a family from Ohio who had stopped him to ask directions to the Hall of Fame, and several other things I forgot the instant he told me. He finally wound down and we managed to be asleep by midnight.

The next morning started like a carbon copy of yesterday. I found Charles at the kitchen table staring at his phone. I chose not to remind him the attorney said he would call today, but only specified it would be when he heard from the police. Common sense told me it probably wouldn't be until late morning at the earliest. Other than both common sense and Charles beginning with the letter *C*, the two had little in common.

After two hours with Charles in the tiny apartment that felt like two of the hours from yesterday, the gods smiled down on us, and Darnell Edelen called. He said if Charles was at the hospital at one o'clock he could see Heather for fifteen minutes and not a second longer.

CHAPTER THIRTY-TWO

Charles, being Charles, insisted we arrive at the hospital no later than twelve fifteen for his one o'clock visit. He had driven, saying that since he lived here, he would know the way better than I. His navigation system knew the way better than either of us and because of its excellent directions and light traffic, we were in the hospital's parking lot a little after noon. I was surprised when Charles suggested we wait in the car until it was closer to the time.

His hands tapped on the steering wheel, he fiddled with the radio dial, and he kept twisting the air-conditioner vent. "Chris," he said as he wiped dust off the dash, "would you go with me?"

"Of course, although I doubt they'll let me." I didn't say Heather was a prisoner and Charles was fortunate to get to visit.

He continued to wipe the dash and rubbed his chin. "They may if you were her brother."

"You want me to lie to the police?"

He lowered his head. "Chris, I need you. I'm scared and don't know what to say to her." He looked at me. "Please."

We bypassed the information kiosk and took the elevator to the fourth floor. No one met us at the elevator door like they had during our first visit. A corrections officer was seated outside Heather's door. We approached and he stood and gave us an intimidating stare.

Charles smiled. "Hi, officer. I'm Heather Lee's fiancée and was told I could see her."

The guard glanced at his watch. "Yes, in five minutes, and for a visit not to exceed fifteen."

The five-minute comment was anal. Charles didn't argue and said we would wait.

The officer looked at me. "Who are you, sir?"

Charles stepped in front of me. "He's her brother."

I didn't lie.

The officer looked at me and glanced at the door to Heather's room. "I was told only her fiancée would be visiting."

Neither Charles nor I said anything.

He shrugged. "Okay. Do either of you have any weapons on you?"

"No," we said, as I visualized us storming the room with guns blazing as we "sprung" Heather from the hospital.

The officer looked at his watch. "Okay, remember fifteen minutes tops. I will be watching through the window so don't try anything."

Heather was in the bed, her eyes closed, and her right hand cuffed to the bed rail. Her face was as white as the bandage on her wrist.

Charles tiptoed to the side of the bed. "Heather, it's me. You awake?"

Her eyes fluttered open and she quickly closed them. "Light. Bright."

Charles leaned close and ran his hand through her curly brown hair. "How're you doing?"

Considering the circumstances, I thought it was a horrible question.

Her eyes opened and she squinted at her fiancée. "Chuckie, I'm sorry. I'm so confused."

Charles continued to stroke her hair. "It's okay. It's okay."

I stayed back from the bed.

Heather's eyes had adjusted to the light and she looked around. "Hi, Chris. Didn't know you were here."

Charles leaned close to Heather's ear. "If the guard asks, he's your brother."

Heather blinked, looked at me, and at Charles. "He is?"

Charles whispered he had to say that so I could visit.

Heather smiled for the first time. "That's sweet." She exhaled, frowned, and repeated. "Chuckie, I'm confused."

Charles glanced at me. I stepped closer. "You'll be fine."

She blinked twice and whispered something I couldn't understand. Charles leaned closer and asked her to repeat it.

"I killed him."

He leaned back like she'd punched him in the nose, and closed his eyes and moved closer to Heather. "Of course, you didn't. Why would you say something like that?"

"I don't remember what happened that night. It was my gun. I hated him." She paused. "Chuckie, I saw me do it. I don't know if I was dreaming it or it's my psychic powers dragging me through it, helping me remember. I killed him ... I must have."

Charles turned to me. His eyes screamed "Help!"

I stepped closer to the bed. "Heather, we believe we know a couple of people who may have killed Starr. You didn't do it. You could help us find who did."

Her eyes sprung open. "Really?"

"Really," I said and realized our fifteen minutes were almost over. "Are you up to a couple of questions?"

"Guess so."

"How well do you know Edwina Robinson?"

"How well? Don't know. Suppose better than some of Starr's singers. You know I even met her in Folly at Cal's. She said Starr sold her the same bill of goods he laid on me. We talked some at the Bluebird and had coffee once, maybe twice. We bitched about Starr. Why?"

"Was she giving him more money than what you'd given him?"

"Let me think. God, it's so confusing. Yeah, she said something about giving him a bundle, whatever that meant. Edwina has lots of money." Heather hesitated. "Whoa, do you think she killed him?"

"Yes," Charles said.

Heather closed her eyes. I thought she was asleep, but she opened her eyes and said, "What about her friend?"

Charles looked over at me, and at Heather. "What friend?"

"Her friend was putting up bigger bucks than Edwina. Something about him going in partnership with Starr. Big plans. Could be confused about some of it. Could be—"

The door opened and the officer firmly said. "Time's up."

I ignored him. "Heather, who was Edwina's friend?"

"She never said, but—"

"Now," the guard barked and stepped between the two of us and Heather.

Now meant now, so Charles and I left Heather's side, thanked the officer for letting us see her. We left the building with more questions about the identity of the killer, and about Heather's mental state.

CHAPTER THIRTY-THREE

Charles had been too nervous to eat before we went to the hospital, so we stopped at a Subway. Charles said he wasn't hungry, but I convinced him he wouldn't be doing Heather any good if he starved. He soon forgot he wasn't hungry as he scarfed down a foot-long chicken sub and repeated, nearly word for word, Heather's disjointed conversation.

Charles swallowed the last bite of the sandwich. "Do you think she really doesn't know if she killed him?"

"She's confused. She was depressed enough to try to kill herself. She's still on meds, and look where she is, not to mention being cuffed to the bed. How would you be under those circumstances?"

"I'd know if I killed someone."

"I'm not certain. She's been drifting in and out of consciousness. Dreams and reality get muddled together, then when you add the trauma of being arrested, plus the suicide attempt, she must be confused. Give her benefit of the doubt."

"I suppose."

"Charles, I don't think she killed him. Edwina is tied up in it.

She either killed him or knew who did. Edwina said "we" went to Nashville, and now Heather said Edwina had a friend with her. We need to find out who he is."

"How?"

An excellent question, and one I didn't have an answer to. My phone rang.

"Well, well," Cindy said by way of introduction. "You fire your secretary?"

"I remembered the phone."

"Good, I didn't want to talk to Charles again."

"You didn't call to tell me that."

"How quick can you get here?"

"Why?"

"I'll tell you when you get back. Can you be here tomorrow?"

Strange. "Let me talk to Charles and call you back."

"Fifteen minutes, no longer."

"Cindy?" Charles asked.

I told him yes and what she asked.

"Why?"

"You know all I know. I don't want to leave you and Heather in her condition."

Charles looked out the large window overlooking the street. He took a sip of soft drink and turned to me. "No offense, but I doubt the chief misses your warm personality so much she's begging you to come home. Don't it make sense that whatever reason she has, has something to do with Starr or Edwina?"

"Yes."

"So, go. I need to stay here in case they'll let me see her."

"You sure?"

"Yes."

I called Cindy, waited while she asked what took me so long to call, and said I'd be there by sunset tomorrow.

I was pleased when I got up the next morning and did not find

Charles at the kitchen table staring at his phone. His bedroom door was closed and I hoped he was getting much-needed sleep. I was on the road before rush hour, and on the Interstate headed to South Carolina before the sun had peeked above the tree-lined roadway.

Seven hours, four coffee stops, one meal stop, and three restroom stops later, I called Cindy to tell her I'd be home in two hours and asked for a hint about why she needed to talk to me. She said it could wait and to meet her at her office. Other than having my curiosity on high alert, I didn't know more than I did when I talked to her yesterday.

I parked a block from City Hall and headed up the steps to Cindy's second-floor office. I had visited her there several times. This was the first time I'd knocked on her door and she wasn't alone. She stood, gave me what seemed like a forced smile, and introduced me to Detective Marshall Grolier, Charleston County Sheriff's Office.

The detective was a few years younger and a few inches shorter than me, had a military buzz cut, and wore a black suit. He reminded me of a mortician. He shook my hand. His expression gave nothing away.

"Chris, Detective Grolier has a few questions. I'll leave you two to talk."

Grolier directed me to one of the chairs in the corner of the room, and he took a seat opposite me. Our knees touched. A notebook appeared from his inside coat pocket, and he flipped through a few pages. "Mr. Landrum, may I call you Chris?"

I nodded.

"Chris, I'm looking into the circumstances surrounding Edwina Robinson's death. I believe you are aware her body was found on the beach."

"Yes, it wasn't an accident, was it?"

"Let me ask the questions, Chris." He scooted to where our knees didn't touch. "How well did you know Ms. Robinson?"

"A little. I only met her a few times. She was a friend of a friend of mine, Heather Lee, and I saw her singing once at Cal's, at Rubino's in Charleston, and maybe at the Bluebird Cafe in Nashville."

"That's all?"

"Are you thinking she killed Kevin Starr?"

Grolier ignored my question. "Chief LaMond tells me you believe Ms. Robinson had something to do with the murder of Starr and you're, umm, nosing in police business."

"Not nosing, asking questions."

"Are you familiar with Olivia Anderson?"

I hesitated. "Yes."

"Have you been to her place questioning her about Edwina Robinson?"

I started wiggling in the chair. I saw darkness enveloping the island outside the chief's large windows that overlooked the Surf Bar. Was it my imagination that it seemed to be getting darker in the office as well? "I did ask if she knew if Edwina had appeared in Nashville."

"And you only had a few conversations with Ms. Robinson, is that correct?"

"Yes."

"What makes you think she had something to do with Starr's death?"

"This may be a bit convoluted, but I know Heather Lee wouldn't have killed him, so I was trying to figure out who might have. Starr had ripped off several aspiring singers and I figured one of them could have done it."

"What ties it to Folly Beach? He was killed in Nashville and from what the police there tell me, he had several enemies. Why here?"

I recounted what Starr had told Heather and Edwina Robinson about why he was in Folly. I shared how he hadn't been at the hotel where he had said he was, how he had lied to his wife about being here.

He put up his hand for me to stop. "You talked to Starr's wife?"

I told him about the meeting at her house and the discussion at the funeral home. The detective jotted a note and told me to continue. I finally told him it appeared to me that someone had framed Heather—another Folly connection. The detective listened. Again, I couldn't tell from his expression if I was making headway.

"Can you explain why she had a note in her apartment that said, *Meet Chris Landrum. Time?*"

"Who?" I asked.

"Edwina Robinson."

I found it hard to swallow. My mouth was dry, but I managed to say, "No."

"Were you supposed to meet her?"

"No."

"What do you think the note meant?"

"I don't know. Could be she wanted to talk about my seeing her perform again."

The detective nodded and wrote something in his book. He touched the pen to his lower lip, paused, and pointed the writing instrument at me. "Where were you the afternoon she died?"

It took me a minute to absorb the question, and a few more seconds to try to remember the answer. "I'm not certain."

"Try."

I looked at my hands griping the armrest, and at the detective. "I was here. The next day I went back to Nashville. I may have gone to the store—really, I don't know."

"Is there anyone who could vouch for your whereabouts?"

My stomach was now in knots. I mumbled, "No."

"Do you have a boat, Chris?"

That I knew the answer to. "No."

"Have you used anyone else's boat lately or have access to one?"

I shook my head. "I suppose I could borrow my friend Sean Aker's boat if I wanted to. I've never asked. Why?"

He was staring at me. "And you're sure you weren't with anyone that afternoon?"

I nodded.

He closed the notebook and stood. "That's all—for now. One more thing, Chris. Don't leave the area."

CHAPTER THIRTY-FOUR

I was numb as I walked down the stairs and gripped the handrail. I was afraid my legs might give way.

Did he think I killed Edwina? I was the only person who was raising a red flag about her death. Why would he think I'd do that if I had killed her?

Cindy was on the sidewalk and motioned me to follow her across the street to the Surf Bar. It wasn't crowded, but the customers were spread out enough so there wasn't a vacant spot where we could be assured of privacy. She pointed to the door leading to the patio. There was one vacant table and I grabbed the chair facing the street. Cindy sat opposite me and we were joined by a college-age server who told us she was Lizzy and would be taking care of us. Cindy told her that her friend wanted a chardonnay and shrugged and said that she was on duty and ordered sweet tea.

Lizzy had gone and Cindy looked around to make sure there was no one close enough to hear. "What did he want?"

I shared Grolier's questions and how it seemed that he was accusing me of killing Edwina.

Cindy lowered her head. "I'm sorry, Chris. I had no choice. He came by yesterday and asked if I knew where you were. He knows we're friends. I told him that when I started pushing for him to start looking at the death as murder and not a simple accident. I told him I wasn't sure where you were and that I'd call you." She pointed across the street to her building. "He was there when I called, so I couldn't say anything. After I hung up he told me he had some routine questions and didn't want you to know ahead of time. He didn't beat around the bush about ordering me not to tell you he wanted to meet. I doubted his questions were routine. I knew you didn't have anything to do with Edwina's death, so I figured it wouldn't hurt for him to talk to you cold. Sorry."

Lizzy was back with our drinks and asked if we wanted to order. I told her I wasn't hungry. Cindy wasn't to be discouraged. She ordered a cheeseburger for me and a house salad with chicken for herself. It reminded me of doing the same thing for Charles when he'd said he wasn't hungry. She told Lizzy I needed the food and if she wanted, she could stand and watch the weight fall off the chief with each bite of salad. Lizzy smiled, like she would at any inane customer remark.

I watched the waitress leave and turned to Cindy. "It's okay," I said, even though a heads-up would have been appreciated. "What I don't understand is why he thinks I had something to do with Edwina's death and then push for him to investigate. He'd already decided it was an accident."

Cindy sipped her tea, said yummy, made a gagging motion, and turned serious. "All I can figure is he started becoming suspicious before you began your crusade. If that's the case, he might have thought that by your saying it wasn't an accident, you were trying to appear not guilty. I know it's circle-like thinking—your buddy William would say circuitous. Since I'm from the hills, I don't know those big words."

She was trying to cheer me. I was having none of it. "Edwina

Robinson was murdered. I knew it and now the cops believe it. Cindy, you know I didn't kill her."

The chief hesitated. I hope she wasn't going to make some smart remark about not knowing I didn't kill Robinson. "So, who did? And, did Robinson kill Starr?"

Our food arrived and Lizzy asked if there was anything else we needed. Cindy said I needed more wine. I declined and Lizzy moved to a family of four on the other side of the patio. The smell from my cheeseburger made me realize Cindy had been right about my needing to eat.

I scarfed down two bites and took a deep breath. "Cindy, I'm still confused. Until Edwina's death, I was convinced she had killed Starr. She may have, so what reason would anyone have to kill her?"

I would love to say Cindy and I solved the various mysteries while I devoured my cheeseburger and pounds fell off her as she grazed on her salad. All we managed to do was to talk in circles—circuitously, in William-speak—and sated nothing except my appetite.

I was exhausted after the drive, my brief, disconcerting conversation with Detective Grolier, and the fruitless discussion with Cindy. The thought of going home and worrying had little appeal, so I headed the short distance to Cal's where I was met by the aroma of stale beer, burnt burgers, and Cal singing his much-performed cover of Hank Williams Sr.'s "Hey Good Lookin'." He was in full stage regalia in his rhinestone-studded coat. His long, gray hair flowed off his shoulders around the sides of his misshaped Stetson.

The room was two tables shy of full and I suspected the busy weekday crowd had inspired Cal to do an impromptu set. He was more comfortable standing behind a microphone than tending bar. His part-time cook was at the grill and Kristin, the waitress, was scampering around the room trying to keep up with drinks. I didn't recognize many of the patrons and assumed most were from a convention at the Tides since they were dressed like they had come from a meeting rather than from the beach. I did recognize a couple sitting at a table near the back of the room. It would have been hard not to recognize Caldwell's six-foot-four frame towering above others in the room. In addition, he was seated with his partner, Mel, whose bomber jacket and camo attire stood out like the Goodyear blimp at a funeral in contrast to the bright-colored golf shirts worn by most of the customers.

Caldwell saw me in the doorway and waved me over and before I lowered myself in one of the two vacant chairs, he asked, "How are Charles and Heather?"

I didn't know if he had heard about Heather's suicide attempt, so I kept my answer generic and said they were both doing as well as could be expected.

"I hope everything gets sorted out soon," Caldwell said.

That told me he hadn't heard about Heather's health.

Mel, not being a big fan of being left out of a conversation, leaned forward. "I'm no stranger to being cornered and crapped on by cops, so I know Charles's little lady can't be doing well. What can we do to spring her? I got it! I could make a couple of calls and get a slightly-used shoulder fired rocket launcher. That ought to do it."

I assumed Mel was teasing, or not. I told him it was up to the lawyers.

Mel waved his hand around and pointed to two or three of the tables. "Don't take me for one of these paper-pushing bureaucrats who don't know a jib from a jellybean. I know it's somewhere in your screwed-up genetic structure to catch whoever killed that scumbag agent and get Heather out of the pokey."

I didn't want to tell him I didn't know what a jib was other than something on a boat, and said I had been looking at suspects.

Two tables of *paper-pushing bureaucrats* sang along with Cal as he began the chorus of Merle Haggard's "Okie from Muskogee". Kristin delivered a glass of chardonnay without my having to ask, and I quickly forgot I was tired.

Mel's chair nearly toppled over when he leaned back; its front legs were off the floor. His crusty, permanently-affixed frown broke momentarily into what I knew was a smile, others would think he had gas. "Told you, Caldwell. I knew Chris'd be on killer patrol."

Caldwell put his arm behind Mel and pushed him forward until four of the chair's legs were where they were designed to be. "You were right."

"Damned right I'm right."

"Anyway," Caldwell said as he turned to me. "You really think Heather's innocent?"

"Yes." I remembered our visit to SHADES and wondered if Caldwell could recall what Olivia had said about Edwina. Perhaps she had said something I had forgotten. I also realized Caldwell and Mel might not know about the drowning. "Caldwell, remember when we were at SHADES?"

"Sure."

"Do you remember Olivia talking about Edwina?"

"Yes, the lady who talked her into trying open-mic nights."

"Did she say—"

"Howdy, Kentucky," Cal interrupted. He had finished his set and was standing over our table. "How're Charles and Heather?"

I gave him the same evasive answer I'd rehearsed on Mel and Caldwell.

"It'll be fine; know it will."

"Is your jukebox broken?" I asked, knowing it provided most of the weeknight entertainment.

Cal grinned. "No pard. I'm doing two sets by popular demand.

Couple of these here conventioneers said they heard me last year and said I could sure do the whole group a heaping favor if I'd share my talents with them."

Mel pointed at Cal. "Crap, Cal. Why don't you do this old jarhead a *heaping favor* and sing some good music, like some funky James Brown. Your prehistoric country songs give me the runs."

Caldwell channeled all of us when he smacked Mel on the arm. Cal nodded to Caldwell, and Mel grinned. No one grabbed a camera quick enough to capture the historic moment.

I figured we had suffered enough foolishness. "Cal, how's your head?"

"Hard and empty," interrupted Mel.

Cal ignored him. "Thanks for asking, Kentucky, it's better."

"Remember more about that night and what you wanted to tell me?"

"It's not all there yet. You'll be the first to know." He looked at the empty stage and over at the bar. "Gotta grab a drink and get back to my fans. Tell Charles and Heather I said hey when you talk to them."

I told him I would.

"What about Edwina?" Caldwell asked, taking advantage of a music free bar.

"Have you heard what happened to her?"

Caldwell said, "What?"

"Why would I care?" Mel asked.

I turned to Caldwell. "She's dead. Drowned a few days ago at the Washout."

Caldwell gasped. "My God. What happened?"

Mel blurted, "Rip current?"

Mel had come close to dying in a rip current more than twenty years ago, and was saved by my surfing-buddy Dude. The two had been the most unlikely of friends ever since, and Mel had rip currents on his mind whenever anything bad happened to anyone in water—ocean, river, or bath.

"That's what the cops said at first. Now they think she may have been killed and someone tried to make it look like an accident."

"I suppose you're trying to solve that one too," Mel said.

I wasn't about to tell them that I was a suspect. "I think she may have had something to do with the music agent's death. Caldwell, that's why I was wondering if you remember anything Olivia may have said about her."

Cal was back on stage. He thanked the group from the hotel for coming and told them to be sure and tip Kristin for all her hard work, and started singing "Rose Colored Glasses."

Mel shook his head. "Where're the Doobie Brothers when you need them?"

Never in Cal's, I thought.

"Remember anything else, Caldwell?"

He looked at his beer bottle and at the stage. "Not really. Olivia and I talked about what she would need to change and I was leaving most of the open-mic stuff up to Cal."

My exhaustion from everything that had happened during the last twenty-four hours was catching up to me. I told my table-mates I was heading home, waved bye to Cal, and the only thing I remembered after falling into bed was the sun shining in the window at nine-fifteen the next morning.

CHAPTER THIRTY-FIVE

I'm no fan of telephones even though they served a purpose, and though I try never to be away from home without mine, I would rather have my conversations in person. I also wasn't ready to drive back to Nashville, so I grabbed my much-maligned phone and punched in Charles's number.

"It's about time you called. Did you run into a bison on the Interstate; run out of gas; throw your phone out the window? Well, I'm waiting for a great explanation why you didn't let me know you made it home."

I held the phone away from my ear and took a deep breath. "Charles—"

"I'm not done. What'd Cindy want?"

"Done?"

"For now."

I told him I had a bison-free trip, had plenty of gas, and still had my phone since he was talking to me on it. I told him about my meeting with the detective, wishing I had hit a bison instead, and about talking with Mel and Caldwell.

"You couldn't find ten minutes in all that to call?"

"Could, but didn't. Sorry."

"Your sincere, heartfelt apology is accepted. Now why in Neptune's name do the cops think you drowned Edwina?"

"Because I pushed Cindy to have them think beyond accidental drowning."

"That doesn't make a lick of sense."

I agreed and shared Cindy's theory that I may have thought the cops would decide it wasn't accidental and by drawing attention to it, would make me look less guilty. Charles said he didn't think the sheriff's office was that smart, and I changed the subject and asked if he was going to see Heather. He said the slow-moving attorney was working on it. I asked him to let me know.

"Like you let me know you made it home?"

The phone went dead.

The temperature was still tolerable, yet was supposed to reach the upper eighties by mid-afternoon. My legs needed to stretch after yesterday's marathon drive, so I headed a couple of blocks to the Folly Pier. Over the years, the Pier had become my prime thinking spot, or that's the excuse I used for visiting the Folly landmark. Puffy white clouds were overhead and a gathering of storm clouds loomed inland. I didn't remember the forecaster mentioning rain, although this time of year pop-up showers could appear anytime.

As with telephones, I was also not a fan of symbolism, but I couldn't help think about how my life since retiring was like the unexpected storms. I was happily retired, living what most would consider the good life, and more often than anyone should be exposed to, I'm confronted with death—death of a friend, or a death where one of my friends was accused of being responsible. These were situations only the police should have to deal with. Did I have to get involved? Of course not. When one of my friends was touched by a tragedy or accused of murder, I was touched as well. I'd nearly been killed on more than one occasion because I stuck my nose into a situation I had no business being involved in. Had I regretted getting involved? Absolutely not.

Here I was again, trying to keep Heather from being convicted of a crime I was convinced she hadn't committed. Not only trying to find out who killed an agent who probably had been killed because of his unethical behavior, but now I find myself the focal point of an investigation into the death of a singer I barely knew. What now?

I didn't know what to do and was relieved when the phone rang and the screen said *Ramsey Promotions*.

"Chris, this is Caldwell. Is this a good time to talk?"

I was pleased someone in my circle of friends could still be courteous on the phone. I told him it was and I was glad to hear from him.

"I just got off the phone with Olivia at SHADES. Thought it was interesting since we were talking about her last night. Anyway, it looks like all my work, and Cal's thinking, are for naught."

"Why?" I asked and watched three surfers riding a medium-sized wave to shore.

"Don't know the details. She'll fill me in when I meet with her in a little while. It sounds like she may have to postpone the remodel and the switch to country. Too bad. After you left last night, Cal finished his set and told me he had come up with a list of things she could do to attract the best open-mic performers around. Some of his ideas were good. The old boy surprised me."

"I learned a few years back not to underestimate Cal. Why's she postponing?"

"Said she's made a bad investment and it was coming back to haunt her. Thought you'd be interested since we were talking about her."

"Thanks, and tell Mel I said hi."

Caldwell laughed. "It'll have to wait. Mel said he can't hear anything because his ears were bleeding from the thorny country cactuses stuck in them at Cal's."

I chuckled and said Caldwell could write him a note. He said he would, but then he'd have to teach Mel to read. I put the phone in my pocket and watched the surfers. I wondered if one of them could be riding Edwina's surfboard.

The storm clouds were inching closer to the beach. I thought about what Caldwell had said. Was it possible Starr was Olivia's poor investment? She had said Edwina gave Starr a lot of money, and hinted it was more than the cost of the demo tapes and marketing promotions. Olivia may be able to give me insights into Edwina's relationship with the promoter. And even if she didn't, at least I'd feel like I was doing something; something to help Heather. Caldwell said he was meeting with her. If I tagged along with him, I could ask some of the questions without looking like I was accusing her friend of doing anything bad. And, it would be safer with Caldwell present.

I called him back. "Hello, Chris. Seems like I just talked to you."

I laughed and said it was because he had. I asked when he was meeting Olivia. He said in an hour and told him I was wondering if he minded if I tagged along. He hesitated, said that I could, and didn't ask why. It was refreshing not to have to explain.

A half hour later, I was barely off the island. Blue sky was to my left, but the black clouds were overhead and doing what heavy rainclouds were known for. Rain pelted the windshield. Another couple of miles and the rain had ended as quickly as it had begun. The more I thought about what Caldwell had said, the more I wondered if Olivia could be tied with Starr more than I had imagined. When we'd visited Heather in the hospital, she said a friend of Edwina had given Starr more money than Edwina had. Hadn't Heather said "he" when referring to Edwina's friend? Heather had also said she was confused. Could the person's gender be one of the things she was confused about? At the first stoplight, I called Cindy.

"Yes, my favorite troublemaker?" the chief said.

I should have Caldwell conduct a seminar on phone courtesies.

"Got a favor to ask."

I heard her exhale. "Of course, you do."

The next voice was Larry in the background. "Hi, Chris."

"Tell Larry hi," I said. "Where are you?"

"Making Larry take me to Harris Teeter. He hates grocery shopping and I'm torturing him for dragging me to hardware hell. What's the favor? It's not legal for a change, is it?"

"Would I ask you to do anything illegal?"

"Yes. What is it?"

"See if Olivia Anderson may be using her maiden name, Mona Alliendre, or if Dale or Kelly Windsor, possibly going by DK Studio, stayed at the Tides in the last few months."

"I already checked on the Windsor's, remember?"

"Yes, but maybe Kelly checked in as DK Studio."

"Gee, okay. Want me to see if the president, the pope, or the Easter Bunny stayed there too?"

"Not yet."

Cindy mumbled something and said for me to hold my nosiness while she got something to write on. It sounded like a glove box clanking closed and she returned. "Okay, names again." I told her and she reminded me she was a simple country girl and asked how to spell Alliendre. I gave it my best guess and she said she would be "seriously starved" after she got the answers. I told her I was on my way to meet Caldwell at SHADES and I'd trade supper for information. "You're danged right you will," she said and was gone.

A couple more miles down the road and I remembered something Cal had said when he was speculating Edwina had been having an affair with Starr. He said Edwina had been angry about Starr taking her money and he had taken much more from someone else. She also said something about *the other woman*. Cal thought it was Starr's wife and how "pesky wives complicated sinning." What if Edwina had been referring to Starr's relationship with Olivia?

If Olivia were involved with Starr, could she have drowned Edwina? If so, why? Was she romantically involved with the agent? After learning Edwina had killed him, did Olivia kill her out of anger? Did Olivia learn Edwina was going to do something to implicate the bar owner and was killed to prevent it? Could Olivia have killed both Starr and Edwina? Or, was I jumping to far-fetched conclusions to get Heather off the hook? There was nothing I knew that could prove any of this. Could I learn anything by talking to Olivia? The one thing I was certain of was there was zero chance of learning anything if I didn't.

I pulled into the SHADES lot armed with a full quiver of questions and a serious dose of apprehension. Caldwell hadn't arrived and the Porsche Panamera was the only vehicle there.

I parked and was waiting for Caldwell when the phone rang and *Ramsey Promotions* appeared on the screen.

"Hi, Caldwell."

"Chris, got a problem. Mel called and asked if I could pick him up at the Chevy dealer. His car was running hot and the service department said it'd take several hours to get the part from the parts house before they could fix it. I'm going to have to reschedule my meeting with Olivia. Hope I didn't inconvenience you."

I told him it was okay and he said he would call Olivia to reschedule as soon as he picked up Mel to keep him from blowing a gasket at the service department. I said that if Mel was going to blow a gasket, the service department would be the best place to do it. Caldwell chuckled and said he'd let me know when the meeting was rescheduled.

Over the years, I had stumbled into a few dangerous situations and had even been ambushed, but never went into a situation that could turn lethal without someone covering my back. It would be foolish to talk to Olivia by myself so I shifted the car to reverse when the bar's side door opened and Olivia stuck her head out. She squinted at my car, seemed to recognize me, smiled, and waved for me to join her.

I cringed and turned off the ignition.

She looked past me toward my car. "I was expecting Caldwell."

She seemed satisfied I didn't have Caldwell with me and waved me in. I told her about his situation and that he would be calling to reschedule and that I was supposed to meet him here.

She wore tight-fitting jeans and a lightweight sweatshirt, much differently attired than in her tailored suit. Lines around her eyes were accentuated by the sunlight and she looked gaunt as she offered me her hand. I gave it a brief shake. Her wrist was still a bracelet collector.

She glanced outside and closed the door. "Why were you joining him?"

Good question, I thought. "He told me he was meeting you and since I had a couple of questions about one of your customers, I asked him if I could tag along. Sorry for the intrusion."

"That's fine. I was here catching up on paperwork. Want something to drink?"

"No thanks."

"Wish you would've brought that charming old timer with you. I loved meeting Cal. It's not often that someone gets to meet a legend."

Legend? I wondered if she'd confused Cal with someone else.

She didn't elaborate and said, "Which customer?"

"Edwina Robinson."

She moved behind the desk and pointed for me to take a seat in one of the two chairs in front of the desk. She sat and shook her head and looked at the black, leather memo pad. "The ocean is so unforgiving. It was a tragic death." She paused and looked at me. "What do you want to know about her?"

"She was a friend of yours, so I hope you won't be offended by what I'm going to say. I think she may have killed Kevin Starr."

Olivia's eyes widened, she leaned forward, but didn't say anything.

I continued. "I was wondering if she'd said anything to you that could help the police figure it out."

Olivia leaned back in her chair and twisted a pen in her hand. "Do the police think she killed him?"

"Not really. That's why I'm asking for your help."

"Back to your question, I'm not offended at all. I didn't know Edwina that well. She was in the bar often. I think I told you that she performed several times, and she wanted me to go country. She considered herself an expert on open-mic nights." Olivia smiled. "She sang at enough of them" Her smile faded. "She had a good voice and was here when I needed her. She'll be missed." She set the pen on the desk. "We weren't friends though." Olivia smiled. "Are you sure you don't want something to drink?"

I declined a second time and was beginning to relax. The more I thought about it, the more I was convinced Edwina was guilty.

"I think I'll get something. Last chance?"

I shook my head as she headed toward the door to the bar.

I was curious if I'd been correct when I spelled Olivia's name for Cindy. I walked to the wall and looked at Olivia's degrees. I grinned when I saw I had the correct spelling, and headed back to my chair when I noticed one of the many photos of Olivia with various people she had hung in groupings around the room. I had been focused on the Wake Forest diplomas during my first visit and hadn't noticed the photo.

The photographer had focused on a group of three people standing on the bow of what appeared to be an expensive, ocean-going craft. Olivia was next to an older gentleman who had his arm around her shoulder. She wore a bikini with a flimsy cover-up that failed to live up to its name. Edwina Robinson was on the other side of the SHADES owner. Edwina held a beer, had a smile on her face, and was leaning against Olivia. Hadn't she just told me she wasn't friends with Edwina? Sharing time on a boat with Olivia appeared to be something more. I had a sour feeling in my stomach. Was I wrong about Edwina? Was Olivia the killer? I needed to make a graceful exit and call Cindy.

Olivia startled me when she returned and coughed to get my attention. I stepped away from the photo and returned to the chair. Olivia smiled but glanced at the photo before returning to her seat.

If Olivia's return hadn't startled me enough, I nearly jumped out of the chair when my phone rang. The screen indicated that it was Cindy. I held up my forefinger for Olivia to give me a second. I wanted to leave the room to take the call, but was afraid it'd make Olivia suspicious.

"Yes, ma'am," I said to the chief.

"Ma'am? What Boy Scout possessed your body? Never mind," she continued without taking a breath. "I hate to admit it. You finally got something right. A woman with the highfalutin name of Mona Alliendre was a registered guest at the Tides for five nights, which happened to be over the same timeframe that the slimy agent *discovered* Heather. And yes, he of guessing right for a change, Ms. Alliendre had stayed there two other times over the last twelve months."

"Interesting."

"Interesting. That's all you can say. I think you're on to something. Sounds like your smarmy agent and Ms. Alliendre, aka Olivia Robinson, were, umm close."

How do I say I need help without coming out and saying it? I hesitated, and said, "Oh, I see."

"Chris," Cindy whispered. "Calling me ma'am, thinking what I found about her was only interesting. Is Olivia there?"

I smiled at Olivia, and with as calm a voice as I could muster, told Cindy, "Yes."

"At SHADES?"

"Thanks for calling. Yes, you're right. Go ahead and have them repair it. Know when they'll be done?"

"Are you in immediate danger?"

"Don't know. See you soon. Bye."

"I'll be there in fifteen minutes."

I hit *End Call*, glanced at my watch, smiled at Olivia, and said, "Sorry for the interruption. They've been having trouble finding a part for my air conditioner." I rolled my eyes. "It's finally arrived."

Olivia didn't smile. My smile ended when I realized she had substituted a handgun for the pen she had had been twirling. She wasn't twirling the gun. It was pointed at my head.

"Chris, we have a problem."

CHAPTER THIRTY-SIX

I couldn't have agreed more. I looked at Olivia but the image of the gun burned into my retina. I wasn't certain how she had planned to solve the problem. What I did know was unless I could stall until Cindy arrived, the outcome wouldn't be to my liking.

I tried to slow my breathing and gave her my best smile. "Olivia, what's going on?"

"You know the answer." She shook her head. The direction of the gun never wavered. "Did you think you could just waltz in here and trick me into telling you I killed Starr?"

"I don't know what you mean. I told you Edwina killed her agent. He had been ripping her off and she had to do something." I nodded at the gun. "What's that about?"

"And I suppose you think Edwina got careless and drowned?"

"That's what everyone thinks. Isn't that what happened?"

"It would've been if you hadn't appeared at the door. Why'd I let you in? Why'd I leave the room and let you nose around? Why'd

I leave that damned picture on the wall? And, why'd I lie to you about how well I knew Edwina? Stupid, stupid, stupid."

I didn't see any upside by acknowledging her questions or agreeing with her about it being stupid, yet had to keep her talking. "You killed both."

She grinned.

"Why?"

"One, I wanted to." She shrugged. "Two, I had to."

A brief answer like that wouldn't kill enough time. "Tell me about it."

"Why should I tell you anything?"

"Why not?" I said, and nodded toward the gun. "You have no intention of letting me out of here."

"You're not that stupid after all."

I nodded and looked around for a weapon. The large executive mahogany desk between us was too heavy to shove into her. The leather letter tray on the desk was outside my reach. Her Gucci briefcase was beside the desk and out of reach.

She watched me looking around. "Kevin Starr," she said. "He walked in here a year ago. Had a rock band blaring out there and I was working the room. He sat at a table by himself, had a half glass of Maker's and water in front of him. Thin, full head of hair, nice looking guy, clean cut, well-dressed. Was little younger than me." She shrugged. "He wasn't the kind of patron I normally get." She sighed. "Was a light crowd and I returned to his table and asked if he needed anything else." She stopped and looked down at the gun.

"Go on."

"He said I could join him for a drink. I made the biggest mistake I've made in years. I sat down. He told me he was a music agent out of Nashville and was developing a chain of bars across the South—he called them nightclubs, sounded classier, I suppose. I had a decent amount of money from my husband's estate and was getting bored with this." She waved her free hand around the room.

I nodded. "And he said he was looking for partners to open these, umm, nightclubs?"

"See, more proof you're not stupid. Yeah, and I fell for it hook, line, and heart. He gave me a sales pitch that could convince a mouse to adopt a pet cat. He came back the next night. In fact, it was the night he met Edwina. He listened to her sing and signed her on the spot. I was happy for her." She hesitated. "Also, I was a little jealous about the attention he was lavishing on her."

"What happened?"

"To make a long story shorter, let's say he and I became much closer over the next few months. I didn't want to take him to the house—I'm old-fashioned about that. Besides, I'd been dating a guy who was so jealous if he got a hint I was seeing someone else, there'd be big trouble. I started getting Kevin and me rooms over in Folly. He liked going to some of the bars there, said he was fishing for talent. Anyway, he brought some partnership papers over and I gave him three hundred thousand dollars—a big chunk of all I had."

I glanced at my watch and realized it had only been five minutes since I'd talked to Cindy. The last thing I wanted was for Olivia to make the long story shorter. "What was he going to do with it?"

"Said he was going to expand the agency. He needed some of the money to provide services for his clients he couldn't do now. Said he should pay for the demos instead of having the clients foot the bill, and wanted to pay off some debts. He would use some of the money to open a Nashville bar. Said it would be bigger and better than anything there."

Some of it was now beginning to make sense. "Did you and Edwina go to Nashville?"

"Several times. Kevin wanted us to get a feel for the city's successful bar business, and he wanted Edwina to start performing at some of the venues."

"The Bluebird?"

"Yeah, that's where Edwina met Heather Lee. She got to liking Heather, and I started getting bad vibes about Kevin."

"Why?"

"I kept asking about the partnership agreement I'd signed. He tried to charm his way around telling me he hadn't filed it yet. He gave some feeble excuses, legal mumbo-jumbo."

"He had your money?"

"And I had nothing except a lying lover."

Her gun hand began to shake. I was afraid she was going to squeeze the trigger. "That's too bad," I said, hoping to calm her.

"Yeah."

"Is that when you decided to kill him?"

"Yes. I had to figure a way to set someone up for it. If the police started looking deep, they'd find a money trail that led to me. I couldn't have that, could I?"

"Heather?"

"It was perfect. Edwina kept dragging me over to Nashville and insisted on appearing at the Bluebird. She was convinced fame was going to be staring at her from the audience. I stood in line with her some of those times. It didn't take a detective to learn Heather had a gun—think someone named Quinn or Gwen gave it to her. Everyone knew it; knew she kept it in her car, the car with the broken lock."

"You stole the gun."

She nodded. "I wanted to give Kevin one more chance to make good on his promises. I met him at an out-of-the-way bar so no one he would know would see us."

"Top Ten Bar?"

"Yeah. He tried to slather his charm on me. I'd had enough of it and told him so. All he did was shrug. That did it. I stormed out."

"And shot him with Heather's gun and put it back in her car."

"The perfect crime, or so I thought."

My phone rang again and I thought Olivia was going to pull the trigger. Instead, she said, "Let it ring."

After five rings, it kicked to voice mail. A minute later an icon indicated that I had a message.

Olivia looked at the screen and said, "Put it on speaker."

We heard Cal say, "Chris, I…whoops, you ain't real. Danged machine. Anyway, good news. Something finally came back to this ancient, pickled brain, something you need to know. When I was talking to you on the phone about what I knew about Starr's killin', guess who was in the bar and close enough to hear me say I needed to tell you? Never mind, you don't have to guess. It was that lady who has the rock bar we went to. Think that's a clue? Well, call when you get this and I'll tell you more. There's not much else to tell. Crap, you don't have to call; that's all I know. Have a great day."

"What more can happen?" Olivia asked. She rubbed her eyes with one hand but held the gun steady with the other. "Now I've got to take care of him."

"You saw him leaving Cal's and bashed his head in?"

"Yeah, thought I'd killed him. Damned hard head. I was in there when he called you and I overhead him saying he knew something about Starr and Folly. I didn't know what it was. Whatever it was it could lead to me. I was supposed to meet Caldwell at Cal's the next night and saw the cowboy coming out when I was headed to the door. There was a scrap of wood next to the building. I grabbed it and smacked him and left. I didn't think anyone saw me. I couldn't take a chance of staying around to make sure he was dead."

I glanced at my watch. It'd been nearly twenty minutes. Where was Cindy? Olivia was getting antsier and I didn't know how much longer I could stall. If Cindy barged in now, what would I do? I could drop down in front of the desk out of Olivia's sight.

"He lived," I said.

"Now I have to do something about that."

"Why kill Edwina?"

"Hated to do it. She was a good kid and always wanted to help. Kevin had made the mistake of screwing her over. He took more money from her than he should have. She got riled and threatened to kill him. Too many people heard her, and the police started to look at her."

"But Heather was already in jail."

"Yes. Some busybody"—she pointed to me with her empty hand—"started asking questions. I was afraid the cops would start questioning Edwina. She knew too much about me. I couldn't wait to see if she'd fold."

"Did she know about your, umm relationship with Starr?"

"She wasn't stupid."

"How'd you kill her?"

"It was tricky. It had to look like an accident. I told her I was going out on my boat and wanted her to go with me. Said we'd swim in the ocean. She loved the water and jumped at any chance to get in it."

"That's how you got her in a bathing suit?"

"Yes. Pretended like the engine was acting up and I told her something was stuck in the prop. She went in the water to see what was wrong. She's a good swimmer so I had to keep pushing her away with a paddle; she'd swim away and I'd go after her and hit her again. We were far enough out that no one was around and nobody could see us from shore. She finally wore down." She sighed. "It took forever. I had to pull her on board and dump her close enough to the beach so she'd wash up and be found. The cops would figure the cuts and bruises were from her being tumbled in the waves and on the rocks."

"They almost did."

"Yeah, until you started waving red flags and the cops found the note in her room with your name on it. They started after you but I knew they couldn't make anything stick."

"How'd you find that out?"

"County cops are in here all the time and one of them knew Edwina had been a regular. Didn't take many drinks for him to tell me—hush, hush, he said."

"How did you—"

She smiled. "Enough. I think my short version of a long story has gone long enough. Now if you'd please stand, you need to head to the restroom. I'd hate to mess up my office."

I didn't know what'd happened to Cindy, but couldn't wait. I started to stand and flipped the leather blotter up at Olivia's as she started to stand. The pistol jerked up as she pulled the trigger. A bullet burrowed into the ceiling.

She grabbed the edge of the blotter and flung it out of the way and lowered her gun hand. I dove sideways and reached for the letter tray. If I could get to it, I could throw it at her.

She fired another round. The bullet ripped through my sleeve but missed my arm. I lunged at her. My stomach rammed the desk. I gasped for breath.

Olivia stared at me, a bemused look on her face. And again, she pointed the weapon at me. I grabbed for it.

Olivia yanked it out of my reach and tripped over the chair. She fell backwards. Her head slammed the credenza. Her eyes rolled up and she slumped to the floor. At the same time, the door leading to the bar exploded inward and Cindy stumbled through the shattered door and tripped. Her knee hit the floor and she screamed a profanity.

Olivia didn't hear her. She was out cold.

I pushed backwards and slid off the desk and collapsed in the chair I had been sitting in. Cindy regained her balance and pointed her service weapon at Olivia who hadn't moved.

"Are you okay?" the chief asked, as Larry came in the room.

I nodded, caught my breath, and said, "What took you so long?"

"Don't go there," She was rubbing her knee and taking deep breaths. "Is she okay?"

"Don't know, better call an ambulance."

Cindy looked around and spotted her phone that had been jarred out of her pocket when she slammed into the door. She dialed and muttered some police-speak into it and turned back to me. I was still in the chair. "We've been here several minutes. Both doors were locked. Didn't figure knocking would be a good idea. The lock on the front door must have been made by a high-school shop student, one who should've flunked. Thank God. Larry had it picked in seconds. I figured you were in here, and I put my ear up to the door." She pointed to the door she had stormed through. "Couldn't hear anything."

"She soundproofed the room so she didn't have to listen to the music from the bar."

"Sound proofers would've earned an *A* in their shop class. Couldn't hear a damned thing. That changed when a gun went off. That's when I decided a quick entry might be wise. And as your buddy Dude would say, 'Rest be history.'"

With the soundproof door in pieces, we heard sirens. Cindy kept her gun drawn, gave me a quick hug, mumbled something about being pleased I was okay, and flopped down in one of the other chairs where she could see the unmoving Olivia. Larry seconded it and went to welcome the troops.

CHAPTER THIRTY-SEVEN

Cindy still had her handgun drawn and another gun was on the floor beside the supine murderer. The first officers to arrive took a moment to evaluate the situation before deciding what to do. It wasn't made any simpler when they asked if the unconscious female had been shot and Cindy said no that she had been attacked by a leather desk blotter and a mahogany credenza. One of the officers asked if the chief would hand him her weapon. Cindy smiled, handed it over, and made another call. The officer smelled the barrel to determine if it had been fired, waited for Cindy to finish her call and returned her service weapon.

The next officer to arrive recognized Cindy and put her on the side of the angels. The first officer to arrive had bent over Olivia and after feeling for a pulse, announced she was alive. Neither cop paid much attention to Larry or me since we were sitting motionless with no weapons in sight.

An ambulance arrived and two paramedics peeked in the shattered doorway before entering. They decided it was safe and headed to Olivia. Cindy rubbed her knee and watched the medics do their thing. She wouldn't admit it, but I knew she was in pain and reeling from her encounter with the door.

The medics were wheeling Olivia out on a stretcher with a police escort when Detective Grolier strolled in, looked at the totaled door, and gazed around the room.

"Chief," he said, and looked at me. "Mr. Landrum." Only four of us were left in the room and Grolier asked Cindy what had happened. She introduced Larry and started to tell the detective what had happened, hesitated, turned to me, and said, "Chris, from the beginning?"

And I did. Nine thousand questions later, I finished my story that started when my best friend followed his girlfriend to Nashville to find fame and fortune and ended with Olivia Anderson confessing to two murders—one that Heather was currently being incarcerated for, and the other where I had been the prime suspect.

Because of those connections, my story would have had little credibility. That was until Detective Grolier called in the crime techs who thoroughly searched Olivia's office. Fortunately for both Heather and me, Olivia was a packrat and had kept copies of the partnership agreement between her and Kevin Starr, and in her business folder, copies of gas receipts that showed she bought gas in Nashville the same day Starr was killed, along with restaurant and hotel receipts showing where she had eaten and stayed, again around the date of the murder.

The receipts and agreement didn't prove that she had killed Starr, but they were enough for the police to go to the DA in Nashville and get Heather a new bail hearing scheduled for next week.

From the hospital and with her hand cuffed to the bed, under advice from her attorney, Olivia refused to talk to the police. She wasn't stupid.

Three days later, the police searched Olivia's boat and discovered blood in a corner of the deck. It would still be several more days before a definitive DNA match could be made, but since it was Edwina's blood type, all bets were on it being hers.

On the same day, Rod, the bartender at the Top Ten Bar, was shown two photos of Olivia and said he may have been mistaken about Heather and that Olivia, "Sure looks like the gal with Starr the night before he got himself kilt."

A week after my near-fatal visit to SHADES, I was on the road to Music City USA. Charges had been dropped against Heather and she and Charles had walked hand-and-hand out of the jail. Charles begged me to come over so the three of us could celebrate with a night on the town.

Heather opened the apartment door and greeted me with a lingering hug and whispered "Thank you." She wasn't as enthusiastic as she had been on my first visit to their apartment, but she had to be exhausted. She was pale and had lost weight, but smiled, something I hadn't seen in quite a while. Charles was behind her and stepped forward to give me an equally long hug.

I threw my overnight bag on the couch and followed them in the kitchen where there were two unopened beers and a bottle of white wine beside a plastic wine glass. The wine bottle was sitting on a square hat box with a red top with STETSON on the side and a rendering of a cowboy herding cattle. The bottle was anchoring a blue string attached to a red balloon floating above the table. It said *CONGRATULATIONS!*

Heather pointed at the balloon. "That's from Chuckie."

Charles popped open the beers. "It's a new hat for Cal. It's an old hat, but hardly been worn and it'll be new to Cal. Found it in a consignment store."

"He'll be thrilled," I said and unscrewed the top on the chardonnay.

Heather said, "Best screwed up bottle of wine seven bucks can buy."

We sat around the table sipping and telling each other how great it was Heather was here and not having supper with thirty-seven women, all dressed alike. Charles asked how everyone was in Folly.

Heather said, "Later. Let's go eat."

"Where?" I asked.

Heather stood and straightened her yellow blouse. "Don't know. I know where we ain't going. Ain't going anywhere there's singing or strummin'."

Next to Charles buying Cal a hat, the biggest surprise came when Charles said we were eating at The Capitol Grille, one of the city's most expensive restaurants, and that he was paying.

After a terrific supper, I saw the bill and told Charles he didn't have to pay. I'd pick up the tab.

"No way, Chris. Heck, I'm flush. I figure I saved a million dollars by not having to bail my sweetie out of the pokey."

It was great hearing Charles joking after what he and Heather had been through.

Heather raised her hand like she wanted to ask a question. "Something else I wanted to say. Think your friend William can give me the name of his, umm, counselor?"

William Hansel had suffered a nervous breakdown a few years ago, and since then had regular counseling sessions and had been pleased with the results.

"I'm sure his counselor could recommend someone over here."

Heather giggled. "Well that's the thing." She turned to Charles. "You tell him, Chuckie."

Charles patted her on the hand and turned to me. "Sweetie's decided she'd rather be a big fish in a small pond instead of a minnow in the ocean. Nashville's a wonderful place, got a lot of good stuff going for it."

I held my breath as Charles paused.

"'Cept it ain't got an ocean; ain't got our friends. We're moving back to Folly."

I stood, waved the server over, and said, "I'm buying the champagne."

ABOUT THE AUTHOR

Bill Noel is the best-selling author of thirteen novels in the popular Folly Beach Mystery series. In addition to being an award-winning novelist, Noel is a fine arts photographer and lives in Louisville, Kentucky, with his wife, Susan, and his off-kilter imagination.

Made in the USA
Lexington, KY
11 April 2018